FORMULA ONE NOEL

A STEAMY CONTEMPORARY HOLIDAY ROMANCE

PERRY HARBOR STANDALONE
BOOK 2.5

CHRISTINA BRAVER

Copyright © 2022 Christina Braver, Three Bs Publishing LLC

All rights reserved.

No part of this book may be reproduced in any form or by any electronic or mechanical means, including information storage and retrieval systems, without written permission from the author, except for the use of brief quotations in a book review. For permissions contact: author@christinabraver.com

This is a work of fiction. Names, characters, places, and incidents are either the product of the author's imagination or are used fictitiously. Any resemblance to actual persons, living, or dead, businesses, companies, events, or locales is entirely coincidental.

Though this story takes place in a fictional location, it is based on an area of the Pacific Northwest that is the traditional land of the Coast Salish. I want to honor with gratitude the land itself and the Coast Salish people.

Cover by: 100 Covers

Edited by: Lynne Pearson, All That Editing, Inc.

ISBN: 979-8-9863614-4-4 (ebook) 979-8-9863614-5-1 (print)

Visit the author's website at www.christinabraver.com

For my friends at FAITH. Whether or not you read steamy romance, you supported me. Thank you!

1

NORA

The perpetual sound of a flatline echoed through the resuscitation room of the Emergency Medicine Department. Everyone's movements slowed as they looked at me. My hands sweated in the blue nitrile gloves, and my hot breath pulsed behind the surgical mask. This was the part I hated about being a doctor. When everything I knew still wasn't enough to save the life in front of me.

What had we not tried? The patient was late sixties, otherwise healthy, and arrived in V-tach with an irregular heartbeat. We applied the shocks in the correct rhythm, pushed the Epi and Bi-carb, and the patient's oxygen levels continued to drop. We'd worked for almost an hour, trying everything the team could think of. This collective of smart and caring professionals was the best I'd known, and it still wasn't enough.

"Dr. Reynolds?" A gentle voice beside me broke through the chaos of thoughts in my head. My colleague, Matt, was an excellent nurse. And he knew, like we all did.

I checked the clock and removed my gloves. "Time of

death, three-thirty-four a.m." I exhaled, feeling the loss of this patient, this woman, in my bones.

My job was to assess symptoms and any potential causes of a condition, work to stabilize, order tests and labs to rule out possible explanations, and chip down to the real presenting problem in order to call for the right specialty consult. I was good at my job.

Most of the time, I liked it, especially when I got to give positive news to family members. We'd identify the problem, and the talented people upstairs would take over. Their loved one would be okay. The sense of relief and energy that filled those conversations was exhilarating. I even had the chance to deliver a few babies, soaking in the reverence of a new life entering the world.

Not this time. I stormed past the curtain and out the room's sliding glass door, frustration burning in my veins. She'd been in the ER before, with unusual fatigue, occasional shortness of breath, and stated, "I just don't feel right." She had a history of anxiety and reported elevated stress due to planning for the Christmas holiday in a couple of weeks.

Dr. Sloane ran all the necessary tests, but nothing showed a potential cardiac issue, and the protocol didn't indicate we should dig deeper. She downplayed the severity of her symptoms, saying it was probably all in her head, and apologized for taking up the doctor's valuable time. Why did women do that, minimize our pain?

Sometimes doctors did everything by the book, and people still died. From my experience in the ER, it seemed to happen more often with women. There had to be something missing in *the book* we all followed.

For a few reasons, most of the standing research on almost anything in healthcare and the resulting treatment protocols were primarily based on studies of men that were then applied to women. As a result, women didn't always receive the best care for them.

We were learning more every day about how women's bodies differed from men's and not just in the parts covered by a bikini. Research was happening, but we needed more.

"Hey, Nora. You okay?" Right on my heels, Jamar, my colleague and friend slipped into the small alcove behind the nurses' station. The radio in the corner played easy-listening holiday music, and colorful string lights lit the sterile white hospital walls the same way they did the light wood counter of the huge desk nearby, the department's hub.

"Yes," I snapped. Always yes. Always okay. I yanked the plug on the miniature speaker out of the wall like it insulted me.

"You don't like Christmas carols?"

"Christmas ... is for miracles and magic-kiss movies on the Hallmark Channel. Not this." I knew I was being unprofessional, which was why I was trying to keep it private, but something about this case pushed me over an edge. I wanted to break something.

"Nora, there was nothing more we could do." Jamar's rich, dark eyes held kindness and understanding. He was an excellent physician, and he felt this loss too.

"This shouldn't have happened, Jamar. There has to be more research on medical conditions and women. Men's and women's bodies are *not* the same."

"And let me say, I am sooo glad—"

"Jamar!" I rolled my eyes and huffed at my friend, releasing some of the mounting anxiety as I felt the smile curve my lips. Jamar was undeniably good-looking, a doctor, and genuinely kind. He never lacked female attention. He tried to act cocky about it, but I could see through him like a window. He was good to the core and looking for *the one*.

I held up my palm to face him and said in a more normal tone, "I know you love women and everything about them, but can you tell me about it later. I'm kinda going through something here."

His face brightened. "There's the Nora I know. It's nice to see you again." He paused and moved closer. "The first time she was here, her HEART score was three. Anyone of us would have discharged her the same way that day."

I sighed. "Because it's what we learned from textbooks and journals utilizing research primarily on men."

Jamar set a firm hand on my shoulder. "Let this one go, Nora. Another one will need you soon enough, *they* deserve all of you." He squeezed my shoulder and ducked out the same way he'd entered.

All of me. Others always deserved all of me.

I rallied, as usual, and pushed through the rest of my overnight shift. Afterward, I sat in the office area for physicians, a small room with a few desks where we did endless charting and had a quick snack before case reviews with residents or an administration meeting we were required to attend. My ten-hour shift that started at seven p.m. often stretched to twelve or fourteen hours by the time I slid into bed alone around eight or nine in the morning before returning for another overnight. The night-shift weeks were the toughest and screwed up my sleep for days after.

Three shifts a week in the Emergency Medicine Department at Birch University Medical Center in Nashville, plus committee meetings and teaching residents, left me exhausted most of the time. Dating was barely a thought sometimes, and thirty-five years old felt like a hundred on these extra-tough days.

My phone rang. I glanced at the caller ID and braced myself.

"Hi, Dad. Where are you?" I kept my voice upbeat, hoping this call would be quick.

"Guatemala City. Beautiful place filled with color and life. Street art everywhere. Wish you were here."

I smiled. Mom and Dad loved to travel, and every city was prettier than the last.

"We have cell service here. I wanted to check in. How are you?" he asked.

"Good. Busy. Christmas and all."

"Oh, right. Out in the field, it's difficult to remember things like that. Not a lot of resources for seasonal decorations in the villages. What have you heard from GDNL?" Dad asked, getting straight to the point of his interest lately.

Global Doctors No Limits was an incredible organization that sent medical teams to the world's poorest communities to provide basic, life-saving healthcare. My parents, both physicians trained in emergency medicine as well, had worked for GDNL for years in cities worldwide and were eager for me to join them. Going along with the plan, I started the application process.

They'd always expected me to do great things as a physician, supporting me in school and helping with tuition and student loans to make them affordable. Every dinner party I attended with them since my teens, they'd beamed as they told their friends that one day, we would be a *dream team* doing good in the world.

"I passed the initial checks and am cleared to send the full application and my CV whenever I'm ready," I said.

"That's great. You could get approved in time to join your mom and me in Africa in a few months. We'll finally be doing this essential work together like we'd always planned."

I swallowed. "I'm not sure I'll be able to start so soon. There are some things I want to see through here."

"Nora, what's happening in Africa is critical right now. What could be more important than that? Those other things will have to wait," Dad said, his tone reminding me of their motto. *Self-sacrifice is usually necessary to do the right thing.*

My heartbeat pulsed, and sweat formed on my brow. I wasn't ready to talk about this with him yet.

"Sorry, Dad. I have a couple of residents here to see me," I lied. "I should go. You and Mom are both okay?"

"Of course. It's been a rough month trying to keep the vaccination supplies steady, but we're making progress. We'll call before we head out again."

Mom jumped in with her goodbye, and *we love you.* I ended the call and concentrated on slowing my heartbeat. I *really* didn't want to disappoint them.

"When's your flight?" Matt stood by my desk, eating an apple.

"In the morning, early. I want to finish my research proposal for the Birch Foundation as soon as possible. Submitting it ahead of others might help me stand out." I would do almost anything to stand out from the competition. Well, one competitor.

Dr. Michael Flores, MD, the MD for massive dickhead, was the other attending from my world who was applying for research funding from Birch. The Birch Foundation had supported many worthy causes since the university campus was nothing but farmland. Descendants of the founder, an excessively wealthy railroad baron, wanted to use their grandfather's ill-gotten gain for good and had solidified the foundation as a leader in research funding across disciplines in recent decades.

With less red-tape and process than grants from the NIH, or other federal agencies, the foundation's Birch Family Grants had become known as a great place to start for those interested in a research career like me.

Exclusive to university faculty and staff, these grants were competitive. Winning meant mentorship from the university's impressive senior researchers and the type of clout that could lead to a principal investigator role in significant studies in the future, like those including expensive clinical trials on both men *and* women. Talk about *a dream*.

If they selected a proposal from Emergency Medicine, it would only be one. So, Massive Dickhead or me.

This was my time, and I was here for it. My interests have always centered on women's health. My time in emergency medicine brought the need for research more into focus. Recent studies found that some serious medical conditions, like heart attacks, were mistakenly diagnosed as anxiety in women. Emergency physicians, and doctors in general, needed a better understanding of diagnoses associated with anxiety, and I wanted any future research I did to start there.

For this project, I planned to do a deeper investigation into physical conditions in women that were thought to be related to anxiety without a clear link. Working with a colleague from Gynecology, the diagnosis I was focusing on in the potential study was vulvodynia, a chronic pain condition marked by discomfort around the opening of the vagina, which impacted sexual health. It occurred in women of all ages, and though there was no known cause, it was believed to be linked to anxiety. Treatment approaches varied but sometimes involved medications to dull nerve pain and, consequently, all sensations in the vulva, unpleasant *or* pleasant.

There had to be a better, long-term solution. Science owed it to women to find a clear cause and an evidence-based treatment.

Tomorrow, I'd head to the small vacation town of Perry Harbor, Washington, seventy miles north of Seattle, to meet with two highly acclaimed sex educators and attend one of their trainings. The two were most known for recommending techniques and approaches to those for whom vaginal penetration wasn't an option. They were respected, and a personal interview would take my application to the next level. Plus, the trip was an excuse to take some time away to concentrate on writing.

"Well, have a safe flight." Matt winked and shifted away from my desk. It felt like flirting. I hoped not because I didn't sleep with coworkers ... anymore. Contrary to current television, emergency physicians and nurses were not all banging each other in empty patient beds between incoming ambulances. But I worked long hours, and these were the only people I had in my life consistently. I'd dated a few colleagues.

Sleeping with Massive Dickhead had changed things. I wouldn't sleep with Matt. Not even *fuck-you* sex, the kind you have with the first option that comes along as a huge FU to the lover before. I didn't have to use FU sex to hurt Flores. I planned to hurt him where it really counted. I was going to win that grant money.

2

WALKER

"I'm sorry, Mr. Hewitt. We don't have any other information on the delay. This storm has turned out to be more severe than predicted, and the forecast is changing quickly. At this point, the flight is just delayed, not canceled."

I nodded at the airline rep. She didn't need any shit from me. Another first-class passenger from my recently landed connection had been in front of me and basically threatened her job if he didn't get what he wanted immediately. Unbelievable.

She'd handled him, but his asshattery had shaken her. She would have a long day. The snowstorm wasn't in her control, but the other people in line all wore facial expressions that showed they thought it was.

Her smile waned as she made eye contact with the next customer. The agent was cute. Young. Light blonde hair and small bones. With the shiny silver tinsel strung along the flight signage wall behind her, she looked more like she belonged at a prom, not at the bloodbath this would soon be. I wanted to stand there for a moment, daring anyone to be shitty and risk getting one of my fancy Lucchese alligator cowboy boots up the ass.

It was the holiday season, a time for people to come together, eat cookies and drink eggnog. It was not the time to condescend to an airline rep because you didn't want to be late for your shopping trip in New York City or some shit.

Entitled people fucking baffled me. Why would they think she wasn't doing everything in her power to get everyone to their destination? That was probably it. She was working for everyone. Entitled people wanted others to work only for them. I knew some entitled people.

I thanked her and, out of habit, rubbed the ache from an old injury to my wrist. I'd broken it in a wreck on turn three at Bahrain a few years ago. Sand had blown across the racetrack, which happened a lot, and I'd thought we'd prepared the car and the tires. But I lost traction and ended up in the wall. The jolt to the wheel snapped the lower end of my radius bone. Fortunately, it was a clean break, and I'd fully recovered, even racing and winning the Formula One World Drivers' Championship for the second time the following year. But lately, the ache lingered, and I worried it had impacted my reaction time this past season.

The gray windows in the airport's gate area were stark against the snow falling heavily outside. A sea of grounded planes sat on the tarmac, their shapes softening in white. It didn't look good for me getting my flight to Bellingham today. It was only a couple of hours north of Seattle, the last leg of a long trip. Monaco to New York to Seattle to Bellingham. If I had to, I'd rent a car and drive, even though I hardly drove anymore, except around a racetrack.

First, I'd eat. Then, I'd make a plan. I shifted the small duffel bag with my laptop, coat, and some essentials inside as I took in my options for food in the busy concourse. As a first-class passenger, I could sit and wait out the weather in the Alaska Lounge if I wanted to. But something about the possibility of spending one more hour hanging out with possibly pampered strangers didn't hold any appeal. Across the brightly lit concourse, a busy restaurant got busier.

Standing at an even 6'1", I saw above most of the crowd to an empty seat near the end of the bar area. Perfect. Out of the way. Though this was the US, the chances were low of anyone recognizing a Formula One driver out of the fire suit emblazoned with the Jaguar symbol and the bright orange logo for the international shipping company, our biggest sponsor; I still wanted to be careful. I wasn't up for it today.

The pressure to perform, to be who the fans thought I was, had become a burden in recent years. I didn't want to let them down. Or my team or my family. My folks had invested a lot of time and money in me. They had expectations. So, I'd always pushed through setbacks. *Hewitts don't quit*, Dad said.

But I was getting older. My reaction time was not the same, and it showed. Younger, stronger drivers were coming up behind me, and I had to make a choice. Go back for another season and *risk* letting my team down by losing or retire and *definitely* let my parents down by quitting. I hoped the right thing to do would become clearer in the next few days.

With a sigh, I squeezed through the growing crowd to the empty seat, thankful for the strict exercise and diet program that kept me agile and fit. Every ounce of weight on or in a race car mattered.

Two women sat on either side of the empty bar-height chair. One was older in stretchy dark green pants, a turtleneck with reindeer hopping across the fabric, and a curly shock of short white hair. She was quietly angled toward the man next to her, who wore khakis with a bright red sweater and very little hair of his own. Two half-empty cocktails sat nearby.

The couple had that look, like they fit together. Like they could communicate with each other without actual words. Not in a hostile way. In the way that came with living with your favorite person for most of your adult life. They knew each other probably better than they did themselves. How did that happen? An image of my ex-fiancée flashed through my mind. I wouldn't have had that with her, even if we had somehow made it to the altar.

The woman on the other side of the empty seat sipped a cup of coffee and concentrated on her laptop. What looked like a scientific journal article was open on the screen with the title "Sex After Sixty: An Integrated Approach to Sexual Health."

That wasn't something you saw every day. I took her in from the side, noticing the slant of her jaw and the deep dark hair held in a thick braid that trailed between her shoulder blades and exposed her pierced but unadorned ears. Her hair shone in the lights above the bar, and my hands itched to loosen it around her shoulders. What would it feel like sliding against my palm?

She wore a soft-looking, red turtleneck sweater that hugged her trim waist and kept her back straight. Slim fingers flew across the keyboard as she switched between the article and another open document, where she added lines of text with quick, sure typing. She appeared determined and laser-focused, and I wondered what she did for a living.

"Excuse me," I said.

She turned, and her expression changed from concentration to blank. Then almost as quickly, her full, red lips curved into a polite smile. Not fake or condescending, but genuinely kind. It had been a while since I'd seen one of those smiles, and from someone who didn't know who I was, what I did for a living, or how much money my father had. I wanted to chase that smile.

"Are you using this chair?" I asked.

She glanced down; her deep blue eyes surrounded by long lashes took in the furniture like she hadn't seen it before.

"No. You can move it wherever you want." She returned to her computer.

"What if I want to keep it here and sit?"

This time when she looked at me, her expression was like surprise. I knew my comment and tone sounded like flirting, and the curve of her lips, slightly bigger now, had me thinking maybe she wanted me to.

"Oh, sure. Sorry, that was what the last guy did with the seat on my other side."

I glanced around her to the small gap there. A group of twenty-somethings crowded together not far away, talking loudly and using the downtime to catch up on their day drinking.

I shifted the tall chair and sat, pulling my duffel bag to rest under my feet. My laptop was safe inside in a prototype lightweight hard-shell case from my dad's computer company. I could throw that thing across the room, and the device would be fine.

The bartender was at the other end of the bar dealing with the growing tide of customers. "Hey, do you see a menu anywhere?" I asked.

She pointed. "It's there, the QR code on the laminated card with the ketchup. You have a smartphone, right?"

"Sure. I don't look old enough to still carry a flip phone, do I?" I grinned. I had a bit of silver at the edges of my hair and in my sideburns, but I'd earned those wrestling turns at high speeds in a car that was barely more than two upside-down airplane wings between four massive tires. It was a dance on the edge of chaos and control.

"Oh, no, I meant … cell phones are expensive. It's inconsiderate to assume everyone has one. A lot of seniors struggle with them, and if I couldn't afford a smartphone when it seems that everyone else could, needing one to order lunch would likely just make me feel worse about the situation. If you want a QR code, have a code, but have a tangible menu too. That's all I'm saying."

I didn't speak. I'd always assumed those codes were a good thing. An environmental shift to save paper or plastic. They were everywhere in Europe, or at least all the places I went had them. But then, those places usually had clientele that could definitely afford a smartphone, even ones encrusted with diamonds. Which existed, by the way.

"Sorry," she said, taking in my confused expression then angling back to her laptop.

"Nothing to be sorry for. I hadn't ever thought of QR codes that way. I hadn't considered them from the perspective of someone different from me," I said.

Another smile. This one was distinctive. It was interesting how she had such unique smiles. This one was happy in an understated way. Another thing I hadn't been around in a long time. Anything understated.

I accessed the menu, and when the bartender approached, I ordered a burger along with a beer. I wouldn't be racing again for at least a couple of months, or ever, and a drink and a burger for lunch sounded good. Adding an extra mile to my run tomorrow would compensate for the additional calories today. As I waited for my food and tried not to read over the slim shoulder of the sex-after-sixty buff, a part of me already considered how to get those lips to do lots of things other than smile.

I was jetlagged. That explained this sudden attraction. Like questions from fans or selfie requests, I hadn't been up for women lately, either. I mean, I could definitely get it up. At thirty-four, I was old in the racing world but still young in the real world. That article she had up on her screen better be accurate. I planned to have sex long after I turned sixty and seventy and eighty if I could.

I liked sex. And there were always girls interested in hooking up with the winner from the winning team. Winning was sexy. Even in my teens, winning the karting races across Europe, plenty of girls were eager to hang out with me.

I wondered what my bar-mate thought was sexy. I shouldn't care. But I did. And that was new for me.

3

NORA

Eyes on the laptop, I reminded myself. No more lectures on socioeconomic micro-aggressions. *Boys don't like smart girls.*

I shuddered at the thought from teenage me. I was wrong. Of course, boys liked smart girls. You had to find the right boy, which took time and effort I didn't have.

Hoping I hadn't completely offended the man next to me, I tried to relax. Ordinary people did this. They sat in bars. They met others and talked to them about everyday things, not pretentious QR codes. At least I hadn't opened with the average number of bowel obstructions I saw in a week. My flirt game outside the hospital was improving.

I noticed the article I was reading from a geriatric medical journal. I was still prepping for my face-to-face with the sex educators in a couple of days. The title jumped out at me. "Sex After Sixty: An Integrated Approach to Sexual Health."

Awesome. Super-hot dude probably thought I was a weirdo or a sex guru. No way I was a guru of anything sexy. I was a bit weird, but not in the sense that he might imagine. I felt weird because I had done absolutely nothing that would be considered weird. Or even impulsive.

Being impulsive was irresponsible. But the idea of being impulsive with this man had heat pooling low. That hadn't happened before.

In college, I was too busy studying to do a lot of … being impulsive. I'd occasionally dated in med school to blow off steam but didn't need the continued distraction. Since graduating, I spent a short time on a dating app that did *not* go well. Once men found out I was a physician, the conversation usually turned to something like, *does this popping sound in my shoulder seem normal?* Or my absolute favorite, *does this rash look like an STD?*

As a result, my romantic life, like almost everything else, had centered primarily on the hospital, where being a doctor was barely worth mentioning on a date. But I'd sworn off dating anyone at work after Massive Dickhead, leaving me without many options, and the months-long dry spell was getting to me. That had to be why my blood was low-key buzzing in my veins.

That had to be why I noticed this guy's cologne, clean with a hint of patchouli, even with all the fried food smells wafting around me. He'd ordered a burger and managed to eat it without getting it everywhere like I would have done in my rush. He sipped his beer, strong-looking fingers grasping the mug's handle.

"Slow reader?" he said, startling me before he leaned in, his sultry scent filling my nose.

"What?" My gaze snapped to his, and caramel-colored eyes sparkled while a small curve lifted the corners of his tempting lips.

"You've been on the same page for a while now. I'm

curious about the rest of Estelle's day with her retired landscaper. What happens after he files his nails? I never knew nail care could be a turn-on, but it sounds like it gets Estelle going."

He'd been reading over my shoulder, and now he teased me about it. But then I heard his words on replay.

"It isn't filing his nails that turns her on. It's that he's preparing for her. He's considering *her* and what she likes and needs from him hours before she sees him. He calls her the night before their date to tell her where he wants to touch her, making her feel desired and beautiful in her body. On the day of, he picks up around the house, puts clean sheets on the bed, lights a scented candle, and takes a shower. It's all foreplay. He's smoothing the rough spots so he doesn't scratch her delicate skin. They're in their seventies. Skin, especially in post-menopausal women, can become thin and fragile because we produce less collagen. He's considering her need for a gentle touch and ensuring he's the man to provide it, which gets him going. He likes knowing he'll be the one making her feel good, alive, sexy because he still can."

The man beside me stayed quiet and shifted his gaze to my lips. I licked them out of nervousness, and his Adam's apple bobbed as he swallowed.

"Sorry again," I said. "I'm used to talking to other ..." I stopped. Did I want him to know I was a doctor? My dating app experience left some scars. And this was a chance to be something else for an hour or two.

"Other?" he asked.

"Other women, friends," I said, hoping he bought it.

"You and your friends read some interesting stuff. Any openings in your book club?" Did he know his teasing grin was also seductive as hell?

I liked his grin, how it bubbled his cheeks and the fine

lines around his eyes deepened. It was enticing but also calming, like taking a deep breath.

I noticed his hair now, dark brown cut short with a few grays blending in at the edges. That must have been why he thought I was making a crack at his age. He looked damn good, however old he was.

"Name's Walker." He held out his hand. "And you're a bit surprising."

At first, I wasn't sure what he said. I blinked to clear my thoughts, which had been heading down a provocative path, wondering how that five o'clock shadow he sported would feel against my palms, my breasts.

We shook hands, and the jolt from his warm fingers woke me the rest of the way up.

"I'm Nora. Nice to meet you, Walker." I attempted a sexy smile, my body seeming to formulate a plan for how to spend these limbo hours waiting for an update about my flight to Bellingham. "Is that a compliment? Being surprising."

"Absolutely. Not much surprises me anymore. So, I'd say it's a great thing." He hesitated like he was searching for something to say. "Your flight delayed too?"

"Yeah." I sighed. "I flew in from Nashville this morning. A snowstorm was a *big* surprise. I thought it rained here all the time."

He chuckled. "I've heard locals say it's a myth, the rain. A lie they tell to keep people from moving here, bringing more traffic and interfering with all the natural beauty."

"Oh, are you from here?"

He paused. "No, Austin. A ranch a few miles out of town. But I've spent some time here too," he said.

He definitely had the cowboy thing going on. I saw it now as I noticed his boots made of what looked like alligator, faded jeans, and a deep blue untucked oxford shirt with a bright white T-shirt peeking out at the collar. He had the tan of a man who worked outside, and the idea of powerful hands gentle on my skin sent an electric bolt straight to my core. What was with my body suddenly? I didn't get zings to my core. I didn't imagine scruff against my skin. It had to be all this reading about the older generation getting it on.

It was exciting, though. I was a long way from the hospital. No one knew I was a doctor. An attractive man was sitting next to me and smiling. He didn't know where I went to school or how many patients I'd saved last month. Didn't know and didn't care. He wasn't my competition. Something about that was appealing, and my belly had butterflies like the time Robbie Berringer, with his sexy thick-rimmed glasses, asked me to prom.

I didn't fight it. With my flight delayed, I had time on my hands. That was unusual, and I took it as a sign from the universe to make the most of it.

"You're a rancher?" I asked. "Tell me about that."

Walker finished his last bite of burger, wiped his mouth with the napkin even though his face was as clean as when he sat down, then folded it and set it on the plate. Precision. That's how I would describe how he moved. Deliberately.

"What would you like to know, little lady?" He winked, and I smirked though a little thrill shot through me. He was laying it on a bit thick, and we both knew it.

"What do you do? An average day?" I rested my elbow on the bar and angled more toward him, trying to keep it casual. Sometimes, I came off like I was interviewing people for a job. I didn't try to, but I was curious about anything new or unknown. That's all.

Walker faced me more directly and pressed against the back of his chair. Out of the corner of my eye, I noticed my computer's lock screen had popped up with a picture of a lush green hillside with a fence row and a giant red barn. How fitting.

His eyes lit as he talked about life on a working ranch. Early morning hours, beautiful sunrises, and riding a horse through tall grass. He spoke of mending fences for days, keeping the cattle fed and happy, especially the pregnant ones, and helping to deliver the calves. He worked with his uncle and brothers on a ranch his father and uncle owned. It sounded like the Hallmark movie I watched last night while I packed. *A Miracle for Noelle* or *A Miraculous Noel.* Something about a miracle and a Noel.

"What about you, Nora? What do you do? I mean, besides reading professional journals about sexy seniors."

Ummm. "I'm a teacher." It just popped out, and it wasn't really a lie. "Biology." Also, not a lie. I always thought if med school hadn't worked out, I'd like to have been a high school biology teacher.

"I can see that," Walker said. "You look like a teacher."

"And what does a teacher look like?" I raised my eyebrow, hoping it looked sexy.

"You have that smart thing going on. Confident, but sort of secretive about it. Like you know your shit and don't necessarily need others to notice."

Huh, that was surprisingly apt for someone who'd spent less than an hour with me. I hadn't always been confident, and I hadn't always not cared about others' opinions, but I was working on it.

He leaned in. "I'm really enjoying talking to you, Nora, but I don't want to keep you from your work. If you need to get back to it," he nodded at my laptop, "I can mind my own business."

He was giving me an out. Checking in. Not pushing or

coming too close. He hadn't done anything that made me uncomfortable. In fact, he'd had the opposite effect.

He stood up, and my heart sank. Had I given off a signal that I wanted him to go?

"I'm going to hit the men's room. Should I take my stuff, or will you be here a while?"

I blinked at him.

"There's nothing dangerous in the bag. I swear I'm legit. Not a bomber or a serial killer or anything like that."

"Isn't that what you would say if you *were* one of those things but trying to throw me off?" I asked.

"Well, you got me there. But it's a bit difficult to prove a negative. That I'm not something, so I guess we have to trust each other."

"You could show me what's in the bag." I lifted a shoulder.

"You want to see my boxers and toothbrush?" he asked and chuckled.

"No, I want to see if that's really what's in there. All unattended baggage must be reported to airport security, and I'm not supposed to accept bags from strangers. The announcement runs on a loop in this place." I twirled my finger in the air.

"I'm on this side of security," he said, his expression confused. "Right. Okay." He grabbed his bag, made of thick canvas, and set it on his empty chair. He unzipped it, and the scent of spice and laundry soap hit my nose as he held it open for me. Inside were neatly folded pairs of men's boxer briefs in dark colors and other clothing items, an old-style shaving kit zipped closed, and a hard-sided laptop case.

I eyed him more intensely. I could usually read most people. Dr. Massive Dickhead being the glaring exception.

I'd certainly been lied to by many people for a lot of reasons. Walker wasn't lying.

"Okay, give me your cell number," I said and unlocked my phone before handing it to him. When he finished, I pinged him and heard the chime from the front pocket of his jeans. "If they call my flight or something, I'll text you."

4

WALKER

Leaving my laptop with a near stranger may not have been the smartest, but I had a good feeling about Nora. She wasn't a racing groupie, a grid girl, or the daughter of one of my parents' friends.

She was different. She had her own thing, and I could tell she liked me. Not the F1 driver or the son of a tech billionaire. But me, the rancher.

Technically, I *was* a rancher *and* from Austin. My family's ranch was home, where I spent my time between racing seasons and where I planned to be when I retired from the sport.

Nora and I were just passing the time, having fun, no risk. I could be that rancher for a day. Test drive my next career. With the current F1 season finished, and my future up in the air, my ranching career might not be that far away.

Racing was supposed to be fun. Then it became like an addiction. The look on my father's face every time I'd won growing up was a big motivator. He'd pat me on the back and tell all his friends about *his* son, *the winner*. It felt good, and I'd worked hard to never disappoint him.

But for the last two years since I'd won the championship for the second time, I struggled to win even a race. That was definitely a disappointment.

I'd been working with one new guy on the team this past year, Lorenzo Messina. It was part of my responsibility as the lead driver. The kid was good, really fucking good, and he was twenty, with two wrists he'd never broken, and it showed. Good or bad, he'd gotten into my head.

I needed to figure my shit out. I was on my way to spend the holidays at my parents' newest house in the San Juan Islands north of Seattle. Peace and quiet, time to think and make the right decision about my future for the right reasons.

When my parents told me they'd bought an island in the northwest corner of Washington State, I was skeptical. But I guessed that was what you did when you retired from one of the world's leading computer hardware manufacturers. A company you started and grew and piloted to the top. My dad still held so much stock in Hewitt Computing that it was a daily challenge to calculate his exact net worth.

He was a billionaire. *I* was not. Wealth, like my folks had, equaled fame. So, a remote home wasn't a bad idea, and what was more remote than your own island? The area was beautiful and not yet completely spoiled by those who had more money than common sense. It wasn't the family ranch outside Austin, but it wasn't an overblown yacht anchored off the coast of Greece, either. It would be nice to spend a couple of weeks there before I headed home to the ranch and the decision I had to make.

Mom had the big idea that we should all meet for the

holidays when she and Dad had come to one of my races in Italy earlier this year. My brothers, their wives, me, and my then fiancée, Claire, were all expected. I wasn't looking forward to being the odd man out now that there was no Claire, but it wouldn't be so bad to have an excuse to lay low and keep to myself.

When I returned a few minutes later, Nora and my bag were right where I'd left them. I slid into the seat, and she turned.

"You didn't make a run for it with my laptop, and I didn't leave you holding a loaded bag," I said, smiling. Not the race-winning photo one, but a real one.

At that moment, both of our phones dinged with an incoming text. With a glance, we acknowledged it wasn't rude to check since we'd both received a ding.

"Damn. Delayed another two hours," Nora said as I read the same message on my app.

"My flight's delayed too. Where are you headed?" What were the odds we were on the same plane?

"Bellingham, it's north of here about—"

"I know where it is. That's my flight too. Alaska 2510," I said, showing her my text.

"Right…. Well, it looks like we're stuck here a bit longer."

Before I could stop it, my smile grew. I was glad to be stuck with her. I didn't know if she was single, but I was going to find out. "How about a drink?" I asked and nodded toward her empty coffee cup.

She assessed the bottles lining the bar and glanced at her watch. It was a few minutes after noon in Seattle. "A glass of wine wouldn't hurt."

"Nope." I raised my hand for the bartender.

"So, Nora. Why Bellingham? You from there?"

She took a deep breath, the move drawing my gaze to

her chest and the round softness there. Quickly, I looked away. Nora was not the type to put anything on display to entice. I needed to be that rancher and remember my manners.

"I'm … visiting a couple of women who are also teachers," she said. "What about you?"

"My folks have a house near there. Family Christmas."

Silence stretched a beat, and we both glanced at the TV above the bar. *Breaking News* flashed across the screen.

"How long do authorities expect I-5 to be closed?" The newscaster from the studio asked some poor intern huddled under the hood of a heavy yellow coat in the falling snow while flashing red lights in the background lit several cars turned and twisted at odd angles.

"Unfortunately, we don't know, but it looks like several hours at this point. Authorities have just issued a state of emergency and request that only emergency vehicles be out on the roads until midnight tonight. If you're somewhere safe, stay there. Back to you, Joyce."

I turned to Nora, and she was a little pale. "Are you okay?"

"What? Oh sure. Sorry. That didn't look good."

"No, it didn't." And closed highways would make renting a car useless if our flight was canceled. There went my backup plan. But that wouldn't be so bad if it meant spending more time with Nora. We could get a hotel.… Whoa. I was going too fast, as usual.

The bartender leaned in to take our order. Wine for her. Jack and Coke for me. It'd been a while since I'd had the *down-home* drink. Champagne or some over-the-top specialty single-malt scotch was the drink of choice at the social events I attended.

Silence again. "Brothers and sisters?" I asked, hoping to engage her smiles and sparkling eyes.

"Only child." She pointed at herself. "You?"

"Two younger brothers. Both work on the ranch."

The sound of bells rang loudly from the commercial on the TV above the bar.

"Favorite Christmas carol?" I asked.

She bit the inside of her lip, thinking. ""The First Noel." I sang it in a church pageant when I was in elementary school. I had to learn *all* the words." She made a stern, parental face. "My mom practiced with me daily. I was so nervous about singing in front of all those people. It's a miracle I made it through. I never did that again. How about you?"

""Carol of the Bells."" I pointed to the TV, where yet another commercial was playing it in the background. "It's beautiful when done by a cathedral choir." I squinted at the techno version currently assaulting my ears. She grinned.

"Favorite food?" I asked, keeping with the favorites game.

"Hmm." She squinted. "That's harder.... Okay, since we just met and soon, we'll go our separate ways, I'm going to tell you the truth. I try to eat healthy, but I love those Little Debbie Swiss Rolls. I've eaten them since I was a kid."

"All the foods in the world, that's your favorite?"

She sat taller. "Yep. You can eat them rolled up or peel off the chocolate coating and eat that first. You can unroll them flat and lick the cream before eating the cake. They're very versatile."

My mind flashed with a different image of licking and cream.

"What about you?" she asked.

"Me?"

"Favorite food?"

Oh, right. "Steak, of course. You can grill it, you can sear it, you can stir-fry it. Eat it with eggs for breakfast, on a salad for lunch, and with a potato for dinner. Also, very versatile."

She laughed. "Surely not all in the same day. That much red meat?"

"Well, no, but you could," I said.

"Okay." She nodded. "Major in college?"

"I didn't go to college." Her expression showed her confusion. "College isn't for everyone."

She blinked. "You're right. Of course. The world I live in, it's all about college."

"That makes sense, helping kids to do well in school so they can get in somewhere good."

She shook her head. "That was elitist of me to assume you went to college. Everyone doesn't, and that isn't a bad thing," she said. "I'm sorry. I seem to say that a lot to you." She chuckled.

I stared, taken aback. I tried to remember if Claire had ever said she was sorry, truly sorry about being wrong, even when things were good between us. All I remembered was how she never took responsibility for doing or saying something that led to a fight or hurt feelings. It had always been me. I was the asshole.

I returned to the present and the beautiful woman in front of me. "It's okay. Taking four years to go to college would have hindered my career success, not helped it. Nature of the work I do."

She smiled. This one was ... sweet. How many smiles did this woman have?

Nora was so genuine and open. Even talking about surface topics like food, felt like I was seeing a part of her she didn't reveal all the time.

I raised an eyebrow in challenge. I was taking our

conversation in a new direction. "Partner or boyfriend or husband?" I sent up a silent prayer for none of the above.

"No boyfriend. Never married. You?"

"Nah, never married either," I said. "Looking at you, I can't believe there's no boyfriend. Recent break-up?"

She leaned away as the bartender delivered our drinks. "Okay, we're getting right into it."

"Why not? You said yourself, we'll go our separate ways soon. We should break some rules. I am. I'm asking a beautiful woman to tell me about her broken heart."

"Instead of what?" she asked. "Trying to get her into bed?"

I grinned. "Something like that."

Her smile was big, and her eyes sparkled. Damn, she was pretty.

"Okay. I'm going with it. I think my only broken heart was my high school prom date, Robbie Berringer."

"He didn't stand you up, did he?" I growled, offended on her behalf. Guys could be dumbasses.

"No, he was a great date and even made it to third base that night." She winked. "But he spent the summer working at a camp for kids, then went to Purdue for engineering school while I went to the University of Minnesota, near where I grew up. It was a short romance, but still my favorite. He wore these dark-rimmed glasses, black like his hair, that he kept cut short. I never saw him take off those glasses, then at the prom after-party, he took them off, and I melted. Or possibly, it was the kiss."

"Interesting fun fact," I said, shifting in my seat. "I wear reading glasses with dark frames to prevent eye fatigue. Got 'em right here in my duffel. Say the word, and I'll put 'em on," I teased.

She chuckled. "No, that won't be necessary. What about you? Broken heart, or did you do the breaking?"

A picture of Claire flashed. Beautiful, polished, lying Claire. I glanced away.

"Oh, I'm sorry to pry. You started this line of questioning." Her words rushed out.

"You're right," I said. "A break-up."

"What happened?" Caution laced her tone, but she didn't squirm like she was used to tough questions.

I inhaled. "She left me. She wanted to be with a winner, and I wasn't winning anymore."

"How do you win at ranching?" she asked.

Oops, too much honesty. "Oh, well, ranching is hard work. There are good years and lean years. I had a tough year."

"I'm sorry. That ... well, that sucks." She took a sip of her wine.

I grinned at her words. "It did suck. It's been several months. Not a big deal anymore." I didn't miss Claire. I missed what I thought we could have been.

Nora leaned closer. "Truth. I slept with a coworker a few months ago." She shook her head. "I know. Not smart. But I work long hours and spend most of my time with the same people. He pursued me, and we had dinner, dates. I thought maybe."

She shrugged and looked down at her fingers resting on her jeans-clad thighs. "Then he let me know he couldn't see me anymore outside of work because he was committing to a relationship with another woman. *And*, to add further insult, I found out he gave two other women the same *I-can't-see-you-anymore* speech."

"He was dating four women and then picked one?"

"Well, when you say it like that, he doesn't sound quite like a massive dickhead. He sounds like the hero in that woman's Hallmark movie."

"No, no, I'm not saying what he did wasn't shitty, especially if he let you and the others think he was exclusive."

"That's the shitty part. All the other women, even *the one*, they knew about me. I didn't know about any of them. He kept me in the dark, but not the others. If I'd known about those other women, I never would have gone out with him. He knew that, so he lied. Mostly, I feel foolish. We have to see each other at work, but I'm not letting it get to me. He can fuck off."

"Absolutely right." I nudged my elbow toward her. "And don't forget. The other girl's prize was a guy who would lie, even if it hurt someone." I raised my eyebrows. "Maybe not such a prize after all."

"I agree," she said. Her voice sounded softer but even more confident somehow as her gaze met mine.

5

NORA

I liked him. I was attracted to him. The fantasy image of him wearing dark-rimmed glasses and not much else was all kinds of good. And with the way his jeans hugged solid thighs, the faded material along the bulge between them, and the slim cut of the button-down, I knew this man had a lick-worthy body.

"So, I have to ask ..." he said.

"Okay." I hesitated. I'd already admitted my dating shame.

"Can we read a little further ... in your article there? I really am curious about Estelle."

I huffed my surprise. "That wasn't what I expected."

"What did you expect?"

"I don't know. I shared my epic fail with Massive Dickhead. I didn't know where it would go from there."

"If that was your epic fail, you're doing pretty well," he said as I woke up the machine and switched to the article we'd been reading earlier. Walker rested his arm on the back of my chair and leaned in, his focus on the laptop. He straightened to look at me. "Is this okay?"

"Um, sure." I returned to the screen but couldn't ignore the heat of his body close to mine. It warmed my blood, and I had to fight a shiver. And that damn scent of his. God, he smelled good.

We had a couple more hours together in a busy airport, and then we'd go our separate ways. We were passing the time. It wasn't real. I was pretending to be a biology teacher, for heaven's sake. My heart wasn't at risk. This was a totally safe place to indulge in some *attraction* for a change.

I scrolled through the scientific article about sex, well, sexual health research, trying to keep my focus on the words and not the man next to me. Silently, we both read about the two people who'd lost their spouses and found passion and tenderness together, exploring how to make the other feel good in their present bodies with the patience and trust that came from wisdom and a lifetime of experience.

The article reported results from a study at the University of Washington in the gerontology department on the physical and emotional benefits of being sexually active later in life. Though not directly related to my proposal topic, the two women in Perry Harbor I was traveling to meet had been contributors, and I was determined to read everything I could find by them.

Walker moved back but left his arm resting on my chair. "Well, that is definitely exciting research," he said once we'd finished reading.

"It is, right? Our culture sends messages and promotes images that sex is only for the young and fit. But a healthy sex life can have many positive effects for older adults, like lower blood pressure and increased mood. Not to mention the benefits of the exercise component and getting your heart rate elevated regularly, something those sixty and older already struggle with. And the idea of being naked with someone can motivate people to eat well and stay fit."

I shook my head. "Why would we, as a culture, want to limit anyone who could benefit from the physical and emotional results of sex by promoting images that say they're too old for it? It's illogical. Healthy seniors lower costs for the rest of us with reduced Medicare spending and lower insurance costs. We should *encourage* sexual health later in life and embolden seniors to have sex, safely, of course."

Walker smiled and glanced at my mouth. "I hope you teach at an all-girls high school. If not, the boys in your biology class haven't heard a single thing after you said *healthy sex life*."

I faltered. His gaze was warm, like a touch. "I don't teach this. It's ... a hobby." My voice was soft.

"Well, I think it's a cool hobby." He straightened and moved his arm off the back of my chair. Instantly, I missed the heat of his closeness.

"What about you? Any hobbies?" I asked, searching for more solid ground.

"Twenty-year-old me would have said sexual health." He grinned. "But seriously, I like to cook."

"Really? Cooking isn't my strength. What can you make?"

He paused, rubbing strong fingers through his scruff. "Lots of things."

"Okay, what are your favorites besides steak morning, noon, and night?"

"I like brownies, my mom's recipe. That's the first thing I ever made by myself, and it always reminded me of home. I also bake a mean biscuit. You're looking at the county fair blue-ribbon winner from the Jackson Elementary 4-H club."

"Very impressive," I said. "Did you learn all your cooking skills from your mom?"

He shook his head. "She and my dad were gone a lot, traveling. So, we had a cook. Miss Del. She taught me a few things too. Then efforts to ward off hunger honed what ability I had. I'm not fancy. Sometimes a man just wants a steak. Salt and pepper. A pat of butter. No crab or blue cheese or bearnaise. A plain, rare, well-aged steak."

"And a Little Debbie Swiss Roll," I said with a nod.

"Naturally." He winked again. Damn that wink.

I had to regroup. "Your parents traveled? I guess I thought ranchers stayed on ranches."

"Ranchers do," he said. "My aunt and uncle work the ranch. Dad worked in tech. Traveled to Europe a lot. When I was fifteen, I went too. They hired a tutor, and we traveled with them. I was into karting. Have you heard of it?"

"Like go-karts?" I asked, and he nodded. "I've seen that K1 place advertised."

"It's a big deal in Europe. Outdoor tracks that are several miles long, twisting and turning."

"Your younger brothers, did they go too?"

"Nah. They stayed home with my aunt and uncle and Miss Del."

"Oh. Well, it must have been incredible for you," I said. "The food. The art. You could read about a great painting, see it in person, and then go to the museum in the artist's home."

"You like art?"

"Sure. Doesn't everyone, depending on the art? I like Van Gogh. There's a tour of his paintings in the US this year. It's the largest collection to tour outside of Europe. I was in Chicago in January and planned to see it there but couldn't. It opened at the Seattle Art Museum last weekend, but no tickets were available for the days I'm here. At this rate, *I'll* probably have to go to Europe to see my favorite paintings."

Walker nodded, a distant look in his eye. "Traveling was great. But I missed normal sometimes, my friends from home. That green grass on the other side of the fence." He smiled sheepishly.

"Well, I was pretty normal growing up, and I can't imagine it was better than Europe. Although, I wouldn't know. I've never been."

"Do you like to travel? When there aren't flight delays." He gestured his head toward the bustling concourse outside the packed bar.

"Not really. I'm a homebody, I guess. I certainly spent a lot of time at home or at the library. Bit of a study nerd growing up." I raised my hand. "The habit stuck. Comfy clothes. Quiet. A good book or a long hike. That's usually all the vacation I need." That was also all the vacation I could afford in medical school.

"I can see the appeal," he said.

"After you've been everywhere else, I guess the only place left is home."

He considered me. "Yeah ... exactly."

The conversation continued about friends, growing up with prankster younger brothers, and favorite movies. He talked about some of his trips to Europe and the things he'd seen. It almost made me want to go. Talking to him was undemanding. It wasn't like most conversations I had where one person tried to outdo or out-doctor the other. Neither of us was trying to prove we were the best and the brightest. I enjoyed it and we ordered another round of drinks as the time stretched on.

My phone rang. "It's my mom. I should take this," I said.

"Of course." Walker turned toward the bar and sipped his fresh drink.

I accepted the call and brought the phone to my ear, all while watching the profile of Walker's neck and the bob of his Adam's apple as he swallowed. Why was that so sexy? I got even more turned on.

"Mom, hi."

"Hi, honey. Checking in again. We're heading out to the villages early. We should be back in a week or so. Facetime on Christmas like usual? Celebrate your progress with GDNL?"

I winced at the mention of GDNL, remembering the disappointment in Dad's voice when I said I wasn't ready yet. I tried to hide it, hoping Walker didn't see. "Christmas, sure. Be careful. I love you."

She said a quick *I love you* and ended the call.

"Making holiday plans with your folks?" Walker asked.

"Not really. My parents are in Guatemala." Walker's eyebrows rose. "They're with Global Doctors No Limits." He nodded in recognition. "They're gone a lot. We try to Facetime for any special days, but that's about it."

"Yeah, this year is the first time in a while my family will all be together for the holidays. My folks continue to travel even though Dad retired a few years ago."

Both of our phones dinged again with a message.

Walker shifted to get his out of his pocket while I read the text in my Alaska app. "Oh, no." I looked at Walker. "Our flight to Bellingham was canceled, and the next one isn't until tomorrow. We're instructed to pick up our bags in a holding area at the end of baggage claim. We can see an agent to re-book or do it online once the credit hits our accounts."

He stretched and searched the concourse filled with worried faces. "Listen." His voice was low and husky and intensified the buzz in my core. "I'm booked in first class. That means I have access to the Alaska Lounge even when it's closed to day pass holders, which it likely is with this crowd. If you let me buy you a first-class ticket, we can both go up there and talk with those agents. The line has to be shorter, and there's free drinks and snacks."

"Oh, Walker, I can't let you do that." My inner voice screamed for me to let him if it meant more time with him, and his spicy scent wrapped around me like a hug.

"Truth. I don't want to navigate this crowd alone. With the roads closed, I think we're stuck for a while. The flight won't be that expensive. You'd be doing me a favor. Plus, there's a concierge who may be able to advise us on hotels for the night. I'm not letting you fend for yourself or sleep in this airport. We're friends. I treat my friends better than that." He grinned, and I swear I felt a rush of wetness. What the hell?

"Well …" I hedged. Could I do this? "Okay, but I'm paying you back. I'll get some cash at the first bank machine."

"Not necessary, but I don't want to take the time to fight. Let's go."

We grabbed our carry-on bags, and Walker left two hundred-dollar bills on the bar for our tab, which wasn't even close to that.

"Um, Walker, I can pay for my drinks."

"I know. But not fast enough. Come on. You can add your drinks to the amount you owe me."

"I will."

I slid off the barstool and shouldered my backpack with my laptop, chargers, and purse zipped inside.

"Excuse us," Walker said to two guys blocking our way. They parted, and he reached back, taking my hand to pull me behind him as he nodded at the men. He repeated the move at least ten more times as we maneuvered out of the restaurant and along the concourse without releasing me. I said nothing. All I felt was the way his hand was holding mine. It was warm and solid with calluses but held mine gently yet firmly. Warmth radiated up my arm, and my awareness stayed right there until Walker pulled me in front of him.

The escalator to the Alaska Lounge above the concourse was like a helicopter lifting us out of a war zone. What was I doing? I barely knew this guy. This was definitely *impulsive*.

My brain flashed with images of Walker and me twisted up in crisp hotel sheets, him touching me and kissing me with the precision he seemed to have with everything else. Had anyone ever taken the time? Not that I recalled.

"Sorry about grabbing you like that. I didn't want to lose you."

"Oh, no, I liked it. I mean, it's fine. I didn't want to lose you either." My voice was breathless. I had never heard that sound coming from my body before.

The edges of Walker's smile curled higher as our eyes met. "I liked it too."

6

WALKER

Damn, she felt good. And I was only holding her hand. I'd let go as I moved behind her on the escalator, but my arm stretched to grab the railing, essentially cradling her back to my front.

This close, her scent overwhelmed me. Something clean mixed with the smell of coconuts in her hair. Standing, I looked closer at her lower body encased in soft denim with black, low-heeled boots. She wasn't too thin. Solid thighs stretched the fabric as she stood tall. I guessed about 5'7" or 5'8".

She faced forward, and again I took in the warm, dark color of her smooth braid, the satin glow of her peachy-gold skin, and the pink flush rising from the edges of the turtleneck. I imagined pulling the edge down and pressing my lips to her hairline, along with a big inhale. I resisted the urge. Barely.

At the top of the escalator, we shifted to the side, and I held out my hand rather than grabbing for hers. It would be her choice this time.

She lifted her gaze from there to my face and smiled as

she slid her warm palm against mine. Something inside me clicked, like wooden puzzle pieces coming together.

Slowly, I pulled her closer to me as we made our way down the brightly lit hall. We joined the small line at the lounge's entrance, but I didn't let go of her hand, and she didn't pull hers away. That was a win in my book.

"If you were in first class, you could have been up here instead of down in the melee. Why did you eat at the restaurant?"

I shrugged. "I wanted a burger, and there was an empty seat next to a beautiful woman. I wasn't passing that up."

She blushed as her smile widened, highlighting straight white teeth, and I noticed a single freckle on her bottom lip. It was like a target. I wanted to bite it.

"Well, whatever the reason, I'm glad you sat there," she said. Me too.

Fuck, she was sweet, almost innocent, but not quite. She was a grown woman. Smart and strong, and confident. Passionate about her interests and ideas. Genuine. It had been a while since I met someone like her if I ever had. I'd met a lot of people who thought they were special. Nora actually was special.

"Do you see a restroom?" she asked, looking around.

"There's one in the lounge. Will that work?" I gestured to the open door as we ambled closer.

"Sure. This is swankier than what I'm used to. But again, I haven't traveled much."

We waited in companionable silence as the line inched forward. Now that I was holding her hand, I didn't have to keep her talking to be close. I could hold her there. And I was enjoying the hell out of it.

A few minutes later, a young boy about eight or nine walked past, holding his mother's hand as he glanced at me. His parents, speaking Japanese, seemed engrossed in conversation, and the boy's eyes went wide. That's when I noticed the cap on his head. Stitched on the front was the shipping company logo of our sponsor, with my car number on the bill. He was a fan.

Turning away from Nora, I slowly lifted my finger to my lips in the symbol for keeping a secret. The boy nodded and gave a wave with his small hand as his parents pulled him onto the down escalator.

Whew. That had been close. I liked Nora liking *me*, the real me, and I wanted more time with that. People usually assumed that my life in F1 was glamorous and exciting. It had been at times. But F1 was also a very small world. The same owners and sponsors and teams, year after year. That glamorous image was only that, an image. It wasn't the real me.

Reluctantly, I let go of Nora as the desk agent greeted me and checked my boarding pass on my phone. "Give her your phone, and I'll take care of this while you go to the restroom," I said and nodded my question to the agent, silently asking if Nora could go into the lounge without me.

"Of course." The woman gestured to Nora, then asked, "How can I help you today?" Her Happy Holidays reindeer pin flashed red at me, and the tinny, extravagant electro sound of a Mannheim Steamroller classic rained down from the speakers above. Usually, I might be annoyed by it, but I was enjoying this day too much to care.

"Our flight was canceled, so I need to re-book."

I flashed my phone again, and the agent typed on her keyboard.

"I had one first-class ticket, but I'd like to purchase two

for the new flight. My friend was on the same plane, so she needs to re-book as well." I handed her my card.

"I have two first-class seats available on a flight to Bellingham tomorrow mid-day. That's probably your best bet with the weather."

"Sounds good. Thank you. Um, any advice on a hotel?"

Her shoulders sagged. "Our concierge has been calling, and unfortunately, all the hotels within walking distance are booked. However, the Sounder train is running, and you should be able to catch one into downtown for more options. I recommend a reservation, though. There's a Seahawks home game tonight, and with the road closures, a lot of fans will likely opt to stay downtown for the night."

She handed me Nora's phone and a paper confirmation of our tickets for tomorrow with a bright smile and a *Happy Holidays*.

The open seating area held a massive gray sofa that twisted and curved around a large fireplace in the center of the room. Smaller seating sets and banquettes lined the back and side walls. The steam table area on the right offered soups, hot sandwiches, fruit, and other grab-and-go items near the counter, where a barista was busy making orders. Beyond that, the bar, decorated with lights and tinsel, was full, and laughter rang out. It was a happy place away from the sea of frowns on the concourse below us.

I glanced toward the restrooms and spotted Nora walking this way as she took in the rich, dark space with no frown to be seen. Her shoulders were back, and her head held high as her hips swayed with each step. Damn. That was some vision. I had a sudden urge to claim her, to kiss her. To caress her slowly and deliberately.

"How'd it go?" she asked.

"Good." I snapped out of my images. "We're all booked for a mid-day flight. Will that work for you?"

"Sure. Thanks again," she said.

"It's not too late for your meeting?"

"Oh, no. My meeting isn't until Tuesday. I was coming up a couple of days early for a change of scenery. I guess I got it."

I chuckled. "Yeah. I guess you did. Um, hotels." I noticed her swallow as she faced me. "The ones within walking distance are booked, but we can take a train into Seattle and find something there. It's early yet. If you want to grab us some snacks, I can make a few calls. Get us both a reservation."

She bit her lip and glanced at the food table. "That sounds great."

"We'll grab our checked bags and head downtown after."

She nodded and, with a sigh, dropped her backpack and coat next to my stuff at an empty spot on the long, curved sofa.

"Nora, you don't have to stick with me. If you're not comfortable," I said, picking up on her uneasiness.

"Oh, no. I'm fine." She waved a hand and walked to the food area.

She wasn't fine, but I had some work to do before I could ask her more about that. I opened my Marriott International app, typed in Seattle, and clicked a couple options before placing the call to the Platinum Elite program concierge. A few minutes later, I'd secured two king rooms at the downtown W Hotel.

When Nora returned, her relaxed confidence was back, and those baby blues brightened as she handed me a hot coffee.

"An eggnog latte sounded good to me, so I got you one

too. Holidays and all. Plus, my internal clock is always off, and my butt's dragging a little."

I resisted the urge to look at her backside. "Yeah, mine too." I accepted the warm cup and took a sip. It hadn't felt much like Christmas yet, but the sweet coffee sure tasted like it.

My body had no idea what time it was. It was the middle of the night in Monaco, and the winter afternoon dark in Seattle made it seem much later here, despite what my watch said.

Nora had brought a plate with slices of cheese and salami, a couple of fruit scones, and a few small, wrapped chocolates. "There's hot food, but I wasn't sure how long we'd be here since we have to grab our luggage."

"This is perfect. I made two reservations, so we're set."

"Great," she said, but the thing in her eyes returned, not discomfort, more like resignation.

"Nora, seriously. If you're concerned, we can go our separate ways. I enjoy being with you, and I wanted to help you, us, both of us. But if you need your space, say the word. I get it. You're a woman traveling alone. I'm a man you just met. Countless bad stories start this way."

She sipped her latte and then kept her eyes on the lid of the cup. "I enjoy being with you too, and I appreciate your help. I don't want you to feel you have to take care of me," she held my gaze, "but ..."

"But ...?"

"I'd like to stick together if *you* don't mind."

Mind? Hell no, I didn't mind. I didn't even try to hide my grin this time. "Then we'll stick together." I ran my hand through my hair and tried to act casual. Stick together with Nora? Absofuckinglutely. I felt anything but casual about that.

I'd dreaded this trip for several reasons, not least of

which was the thinking I had to do about my future. But since the lovely Nora turned that first mesmerizing smile on me, I'd barely remembered I was an F1 driver, much less that I had a career decision to make.

"THERE'S MINE. JUST THE ONE," Nora said as I pulled the reasonably sized light blue suitcase with the orange ribbon out of the pile of luggage. I'd already found my black hard-sided case about the same size. We stepped aside and showed our claim tickets to the attendant who had the unfortunate job of trying to manage the chaos of canceled flights and frustrated passengers looking for their bags stored in the large sectioned-off area. With my duffel latched on my roller bag, I gripped the handle and reached again for Nora with my other. The ache in my wrist was barely there.

Quickly, she took my hand and squeezed, like she'd done it a million times before, and we made our way through yet another throng of people. Up the escalator, across to the parking garage, and out to the walkway that signage said would take us to the elevated Sounder Light Rail Station. Nora stayed close as the falling snow and cold drifted into the semi-open breezeway.

Once on the boarding platform after buying our tickets for the turnstile, the crowd grew tight around us, and Nora huddled closer to my side. Her soft breasts brushed the back of my arm, and the pinkie finger of my hand holding hers rubbed along the fly of her jeans for a split second as she shifted to let another person into the space.

My finger twitched, and I felt her warmth. I couldn't be more than a centimeter from that sweet spot. I swallowed and tried to get a grip for the thousandth time today. This woman was getting to me fast.

In the corner, someone in a full Santa suit played a one-man-band version of "Jingle Bells" like his life depended on it. Maybe it did.

"Hang on. I'm gonna drop a bill in his bucket." I didn't want to pull out my wallet in this crowded space. That would be like asking to get it lifted. I had a couple more hundreds stored in the inside pocket of my coat for quick access, and I reluctantly let go of Nora's hand to grab one as I turned away. I squeezed through the horde as the rumble of the train sounded its arrival.

Shit. The crowd shifted tighter, pushing me and my luggage farther back and away from the train. Away from Nora.

"Walker?" Nora rose and shouted above the crush of people.

"Get on," I shouted back. "I'll board back here and meet you."

The doors opened, and the wave pushed inside, taking Nora with them while simultaneously moving me away. Shit. Shit.

The bells tolled, indicating the doors were closing. Hell no. Not without me. Spying a crease, I pushed hard and bumped into a couple of guys as I drove to the goal, the win, the checkered flag. The train car appeared packed, but I kept my eye on the prize. No mercy, exactly like the track. I wasn't letting Nora slip away from me now. Not since she said she wanted me with her.

7

NORA

I stood again on my toes, moving with but trying to see over the people pushing me into the train. Walker said he'd board the next car and find me after. But he was still on the landing. My heartbeat raced.

What the hell was happening? I was freaking out because we might get separated? I'd known the man for like five hours. We weren't Rose and Jack on the sinking *Titanic*, a movie we both liked. Mostly the second half, he said, while I preferred the first half, but it was the same movie. We had that in common and more.

My reaction wasn't logical. But then, we'd been in a sort of foxhole together. The holiday travel type of foxhole with disgruntled crowds, sweaty strangers, canceled flights, and someone seriously butchering "Jingle Bells," all backlit with colorful twinkle lights and over-produced instrumental versions of carols filling my ears, and not in a good way. All that cheer would usually make the craptastic aspects of a bad day seem worse. But then, it hadn't been so bad, and that was because of Walker.

The doors closed. I stretched and searched. I didn't

spot him on the landing anymore, but the crowd had shifted again. My phone dinged, and I pulled it from the inside pocket of my coat. Walker. Right, we exchanged numbers when he went to the restroom. God, that seemed like days ago.

Walker: Take the train to Westlake station. Then wait there. I'll find you.

That famous line from *Last of the Mohicans* flashed in my mind, and I chuckled.

Me: Are you sure you aren't trying to ditch me? [winking emoji]

Better to keep it light instead of clingy and freak him out. I wasn't sure what was going on with me and this sense of loss at being separated.

Walker: No way. Not ditching you. The sign says the next train is in fifteen minutes. Sorry about this. I'll make it up to you.

Me: Nothing to make up. It's a forty-five-minute ride. It's fine.

Walker: Not for me. I'd be holding your hand again right now if I'd made it on that train. Might even have my arm around you, pulling you closer. Protecting you from the crowd. Friendly. [big grinning emoji]

The actual smile on my face matched his grinning emoji.

Me: Nice.

Me: The crowd's not so bad. Though, everyone looks like they ate something sour, except this one kid, probably two years old. He's pressed to the window, wide-eyed as the lights fly by. It does sort of remind me of the Peter Pan ride at Disney.

Walker: Never been to Disney.

Me: What? Went to Europe but never to Disney. How is that possible?

Walker: My family took a trip. I didn't go.
Me: And that's why you hate your family now. Got it.
Walker: Ha. No, it was my choice. I had some karting stuff going on.
Me: Karting stuff? Better be some freaking good stuff. Do you ever stop and look around for a minute? Check your credit cards and keys, then realize what you're missing is a trip to Disney?
Walker: Wow, you're really into the mouse.
Me: No. It's not that. I'm surprised. All this time we've been together, most of the five hours I've known you, I assumed you had it all.

The three dots appeared as he was typing. My heartbeat thumped as I waited. Had I said something wrong? Then the dots stopped and returned a second later.

Walker: No one has it all. Not possible. Believe me. I've seen people try. My goal is to have enough.

Well, damn. My colleague Amber said that a lot, and it always made me smile, but I never had the urge to say it, too, until now. Because that statement from him, insightful, poignant ... right, it lit something inside me. My blood heated as the butterflies took flight in my stomach for real this time.

Me: And do you? Have enough?
Walker: I'm working on it. You?
Me: I'm working on it.

LEANING against a pole in the middle of the train car, I steadied myself as the lights and snow whizzed by. I was heading into Seattle for the night with a man I'd only known for a handful of hours. Impulsive, yes. Risky, maybe. But something about Walker put me at ease. And clearly, I needed to get my game face on.

When he said the word *hotel* earlier, that vision of us in rumpled white sheets had roared back into my mind, only to be doused with the offer to make *two* reservations.

He'd seen my hesitation and thought I didn't want to be with him. What I didn't want were separate rooms. And that was crazy. He. Was. A. Stranger. Sort of.

Checking my watch, I thought of Jamar. He'd asked me to call when I arrived in Perry Harbor. We were friends. We'd entertained the idea of having sex once for about thirty seconds but decided being friends was better. Honestly, I wasn't Jamar's type. He grew up with a smart, Black woman for a mother and wanted a smart, Black woman for a wife. We both knew it would only be temporary if we slept together, and friendship was more important. With the closeness of the crowded train car, I decided to text rather than call.

Me: You there?

Jamar: Watching a movie. Alone. It got up to fifty today. Winter in Nashville. So, I rode forty miles. Still working on the safest route to the Trace.

I was a hiker who sometimes biked. Jamar was a hardcore biker training to bike the entire historic and park-like Natchez Trace next fall. All 444 miles across three states from Nashville to Natchez, Mississippi.

Jamar: What's up? You make it to that island?

Me: Not yet. Snowstorm. My connection was canceled. I'm re-booked for tomorrow.

Jamar: You OK? Need something? Some company for a bit?

Me: Actually, I have some. Which is why I'm texting you.

Jamar: So, you picked up a dude along the way. Good for you, doc. Get Flores out of your head.

Me: Here's the thing. The hotels near the airport are full.

Before I could type the next bit, he replied.

Jamar: Let me guess. There's only one room, and you have to share it.

Me: Not exactly, but I can't believe you thought of that.

Jamar: You made me watch that TV movie last year. Some of the shit you watch, I don't know.

I could almost see him shaking his head.

Me: It's fantasy. It's happy. What are you watching? A documentary on space exploration?

Jamar: What do you want? Razz me about my entertainment choices?

I took a deep breath.

Me: The guy, he booked a separate hotel room for me, and I'm thinking of not using it.

Jamar: Uh huh.

Me: And I'm telling you my plans in case I turn up missing. You'll know I was last seen in a downtown Seattle hotel with a man named Walker Hewitt from Texas.

Jamar: Got it. I'll keep this text for the record. Did you Google him? Anyone with that name escape from prison recently?

Me: Of course I Googled him. There are like fifty Walker Hewitts. I skimmed the list. No top story about a jailbreak. And that's the name on his boarding pass, so it's his real name.

Jamar: Okay, I have the info. You have a good head on your shoulders. What does your gut say?

Jeez, my gut said I should rip his clothes off the first chance I got.

Me: My gut says do it. I'm not getting any bad vibes, and that's weirding me out the most. He's given me several opportunities to go my own way. My hand effing tingles when he holds it.

Jamar: He held your hand? That's some heart-eyes shit right there. I can see why you're thrown.

Jamar: But I trust you, Nora. Trust yourself. Tell him you told this big dude at home all about him and that I'll rain down terror if something happens to you. I'm an emergency medicine physician. I have a particular set of skills.

I laughed.

Me: Jamar, you're the best girlfriend I could ask for.

Jamar: That's sexist. Men care. Men have feelings. I'm not just a talented doctor with an enormous cock, Nora.

I laughed again at our regular banter. People on this train were going to stare.

Me: You're right. I'm sorry. Me, of all people, should know better.

Me: I'm gonna do it. I'm gonna spend the night with him. You have the name. I have an airline-safe can of mace in my checked bag.

Jamar: You got this.

THE WESTLAKE LIGHT rail station was under the city, out of the weather. I moved closer to the long escalators up to the street level and noticed an advertising kiosk off to the side.

Of course, it was filled with images of the Van Gogh exhibit I would never see. Meeting my parents in Chicago for a New Year's reunion hadn't gone as I'd expected. I thought we'd stop by my med school alma mater, eat at incredible ethnic restaurants, do some shopping, and I'd go to the exhibit. Maybe I'd convince them to join me.

Instead, there was a free clinic on the south side that GDNL supported, and they had volunteered us for all three days doing well-child milestone visits, key preventive care that many struggling families couldn't afford. When the choice was between preventive healthcare or food for your kid, food won every time.

I was glad I could help. It was important work. Much more important than seeing an art exhibit. Self-sacrifice is often necessary to do the right thing.

Moving to the wall near the kiosk, I leaned back to stay out of the way of coming and going passengers. I started to text Walker but had no signal in the tunnel. All I could do was wait for the next train and hope he showed.

My mind drifted over the hours I'd spent with him and the conversations, his grin and firm jaw, and how his caramel eyes sparkled like they were golden sometimes. He smelled of sweet spice and luxury and had a scar along his chin that the scruff couldn't hide. I wanted to know how he got it. I wanted to know a lot of things about him and his body.

Did he want to know me too?

His lips looked soft and warm, and I imagined tasting them. How would he kiss me? Wet and hurried or deliciously slow? Did he like his tongue sucked? Would his mouth pull me in the way his words did?

All that imagining had more heat pooling in my core as time passed. The next train arrived, and I straightened. The doors opened, and a rush of people headed for the escalator. I rose to my toes again, straining to see above the crowd. I didn't see him.

Quickly, I glanced around the station. Was there another escalator? Another side? Turning back, I suddenly found myself wrapped in a warm embrace.

"Thanks for waiting." It came out with a sigh and a rumble I heard and felt as his chest pressed into mine.

He didn't release me right away but held me to him with one arm. I had one hand on my bag, and my free arm circled his back while I breathed him in and closed my eyes. I felt him draw back to face me. "Nora."

I looked up at him and those kissable lips I'd been imagining. His gaze dropped to my mouth as he leaned in.

"Tell me to stop, and I will," he said. His warm breath caressed my face, already moving toward his.

"I'm not stopping you." I exhaled and felt the firm press of his mouth against mine.

Warmth and electricity surged through me, and I pulled him closer. He did the same and traced the seam of my lips. I opened on a moan, and he dove inside, his warm velvet tongue caressing, searching. Our tongues tangled, then I lightly sucked his.

He groaned and kissed me harder before pulling back. "Fuck, Nora." He pressed his forehead to mine, then straightened with a jerk and glanced at the people surrounding us.

Right, we were in a busy train tunnel. White twinkle lights, a hundred glittery snowflake cut-outs hanging from clear wire attached to the tunnel's ceiling, a sea of Seahawks jerseys and flags with the number twelve on them. Families with kids. Twenty-somethings hooting at us.

I grinned at him, and he laughed. "It's nice to see you again," he said.

"Yeah, it's nice to see you, too."

He grabbed my hand, "Come on," and moved to the tall escalator.

On the street, he took out his phone. "The hotel is a few blocks this way. You okay to walk? I'm not sure an Uber or a cab is happening."

I glanced down the street toward the waters of Puget Sound and saw a couple of cars inching through an intersection on a layer of packed snow.

"Walking is fine." I grabbed a knit hat out of the side pocket of my backpack and shoved it on my head, covering my ears that were left exposed by my braided hair. I zipped my coat as Walker did before he slid on a Rangers baseball cap he found in his duffel. Before he closed the bag, he pulled out a pair of gloves, and I realized I'd forgotten mine.

"Do you have gloves?" he asked.

"Oh no. It's fine." I shoved my free hand into my coat pocket.

"Here, you take one, and I'll take one." Then he grasped my bare hand with his bare hand, and I didn't even notice the cold.

Together we shuffled along the sidewalk, the snow quickly packing to ice. Most buildings had awnings that provided cover, and walking close to the walls meant clear concrete for most of my steps.

Our roller bags were less roll than drag, but we were making progress, and my hand was in his. Something I was quickly becoming attached to.

No. It was something I was enjoying for the moment. This wasn't real, and it wasn't forever. I was indulging in this surprising attraction for one night. Nothing more. Nobody had to know I did this thing *just for me*. Flirting, kissing, and hopefully a whole lot more good stuff. *Merry Christmas to me.*

8

WALKER

I liked snow. Skiing in the Alps was great. But right now, I was kinda pissed at it. If it wasn't snowing, I'd already have Nora inside the warm hotel. I would have bought her a scotch and asked her to dinner. Asked her for a lot more, if I was being honest.

But then, if it wasn't snowing, we would have boarded the same plane to Bellingham and never met. I never would have felt her soft, trusting hand in mine. Never felt the press of her curvy body or the electric touch of her lips. And when she sucked my tongue, I wanted to strip her naked right there in the station and kiss her everywhere.

It was all I could think about when I pressed my forehead to hers.

I was sorry we'd been separated, but if the time apart led to that mind-blowing kiss, I'd do it again. I'd fucking plan it.

Except for the expression on her face when the train arrived, and she was pushed inside by the crowd while I was pushed away. It stayed with me, and I wanted to make it up to her, whatever caused that worried look. I had a great idea brewing after a couple of calls and texts to the right people while the train glided along. All I needed was final confirmation. It was early, not yet six o'clock. We had all night.

The walk to the W Hotel traversed mostly level city blocks. The pitch of some streets that ran down toward the waterfront was like a ski run. I was happy to avoid them.

Every tree lining the sidewalk glowed with white lights in the falling snow. Festive displays shone from the windows of businesses, and a colorful merry-go-round spun to tinkling music in a large open space across from a cluster of brightly lit stores. Finally, this felt like Christmas.

It was strangely quiet without many cars on the roads. A smart person out in this weather in a city with these steep hills was walking. We passed restaurants and bars. Warm air and the noise of fans watching the Seahawks football game filtered out to the street with every opened door.

"Not much farther. You okay?"

Nora nodded. "I'm good. I'm getting some exercise, and these boots aren't too slippery."

No complaints, only the bright side. She hadn't complained once this entire day. Not about the delays, the flight cancelation, the crowds, or the train debacle. Nothing. Except the QR codes. That memory made me smile.

In my racing career, I'd been with countless people who demanded the best and accepted nothing less. No exceptions. They rarely complained because they rarely had anything to complain about. Today, Nora had plenty and hadn't said one negative thing.

Damn, I liked her.

Like a beacon, the tall coal-black building rose in the sky.

"This is it," I said as we stepped onto the wet concrete of the shoveled and sanded sidewalk.

A doorman greeted us, and we stomped snow from our boots on the rough outdoor mat before entering.

"You still okay? Frozen?" I asked.

"I'm good. Cold. But good." She grinned with a slight shiver as the warm air hit us.

The lobby was a burst of brightly colored chairs and wall hangings on one side, with dark windows and black marble on the other. A sleek and curved gray leather banquette hugged the bottom of an enormous gas fireplace surrounded by stainless steel panels that made up at least half of the darker wall. A large Christmas tree stood in the corner, glittering with bright lights and silver decorations that reflected all the colors around it like a prism.

It looked like an oversized living room hosting a holiday rave. It was *a lot*, but the VIP concierge for Marriott International said this place had wonderful views and great service.

Off to the right were a bar and restaurant. Thankfully, the colors were more muted in there. Maybe I *was* getting old.

Tucked to the side was the small check-in desk. A man spoke with one of the reception staff in a pleading but gentle voice while a woman I assumed was his wife stood beside him, her elbow propped on the counter, clearly exhausted and possibly worried.

"I'm sorry, Mr. Williams. The hotel is fully booked. With I-5 closed and the Seahawks game, we have nothing available."

"I see." The man glanced at the woman. "We'll find something, Hon. Or it'll be an adventure. Stay up and drink coffee in an all-night diner like when we were in school."

She returned a weak smile.

Nora stepped forward. "Mr. Williams?" The man turned.

"Hi. I'm … Nora. I couldn't help but overhear. You need a room?"

"Yes." He sighed. "My wife and I, we've called several places, and nothing is available. Our car is stuck on Seneca." He thumbed behind him.

Nora nodded, listening, encouraging him to continue.

"Our daughter-in-law had a baby last night at Swedish Hospital, not too far away. Leaving today, we took a wrong turn onto a one-way street and ended up downtown. I hit a patch of ice on the hill and slid. Fortunately, we skidded into an open side of the road, so no damage was done, but our luck ran out there. We're not getting out of the city tonight, and our son should stay with his new family. Andrea, his wife, had a rough go of it."

"I understand." Her voice was confident, almost practiced. "Um, we have a reservation for two rooms, but …" she looked back at me and raised her eyebrows in question. "We don't really need them both," she said to me, her tone carrying a hint of question.

"No," I said, surprised and not entirely smooth. "No, we don't."

"Your name, sir?" the reception manager asked.

"Walker Hewitt," I said, lowering my voice. No one here knew who I was, but old habits.

The manager tapped on the keyboard in front of her. "Yes, Mr. Hewitt. Um. Of course." I could always tell when someone realized my family's wealth or the status it bought me. She'd seen my Platinum Elite account listed with the reservation, a mark reserved for celebrities, billionaires, world leaders, and the like. It meant extravagant special treatment and the restraint necessary to maintain my privacy. "Yes. We have your rooms ready for you."

I nodded at Nora and her sparkling baby blues that had me hoping. If she wanted to share a room with me, I was ready to go.

"We'll only take one of those rooms," Nora said. "That leaves the other available."

"Please register it to Mr. Williams," I added. "And leave it on my card. He and his wife are my guests."

"Of course, Mr. Hewitt," the manager said.

Mr. Williams sputtered in surprise. "Son, I can't let you do that. We can pay. I'm grateful you would help us like this." His wife stood straight, her eyes wide, her hand over her heart.

"It's my pleasure, sir." I leaned in. "I paid for the room mostly with points," I lied. "It's not a big deal. Have a nice dinner. Celebrate. Congratulations on your new grandchild."

Mr. Williams shook my hand, his expression telegraphing his sincerity. "Thank you. Really. Thank you."

"You're welcome. Happy Holidays." I nodded.

"Happy Holidays," they said in unison.

The manager had been whispering to her colleague. No doubt explaining my status and getting Mr. and Mrs. Williams set up in our extra room. *Our* extra room.

"Here are your key cards to the corner suite," she said. "Information and Wi-Fi logins are all listed there. If you require anything additional, as you know, please call. We're at your service."

"Thank you." I turned to Nora, who was beaming now. Yeah, I knew that feeling. Taking her hand, we strolled toward the elevators.

"Thanks for your suggestion," I said. "But what if I snore or hog the covers?"

She grinned. "What if I do?"

THE BLACK, heavy door whooshed closed as we entered the spacious suite and removed our coats.

"Oh. Wow. Walker, look at this." Nora rushed across the large sitting area and squeezed between the sleek desk and table to get closer to the far window. She stood, looking out at the sparkling lights and the city streets twenty-four floors below. Colorful lights decorated the tops of cranes on nearby buildings under construction or made out the shape of a shining star atop one of the other skyscrapers.

"And here." She rushed into the bedroom area where more lights winked from more tall buildings. "This is incredible." Like a wide-eyed kid, she brushed past me and into the ensuite, then gasped. "This tub. It has a view. I'm taking a bath later. *That* is happening."

I chuckled. Anything she wanted, that's what would happen tonight. More kissing and more touching, yes. More of her skin and her hair down around her shoulders, God, yes. I wanted slow *and* fast with Nora. F1 races weren't all a straightaway at 200 miles per hour. There were twists and corners. You slowed, changed the pace, and I wanted that tonight with her.

She had suggested we share a room. She held my hand and kissed me with her whole body. I had every reason to believe she and I wanted the same thing tonight, but I needed to hear her say it. The sitting area held a large sectional sofa, and I took a seat, realizing I hadn't sat down since the airport.

"Hey, Nora."

She appeared from around the corner, her leather

boots already off and her feet now sporting the bright white slippers provided by the hotel.

I grinned as I gestured to the sofa. "Come sit for a minute."

"Sure." She strolled across the room and sat with an exhale at the opposite end. "Oh, that feels good."

The breathiness of her voice and the words about feeling good went straight to my dick. Not now, buddy.

"Listen, we didn't really talk about this. I want you to be comfortable. I can sleep on the sofa. Say the word."

She smiled. This one was new. This one was ... sexy as hell, and she had a hungry gleam in her eyes. She crawled across the cushions. Damn. That little move would not help my dick situation.

"What word is that?" she asked, her voice barely more than a whisper and her mouth inches from mine. "I want to know because I don't want to say it accidentally."

"Nora," I pleaded. "I'm trying to be the good guy here, and you are making it har—um, difficult."

She snickered and sat back, though I could still smell the coconut in her hair and see the faint blush rising on her cheek.

"Okay. I did push this on you." She schooled her features and passed a hand over her braid. "But with the kiss, I thought—"

"Wait. First, I'm happy about this. I hope you let me sleep in that bed with you, wrap you in my arms, and kiss you again, possibly more, but I'm not expecting it. I enjoy spending time with you. This is the best canceled flight scenario I could've imagined. But you don't owe me anything and are safe with me."

"I believe you. Look, I'm a smart woman. I know this is impulsive, and I never do anything impulsive. I'm intentional and specific, and calculated. Always." I could relate.

"This night with you is like an unexpected free pass. A chance to do something different for a few hours. You've had opportunities to set off my creep radar, and you haven't. So, how about we don't decide sleeping arrangements right this second?" she suggested as her stomach growled. She covered her mouth with a laugh. "Clearly, I need to eat."

I paused and noticed the silver in her blue eyes near the pupil and her skin flush from the cold air. Definitely the best canceled flight scenario. And a chance to be someone different for a while sounded perfect.

My real life, my priorities, my career choices, would all be waiting for me on the other side of whatever this was.

My phone dinged with an incoming text, and I did a quick check. It was the confirmation I'd been hoping for in my plan to do something nice for Nora.

I stood and reached out a hand. "Come on. Let's get settled and then head out for some food."

9

NORA

As we rolled our bags into the open bedroom, Walker handed me one of the two large water bottles from the minibar. Pausing, I gulped down a long swallow. I was dehydrated. It was a familiar feeling. Every day in Emergency Medicine wasn't crazy, but on some shifts, I barely had time to pee, much less eat or drink.

Walker grabbed a dark wooden luggage rack and set it on the side of the room. "Is this okay?"

"Oh, sure." Then, before I could lift my bag, he'd placed it on the rack and did the same for himself on another one. God, it was sexy how he took care of me.

In the enormous bathroom, I washed off the remnants of my morning makeup and reapplied, keeping the look natural. I changed out of my thin red sweater and into a heavier one. A weave of tans, browns, and creams in a chunky loop highlighted the pale gold undertone of my skin. It was another turtleneck, but it was loose and bulky, inviting me to snuggle into it.

I smoothed along my thick braid and tucked a couple rogue strands back into the pattern. I had a love-hate relationship with my hair. It was coarse and heavy, requiring special products and over an hour to blow dry. Such a waste of electricity; I rarely did it, usually opting for the French braid. But it didn't frizz or break and tended to stay sleek and straight when it was down without too much effort.

Back in the bedroom, I noticed Walker had slipped on a navy sweater over his dark blue untucked button-down, which added to his sophisticated masculine vibe, even with the muted blue-gray Adidas sneakers he was wearing now. They were probably better in the snow than those alligator boots.

"You look ... great," I said and quickly turned to lay my discarded red turtleneck on my open suitcase.

"You too," he said and rubbed his chin. "I'm thinking about shaving."

I stared at his lips set against the dark scruff of his way-past-five o'clock shadow and slowly shook my head, wondering again what it would feel like against my skin, except this time it wasn't my breasts, it was my thighs.

When I met his gaze, something deeper smoldered there. "If you want me to feed you, hell, if you want me to let you out of this room before morning, you can't look at me like that."

I peered down at my feet and bit my lip to hold back the smile. Imagine that. Me. Dr. Nora Reynolds. Studious, boring, easy-going, smart girl tempting the kind, generous, hot as hell, rich guy. Miracles never ceased.

He moved closer and lifted my chin with a finger. Holding my gaze, he brushed his thumb below and pulled my lip free as he leaned in to take my mouth in a gentle but all-consuming kiss.

Well, damn.

. . .

Dressed more warmly, a walk in the city sounded lovely. The air carried the smell of seawater and cold. Walker had called the concierge for restaurant recommendations while I had been changing, and we set out, deciding to choose in the moment when we found the right one.

The snow had stopped, but my weather app said more was on the way. This was a brief reprieve, like the eye of the storm. The muffled sound of tires on packed powder occasionally broke the silence. The city seemed deserted yet filled with lights and color and quiet just for us, except for the occasional *Sea ... Hawks* chant coming from a bar.

Walker held my hand and kept me close, our frozen breath mingling in front of us as we passed the symphony hall.

"The first place they recommended is there," he said, pointing across the street to a cream-colored building. It had large windows framed in black, and warm light poured out to the sidewalk, pushing back the frosty night. "It's Pan-Asian. A specialty here. Good wine list too. What do you think?"

"Sounds great. I've never been to the West Coast. I want to soak up what I can."

Walker's expression was all joy as he pulled me tighter to his side in the middle of the crosswalk.

The door opened, and the warm aroma of spice and meat hit my nose. My stomach rumbled.

"Down tiger. Let's get you fed." Walker turned to the host and spoke.

"We don't have a table, but I could seat you at the kitchen bar right away." He pointed toward a large semi-circle near the bustling area in the back.

Walker raised his brows at me, and I nodded. I'd sit anywhere I could eat something flavored like the tantalizing scents filling the air.

At our seats, we shook off our coats and placed them on the chair-backs.

"I hope I'm dressed okay," I said as I sat.

Walker slid into the seat next to me, his body moving with such precision and calm. It was so damn hot. Doctors were precise and at least calm on the outside. But it was different on Walker, and it worked for me.

"You're perfect," he said, and I felt the blush warm across my skin, still cold from our walk. "Plus, I think everything is casual here." He was right. A handful of glamorous-looking couples were scattered throughout the restaurant, most of them older, but everyone else was dressed like Walker and me. Weather appropriate.

"This is nice. I can see the action in the kitchen," I said.

"It is nice." Walker shifted closer and placed his hand on my knee, his expression warm and tentative. It was the first intentional contact *below the belt*.

I gave him my best attempt at an inviting look and pulled his hand higher on my thigh. Nothing indecent, but enough to send the signal that I wanted him to touch me. The sexual energy pinging between us since that kiss had me practically vibrating.

Never before had a man affected me like this, and I was not wasting it. A free night with no rules and no regrets.

Walker's expression didn't falter, though that golden spark in his eyes shone brighter as he gently squeezed my flesh under his palm. Yeah, I liked this seating arrangement for several reasons.

The service and the food were wonderful, and the wine was almost as intoxicating as the man next to me. We started with the lettuce cups. The flavors of salty dried fish, sweet chili, and tamarind combined perfectly with the crunch of jicama and peanuts and the bright, fresh lime and cilantro. I moaned at the first bite.

Walker's eyes blazed, but he didn't make a sound. He calmly made his own lettuce cup combination and popped it into his mouth.

All the food was equally moan-worthy. We decided on two specialty dishes, roasted duck and seven-flavor beef. Sampling a bit from each other's plate, I wondered how it would be to have more dinners and days like this with Walker. His easy smile and gentle hand.

It would be wonderful, that's what. For a moment, I was jealous of the lucky woman who would capture his heart and get to keep him. It couldn't be me, so I planned to make this night, this time-out from reality, my every fantasy.

I was pleasantly full, and the memory of the delicious flavors lingered. Walker topped off each of our wineglasses with the last of the silky red blend the waiter had recommended.

"I don't think I have room for dessert. Those chocolates in the minibar are about all I can handle," I said, patting my stomach.

Walker leaned close and placed his hand back on my thigh. "We can do better than that." He'd squeezed my leg several times during dinner. Or he'd slid his palm along my jeans-clad thigh, inching a bit higher each time he paused for a sip of wine. I was buzzing with anticipation. Share a bed? Hell yes.

Walker asked for the check and handed his card to the waiter with the request.

"I can pay my part," I said.

He shook his head. "No, this is a date. I'm sorry I didn't make that clear. I'm paying for dinner, babe."

Babe. Gah. Why did that one word, whispered seductively and low, make me want to straddle him in his chair, grinding until this fire in my blood settled?

Back out onto the street, Walker again took my hand. "You mind if we walk this way?" He nodded in the opposite direction of our hotel and the big cushy bed I wanted to be in with him, not sleeping. My internal clock was still on nights, and I was more awake now than I'd been at noon.

"No, I could use a walk after that meal."

"The hotel said with the football stadium nearby, and the holiday, there would likely be a few shops open at Pike Place Market. I thought we could check it out."

The hotel was correct. The Market was only open in the daytime, the stalls now empty with deep green canvas pulled over the bins and shelves. But several stores close by were lit with bright lights. The famous neon red Pike Place Market sign split any remaining darkness. I snapped a photo, and a man approached.

"I could take one of the both of you?" he said. I raised my brows at Walker in question. Would it be okay to have a record of this night? This break from our real lives.

"Thanks, that'd be great," Walker said, and I handed my phone to the man. He stepped back and to the side, looking in the distance, and for a moment, I was worried that was the last time I'd see the pricey device. But then he studied us a bit before he started shooting, some with flash, some without. His companion, a tall, thin man with the bluest eyes on the planet, stood nearby, grinning at us.

"Thank you," I said as the man handed back my phone.

"Happy Holidays." He waved and walked toward his friend.

I opened the pictures. They. Were. Awesome. Unbelievable. WTF?

I jogged to catch up with the couple. "These pictures, they're incredible."

"Thank you," the man said. "You're great subjects. The energy between you two, that's what you see in the photos. That's all you. I just captured it."

I was stunned. "Merry ... Merry Christmas," I said, awestruck at the man's words.

"Merry Christmas." He nodded and took the hand of the other man, who snuggled close, and they turned to walk up the hill.

"Oh my gosh, Walker." I showed him my phone and flipped through the shots, about ten of them, the next more beautiful than the one before. Light reflected in our eyes. Crisp, clean snow at the street's edges. The deep grayish blue of the night sky behind us. The smile and face of the man beside me. Wow. I shared all of them to Walker's number.

Near the entrance to the Market and the stall where they threw the fish, delighting tourists as I'd seen on some Travel Channel show, there was an Italian grocery. "I need to run in for a second," Walker said and gestured toward the door.

I paused. "You go ahead. I'll meet you there." I nodded to the newsstand at the end of the covered corridor.

Every magazine imaginable was tucked into rows of shelves and held in place by a thin wire stretched across the length, so the edges flapped in the frigid breeze.

Magazines had always been a treat, an extravagance. Growing up, I studied daily and took extra prep classes in the summer. Reading for entertainment wasn't something I had time for. With the help of my more worldly roommates in college, I'd discovered I rather liked reading a magazine now and then. I perused the headlines, which were always the same.

"Ready?" The deep timber of his voice rolled across my skin a while later.

"What did you get?" I asked.

"Another bottle of that wine we had with dinner and some very rich Italian chocolates I like."

Mmm. "Perfect," I said and melted against him. The handled brown paper bag in his hands crunched between our legs.

We headed back to the hotel. A different route along First Avenue. Walker turned to cross the street, up a hill toward our hotel. The Seattle Art Museum and a huge banner announcing the Van Gogh exhibit were on the corner.

10

WALKER

Nora sighed next to me as she eyed the sign for the art exhibit. I hoped she didn't notice the Hewitt Family Foundation logo on the banner's edge. The foundation gave a shit-ton of money and expected prominent placement as a named sponsor in every city the show toured, but I wished the name was smaller right now.

"Let's see if we can go in." I pulled Nora away from the sign and started up the sidewalk beside the museum.

"I wish. It's obviously closed," she said, a slight sag in her shoulders that I didn't like.

"We could ask."

She looked at me like I told her I could fly. By some definitions, I could.

"Ask who? It's completely dark in there."

"We can ask security," I said with a nonchalant shrug.

"Walk up to the door and say, *hey, I know you're closed, but could we come in any way? We won't steal anything.* They'll call the cops."

"Maybe not. Look at where we are. This town is filled with over-the-top tech people. We couldn't be the first to ask." Plenty of over-the-top people in F1 asked for the moon and usually got it.

"I don't see any security staff," she said, peering through the tall, darkened windows to the museum's lobby stairs.

"Yeah, me neither." I had to get her to Second Avenue. That was the door where they were expecting us. "There." I pointed. "Delivery entrance and loading dock. I bet that's where they are."

"Walker, you're nuts."

"No, I'm persuasive." I gave her the side eye.

"Right." She chuckled.

"Come on. What does it hurt to ask? You stay here, under the awning, out of the wind. I'll do the asking."

"Fine. But I have no bail money if you get arrested." She shoved her hands in her coat pockets and leaned against the cold stone wall by the loading dock side door marked Employee Entrance.

I knocked and gave the guard my name and ID first thing. He nodded in recognition. His name was Clint. The Museum Director's personal assistant told me when she texted earlier to confirm we were all set for a private show tonight. I'm glad she did. Nora crawling across the sofa in the hotel room almost made me chuck the entire plan and make it up to her with my mouth on her body. I still intended to do that if she'd let me.

Clint introduced me to the other guard on duty, Jasmine, and their supervisor, Tony, who'd stayed way past the end of his shift to help me out.

"Thanks for the steaks," Tony said. "The Capital Grille always does them right. Even takeout."

"You're welcome. I'm glad you enjoyed it. Buying you all a nice dinner was the least I could do."

"No problem. When Marilyn called and said one of

the show's signature sponsors was coming for a private tour, I figured it was a good chance to catch up on end-of-the-year paperwork. Museum's closed Mondays so I can sleep in tomorrow. Plus, this way, I probably won't have to work between Christmas and New Year's. That'll make the wife happy," he said.

I had several hundred-dollar bills in my pocket that I hoped would make all their partners even happier.

"Well, thanks for staying to help me surprise my girl. She has no idea. Actually, she thinks you guys are calling the cops right now."

The guards chuckled.

"Okay. I think we've made her wait a believable amount of time. You all good with the plan?"

Three heads nodded. "We don't know you. I was here working late anyway, and you talked us into it," Tony said.

I grinned. "Right."

"I hope your girl buys it. We'd never do this if your family hadn't been a key sponsor. Marilyn and the museum board would fire us all."

"I'm banking on her excitement about the exhibit interfering with her sound judgment."

"We're in," I said, returning to Nora, huddled against the building.

"What? You're kidding me." Nora's eyes rounded in surprise.

"Nope. Never underestimate the power of holiday miracles." I grinned. "There are rules, though. We're restricted to the special exhibition hall where the Van Gogh thing is, and a guard has to walk with us. The supervisor was here, working late for the end of the year, and he agreed since, technically, they have extra staff on site."

"Are you serious?" She placed her hand on her heart.

"Yep."

"So, I'm going to see the exhibit?" Her eyes sparkled, and, at that moment, I would have given any amount of money to make this possible.

"You are. If you hurry. Let's get in there before they change their minds. The security cameras will record us. Can't do anything about that. But if we don't cause a problem, no one will have a reason to check the footage. Plus, I slipped them a few bucks."

"Walker, a bribe?"

"No, a gift. The supervisor has a family. Wants to splurge this year. Now he can."

"What if he gets fired?" she asked, stopping in her tracks.

"He's the supervisor. No one's getting fired." I knocked again, and the guard, Clint, let us both in. The expression on Nora's face was a mix of excitement and unease.

"Welcome," Tony said in greeting, probably wanting to soothe that look as much as I did. "This is highly unusual. But ... it's the holidays, and your boyfriend said you were a huge fan and had missed the show in Chicago. He said you'd follow all our rules."

Nora nodded. No reaction to the word *boyfriend*. "Absolutely. We will. I don't know what to say." Her words came fast.

"Happy Holidays," Tony said.

"Happy Holidays." She beamed.

SLOWLY, Nora walked the cavernous space of tall, clean white walls and honey-colored hardwood floors that clacked lightly under her boots. Clutching my hand, she read each placard by every painting, occasionally adding stories I didn't know. Van Gogh suffered from mental illness with debilitating symptoms and spent time in institutions. The paintings made during those years differed from the others. Nora pointed out the changes in the colors and strokes.

The shapes, the light he painted, the composition of darkness or brightness reflected his internal state. It wasn't merely swirls and lines that sold for millions at auction. They were the story of a talented man who loved and suffered and ultimately took his own life from a suspected broken heart.

"Experts believe he was color blind. That's why the colors he used were so bold. He needed the vivid contrast so he could see the differences in shade and shapes," Nora said, shaking her head.

She was beautiful. Her expression was thoughtful, and a slim finger rested against her delicious lips as she considered each painting. Reverence. That was what she showed for each one.

Clint, who had walked the space with us, and I exchanged looks as Nora treated it like a church. No way she'd ever do anything to harm this work. I think she'd die first; he saw it as well as I did.

"Oh. My. God. Walker! That was ... I don't know what that was. Can you feel it? Aren't you more alive ... having seen all that beauty? God, I am." She giggled, then covered her face with her hands like she was holding in the visions filling her mind.

I'd seen plenty of famous art in Europe, but never that way. Not even close.

"Thank you." It came out with her breath on an exhale. She clutched my hand as if it was the only thing tethering her to earth.

The snow started again, gentle flakes floating down like

calm as we stood on the sidewalk outside the museum after almost two hours spent looking and reading and considering. Nora closed her eyes and lifted her smiling face to the sky. Her expression was quiet, tranquil, and satisfied with life.

I'd made that happen for her; it was better than a race win.

Nora turned to me. "Thank you, Walker."

"You're welcome," I said, and then she kissed me. Sweet at first, but it soon changed to hands grasping and clutching to get closer, breath pumping into the night air.

"Walker?"

"Yes, Nora," I exhaled.

"Take me back to the hotel. Show me something else beautiful and full of life."

11

NORA

"Let me take a quick shower, then you can have that bath you mentioned," Walker said, guiding me into the suite. With the room still dark, all that was visible were the twinkling lights of the city outside, like we were floating above it.

I *was* floating, buzzing with energy from seeing that breathtaking art. Paintings I'd only ever read about or seen on postcards. I couldn't believe he'd done that for me. Noticed what I wanted and somehow made it happen. No one else had done that for me in years, maybe decades, not even my parents.

I would thank him with my entire body. One *miraculous* night.

Walker flipped on the light near the sofa. I didn't want a bath. I wanted to feel him next to me, hear his voice in my ear, touch him, kiss him. But it had been a long day, some of it on a plane. A soak would be good for me and help to settle my nerves about what I hoped would be hours ahead of us.

He stood close and cupped my jaw with his tender

palm as he gazed at me. "There's no hurry, Nora. We have all night. Take your time. If you let me touch you the way I've been thinking about, I want you completely relaxed for it."

Oh. My. "That sounds wonderful." My breath whooshed out on an exhale, and his grin was lazy and suggestive before he brushed a soft, sweet kiss across my lips.

"Start relaxing. I'll be quick, and it'll be the last thing that happens quickly tonight," he said, then turned with a wink.

I swallowed. So. Damn. Sexy.

Ten minutes later, I spun from the window at the sound of an opening door and spotted Walker by the bed wearing nothing but a towel, the relief map of his chest and abs on full display in the bedside lamplight. I had sat mesmerized by the snow and the lights and the unbelievably lucky man who got me into that exhibit and thought about how he was about to get luckier.

Seeing him there, clean and wet, muscles shifting and bunching, I knew we were both getting lucky. I stood from the sofa and moved closer. He looked up, and I heard water running in the bathroom.

"I started your bath," he said.

"You did?" My voice was breathless. All the things he'd done for me today. And now this. I thought I'd melt into a puddle right there. Who was this guy? No one had ever treated me this way, like I was his world, even if for only a night.

"I didn't add anything to the water," he said. His voice stirred me as he moved closer. I inhaled his clean, masculine scent and tried not to ogle his fine form. "Take your time. I'll open the wine and let it breathe."

"Will you bring me a glass when it's ready?" I asked, telegraphing my permission.

His Adam's apple bobbed. "Absolutely."

I practically floated into the bathroom, holding a pair of pajamas and the sexiest underwear I had. It was a lacy, cheeky style in a pale cream I wore with leggings. Most of my other stuff was built for comfort. No time to deal with ill-fitting undies in the ER.

I checked the water temperature and examined the sample bottles of products on the nearby ledge. Bath salts were my usual, and the hotel's were scented with sweet birch and lavender, which I loved. I wasn't a bubble bath girl; too soapy on my skin. Without bubbles, Walker would see my body when he brought in the wine.

No rules. No regrets.

I added the salts to the swirling water and undressed. When the tub was full, I lowered the lights to a soft twilight with the slider switch nearby and sunk into the steam. Resting my head against the curve of the tub, I peered out into the dark sky. Lights from taller skyscrapers shimmered above like stars. It was mystical and serene. I was a million miles away from emergency medicine, Dr. Flores, and the competition for grant dollars.

I released a deep breath. Walker wanted me to relax, but the images of him shirtless flashing through my head were anything but relaxing. I imagined his breath across my skin, his muscled chest hovering over mine, and the sweet pressure and stretch of taking him inside me. My hands moved on their own, stroking and gliding across my skin the way I yearned for Walker's to do.

"Nora?" The light knock brought me out of my fantasy.

No regrets.

"Come in if you have wine." I hoped my tease would hide the flutter in my voice.

The door opened, and Walker entered wearing navy and black plaid pajama bottoms slung low and his version of the hot as fuck, dark-rimmed glasses.

"Nice glasses," I said, trying not to drool at the picture before me.

He winked as he approached. "I brought your wine." His stare shifted to the edge of the tub and the lack of bubbles, leaving my body open to his gaze. "Tell me to stop, and I will."

"Not stopping you." I stared up as he came close and lowered the glass to me.

His gaze roamed like a caress. My skin flushed from the heat of the water, plus the heat in his eyes as he spoke. "You're beautiful." His tone was laced with something that sounded a little like awe.

After years of changing clothes in front of men and women alike in the locker room, I'd mostly worked the instinct to cover myself out of my system. But this was different, and I had to resist the long-gone urge.

Stepping to the side, he reached for one of the fluffy hand towels and unrolled the tight bundle. He re-rolled it more loosely and bent over me. "Lift your head."

I sat forward, shifting the water at my breasts.

"Lie back," he said, and when I did, my neck came to rest on the cushion of the fluffy cloth.

He held my braid out of the way. "Do you take this out at night?" he asked, sitting on the deep edge of the tub near my head. His gaze returned to roaming my body.

"I do. Usually the last thing. My hair is unruly, especially after brushing."

"Unruly, huh? I'd like to see that." He slid the braided tail between his fingers as his eyes met mine, the caramel color of his now darker in the dim light. "May I?" he asked.

I swallowed. "Sure."

"Where's your brush?"

"You want to brush my hair?"

"Yeah, if that's not weird. I've been eyeing it all day, wondering what it would be like to run my hands through it."

"All day?" I was a little breathless.

He leaned close. "Yes, Nora. All day." His voice was low and rumbled deep in his chest.

That sizzle in my core overtook my shyness about being naked with him.

"It's ... there. It's in my blue toiletry bag," I stammered. My blood simmered, my nipples pebbled, and my sex pulsed. The man had barely touched me. Wow.

Walker returned to his seat on the ledge. He lifted my braid and removed the elastic at the end as I shifted, angling my body to give him better access. Slowly and gently, he unwound my hair. When he reached the part near my skin, he let his fingers sink deeper to massage my scalp as he worked.

A moan escaped my throat. "God, that feels good."

"I agree," he said, smoothing the brush down while I melted. This man was going to ruin me for all others. If he fucked me the way he touched me, the outcome would be nothing other than total ruination. And I couldn't bring myself to care.

His long fingers, calloused and rough, were tender as he separated the heavy mass into pieces rather than attacking it all at once, as I'd expected. He knew what he was doing. Maybe an old girlfriend had similar hair. I ignored the edge of jealousy. No room for that now. There was only tonight. And tonight, he was mine.

"How did you learn to brush thick hair?"

"If I tell you ... you have to promise not to take it wrong," he said.

"Old girlfriend?"

He chuckled. "No. Growing up in Austin and working on the ranch with my uncle, my job was to braid the horses' tails. It helped to keep them from getting knotted with burrs, prickly little balls they pick up in the tall grass that were a bitch to remove. I was the oldest and knew best how to not get kicked by the horse. And I liked doing the braids. It relaxed me. I'm not sure why. I never wanted to be a hairdresser or anything, but I could see the appeal."

"Is brushing my hair relaxing you?"

"In some parts of my body. Others, not so much." I heard his grin, and then the quiet stretched between us as I soaked in his caring touch along with the warm water.

"I should let you finish in here and drink your wine." He stood and set the brush back on the counter by my bag. Precision.

"Thank you, Walker. That was ... wonderful." I brushed a loose lock behind my ear, and he slipped out the door with a wink.

12

WALKER

I snicked the bathroom door closed behind me and exhaled. Fuck. Me. She was gorgeous. Her breasts were full and topped by sweet, pink buds. Her waist rounded out to her hips, bracketing that small patch of dark curls at the apex of her firm thighs. And her hair. She'd been a goddamn vision with it flowing around her shoulders, nearly grazing the top of the water. She was smart and fun, lush and beautiful, and all mine for the night.

I couldn't believe I had told the story about the horses and my childhood. But she didn't seem to get upset, and it had been relaxing to glide my fingers through the silky strands and breathe in the coconut scent. A man could get used to that. This man could.

Would someone like Nora, who was real and beautiful and easy to be with, ever choose me? Not the flashy F1 driver who could show her the world, but the Texas rancher who would love her with everything in him.

There would be competition. Men everywhere must fall at her feet. She was exceptional and deserved the same. I'd been exceptional once, confident I'd win the girl or the successful driver would. But there was a *very good chance* I'd never be that driver again. I needed to make tonight exceptional.

Earlier, while she soaked, I opened the wine, turned down the sheets, and pulled up an old playlist on my phone, which I plugged into the portable speaker in the room. Music, sedate and low, hung in the background. I called the front desk to confirm a late checkout, in case we slept in, and found condoms in my suitcase from a trip several months ago.

When I was younger and dumber, I'd gotten around plenty. But not anymore. I was always careful with my health and got checked regularly to be sure I was keeping my partners and me as safe as possible. But those appointments had slowed in the last year or two. I'd been committed to Claire. After her, I tried to ease the loneliness with another, but it never worked. I quit trying. Nora was the first woman I'd wanted to worship in a while.

Sitting back against the headboard, I grabbed the tiny bottle of lotion I'd snagged from the bathroom earlier and rubbed half of it into my rough hands. I wanted them to be gentle on her skin like Estelle's retired landscaper turned lover from the article today.

A bit later, Nora opened the door and stepped out wearing a silky pink tank top that didn't hide her peaked nipples and pink flannel pants that looked worn and soft. I grinned at her from where I sat, filing my nails. The single nail file had been in an emergency travel essentials case one of Dad's personal assistants gave me years ago. I didn't think it was an emergency essential, but I'd been wrong.

Nora licked her hypnotic lips, and her eyes sparkled. "Such sexy glasses. What are you doing?"

"Preparing for you. Thinking about how I get to be the man to touch you and make you feel good tonight."

She didn't look away but silently walked across the room to my side of the bed and set her almost empty wineglass on the bedside table. "What do you need from me?" she asked.

"For you to let me."

She took the file from me and placed it next to her glass. Then she removed my glasses before smoothing her hand down my chest.

I threaded my fingers through hers and pulled her on top of me. With one arm cradling her against me, I rolled us. My dick, hard and eager, nestled between her legs.

"Is that a yes?" I asked from above her.

"Yes," she whispered as she lifted her lips to mine, encouraging me.

"This could take a while," I said.

"God, I hope so." She moaned, and I smiled. Making her come was going to be fun.

Her kiss was slow at first but morphed quickly into something hungry. I met her bite for bite and suck for suck as her hands clutched my back and pulled me tighter between her parted thighs.

Cupping her face, I held her as I nipped and kissed her neck, surrounded by the sweet scent of her hair and her skin. Her chest pumped as her breathing grew rapid. I wanted her relaxed. I read once that a woman orgasmed strongest when she was completely relaxed before the build, and something about Nora told me she needed a great orgasm if anyone did.

I kissed along her collarbone and dipped my tongue into the hollow of her shoulder. "Relax, babe. Deep breaths."

Her movements slowed as she tried to slow her breathing.

"That's it, good," I said, kissing across her chest to her other collarbone, lavishing it with the same treatment.

"If my stubble is too rough, tell me. I'll shave."

"Say the word?" she asked, her tone mocking, but her fingers caressed my cheeks as she stared at my mouth.

"That's right. I want to take my time, kiss you and taste you, and I want it to feel good, not rough." I paused. "Unless you like it rough. Do you?" I raised my eyebrows, realizing I didn't know what she liked.

"No. No, I think I'd like it slow if you want to show me."

"No one's ever fucked you slowly, Sweetheart?"

She shook her head. "Not like I think you're going to do." Her voice was hushed, unbelieving, but I would show her she was right.

I rarely got to go slow. All the women before Nora knew I was a driver. Someone who pushed limits with speed and danger and control. They wanted me to fuck them that way, too. Fast and hard and dangerous.

Then, I realized I drove fast and dangerous. I didn't really want to fuck that way. But expectations and performance were part of my life, and I didn't disappoint. Tonight, with Nora and the lack of those expectations, I planned to go very slowly.

I rolled off her to my side. "Can I take this off?" I asked as I toyed with the edge of her silky top. Nora wiggled, helping me inch the fabric up before she lifted her arms for me to pull it clear. With another brief kiss on her lips, I rose to see her head resting on the pillow, her thick, dark hair fanned around her, and her skin pale in the low light.

"So beautiful," I whispered. My fingers smoothed along her neck. "So soft."

I leaned in, my mouth following my fingers as I

touched and teased the sweet valley between her breasts, then cupping them and testing their weight in my palm. My thumb ghosted across her nipple, barely scraping the delicate pink, and she sighed.

"Do you like that?"

"Yes." She arched toward me, and I lowered to take her in. "God, yes," she said and combed her fingers through the short hair on the back of my head.

Electricity buzzed through my body from that one touch. I needed to pace myself. She felt too damn good.

13

NORA

I was on fire, but it wasn't a blaze. It was more like coals glowing orange after the flame died down. Those coals were much hotter but looked innocent and peaceful on the surface.

That was Walker. His gentle hands caressed while his lips and teeth teased one nipple and then the other. The deliberate slowness had my blood roaring in my veins. I was already climbing. After the looks he gave me, my imaginings in the tub, and the feel of him brushing my hair, something so intimate and tender, it was no surprise the reality of his touch on my skin overwhelmed me.

"Slow deep breaths, babe. Relax." His tone was soothing as he whispered against me.

"If you want me to relax, why are you lighting me on fire with your mouth?"

I felt his whiskers against my breast. "I'm glad you like it. I do too, and there's more of you to taste and suck before you come. So, slow deep breaths, please."

"Oh, fuck." I exhaled, and he chuckled softly as his mouth returned to my body.

Fine, he wanted to kill me with pleasure. I would hold on as long as I could. Gripping the sheets at my side, I slowed my breathing.

"Good, you're doing great," he said, caressing my stomach, inching nearer to the waistband of my flannel pants. Why did his words of praise get me so hot?

"I want you to know I'm healthy. No issues to worry about," I said, glancing at his hand creeping lower.

His warm eyes rose to meet mine. "Me too. I would never do anything to hurt you or risk your health."

I cupped his cheek, his rough, stubbly chin titillating my flesh and sending sparks to my clit. "I believe you."

Quickly, he rose and pressed a gentle kiss to my mouth before returning to his efforts with my pants. "Can I take these off?"

"Yes." I concentrated on slowing my breathing as a single finger dipped below the waistband. Achingly slow, he caressed lower, taking the fabric with him. Working together, I lifted my hips and shimmied as he pulled them off. All that remained between us were my lacy undies and his PJs.

"Can we do that again with yours?" I asked, a tease in my voice, as I slid a hand down his side.

"We can try, but there is no way my wiggle move will be as sexy as yours. And ... I'm not wearing anything under mine."

"Good," I said.

"Go for it, then." His tone lightly challenged.

I rolled to face him and leaned in to skim my tongue across his firm, flat nipple as my hand wandered around to grip an ass cheek. Damn, that was solid, along with his sculpted abs and pecs. Not bulky. Defined. He must work hard or run daily.

As I tugged the fabric lower, I slipped my fingers under

the waistband to find warm skin and rough hair on his thighs. He lifted his hips in a side plank move he made look effortless, and I pushed the pants lower, freeing his stiff cock to thump across his stomach. He moaned, or I did, or we both did, and I helped him kick the offending clothing off and onto the pile of my discarded clothes at the bottom of the bed.

Leisurely, I danced my fingertips along his thigh, over his hip and abdomen. I grasped his hardness at the base, then stroked up to run my thumb along the ridge of his crown. He sucked in air as I teased the underside right below the head. This spot was usually the most sensitive part of a man, and I rubbed it with gentle pressure in a constant rhythm. Walker closed his eyes as his hand gripped my waist like he needed to hold on.

"Do you like that?" I asked, echoing his words from moments ago, and he shuddered.

"Yes. Hell, I might like it too much." He glanced down. "That's a picture. Your sweet breasts framing your hand below as you stroke me." He gave me a tender kiss. "You are so fucking hot. And your hands are incredible."

His voice was deep, the words dusting across my cheek as I imagined him stretching me, filling me.

"I want you inside. I can't wait much longer," I begged.

"Then I should get back to work." He winked and covered my hand with his, briefly pulling it to his lips.

In a swift move, he nudged me to lie back as he reached for pillows at the top of the bed. He slid a couple low under my hips, lifting me, angling me to him.

He traced his fingers along the lacy edges of my undies. "Can I take these off?"

"Please." I exhaled it like a prayer.

He placed a kiss below my belly button, then pulled the pale cream fabric down and off before he guided my knees open and sat back at the bottom of the bed. With a sly grin, he stared for a moment. I was completely exposed to him.

With that seductive expression, he crawled closer and lifted my leg to kiss his way up, above my knee, to my thigh. He stopped there and returned to give my other leg the same treatment.

My hands caressed my breasts, alternating between pinching my nipples and grazing over them as he watched.

"So hot, babe." His voice was strained as he dove closer, lifting my thighs to slide his arms underneath. The result was my legs resting over his shoulders and his forearms cradling my sides with my sex lifted to him like an offering.

He kissed the top of each thigh, nipped, and sucked each crease where my leg met my center. I closed my eyes to absorb the delicious sensations. Unrushed, he placed delicate kisses around my opening and above my clit before he finally, gloriously, covered my sex with his warm wet mouth.

I moaned at the pleasure of his flat tongue fixed against me. I wriggled, climbing higher as he resumed his private licks and sucks. Awareness of him vibrated and filled me to the point I writhed with it, but his hands grounded me to the bed as he took his ever-lovin' time exploring.

"The way you taste, the way you smell. God, it makes me crazy. I'm struggling to focus on your moans to learn what you like the best."

"I like it all. I like it all the best." The words were short, my breathing deep and labored.

"I don't think that's true, babe." His hands came up, his arms wrapping around my thighs and helping his shoulders spread my legs wider. Then, using his thumbs on the sides of my pubic bone, he pulled the skin tight, stretching my outer and inner lips, opening me to him even more.

"I think you like this." He licked along my seam and over my clit and hood. I moaned. *Slow, deep breaths*, I repeated in my mind.

"But I think you like this best." He licked my exposed clit, then wrapped his lips around me and gently sucked.

"Oh, shit." I bucked at the surprise, the pleasure too intense. But he was ready for me. His hands held me in place as the onslaught continued with the constant, gentle pull of his mouth on me.

Unaware if I could handle it, I begged. "Please. More." My hands gripped and bunched the sheets at my side.

He added a hum to his ministrations, and I was falling, the waves of my orgasm crashing into me as the world stopped.

Oh. My. God. Never before. Never like that. I'd had sex. Good sex. Maybe even great sex when it was with men I cared about, spent time with, and knew well. None of them had ever known this about me. How to use their mouth to make me fly.

Walker's grip loosened as he lapped at my center, drinking me in. His groans and inhales mingled with mine.

"Inside me. Please." I gasped for air.

"Hang on, babe." He slipped away from me and off the bed before he returned, rolling on a condom. Once again, he crawled from the bottom, except this time he didn't stop until he'd removed the pillows and settled on top of me, our mouths fused, tongues tangling and sucking, my flavor and scent joining with his.

My hands circled his back, and I curled into him while I spread my legs wider.

Breaking the kiss, he rose to sit on his knees, dragging

his hands over my body, flushed and buzzing. He stroked his swollen cock twice as his eyes took me in. Then, leaning over me, he lined himself up with my entrance and sank inside.

His face held concentration as he bottomed out and paused, letting me adjust to his size.

"Slow deep breaths," I said, teasing him.

"So fucking good, Nora. Like you were made for me. I want this to last. Not coming quickly, remember? But damn, babe, you're unreal."

He rose to his hands, breaking some of our skin contact, but the angle and his weight pushed his pubic bone against my clit. I knew there were hundreds of nerve endings not only in the part of me that was exposed but connected deeper inside and in the surrounding area of my sex. With this angle, he ignited all the pleasure spots at once.

My hands roamed his chest and abs, taut with effort as he moved slow and steady. He held himself above me, his focus on mine as his rocking rhythm drove me higher again.

"Yes, Walker." I pulled my knees to his sides, and he ground down harder, faster, deeper. My breath panted, my heart raced, and I was there again. Stars exploding, my walls milking him as he swelled and found his own release with a guttural grunt that sounded as sweet as any bells.

Still buried inside, he gradually lowered himself back to me, chest to chest, warm skin to warm skin. Neither of us spoke. The light music in the background reached my ears, and the sound of our calming breaths.

He was so comforting and heavy, surrounding me with something that felt like how love should feel. It wasn't love. We just met. He wasn't my future. But for a moment, I would pretend he was.

14

WALKER

The bed shifted, and the warm, soft woman in my arms rolled to face me, her sleepy head burrowing into the seam where my shoulder met the pillow. Her breathing was even and steady. She was asleep. I wanted her to rest, but I also wanted her lush body again before I had to let her go.

She was incredible. And I'd known some incredible things.

After the first time she blew my mind with her sweet body, she fucking did it again with her sweet mouth. Every kiss from now on, when she sucked my tongue, I would feel it on my dick. No question.

I opened my eyes and checked my watch. It was early. We'd left the shades open, and in the pre-dawn darkness, it snowed gentle flakes that hit the window and melted to form rivulets down the side. I pulled her closer, cocooning us under the covers, her naked skin silky against mine.

"Mmm. You smell good," she said, kissing my shoulder near where she'd buried her nose.

I slid my hand between us to tease the small patch of hair at her apex. "*You* smell good."

She squirmed, bringing her top leg over my hip, and opening her body to me. She didn't have to ask me twice. I glided a finger along her tender folds.

"Are you sore?" I hadn't held back last night. No way I could have. She was a fantasy come to life. Smart, fun, and curved in all the right places. I liked killer curves on the racetrack and off.

She answered my question by grasping my dick.

I buried my face in her neck and shoulder. Her hair, wild and unruly as she'd called it, lay soft against the pillow. With my arm under her and my other hand now gripping the leg draped over me, I held her to me and rolled to my back, pulling her on top. Her head and that silky mass of hair came to rest on my chest.

"What time is it?" she asked.

"A little after six." I gripped her other hip, now resting above mine, exactly where I wanted her. My morning wood was a bit extra today, no surprise. I pushed my dick against her, and she spread her legs.

"You got something for me, big guy?" She whispered into my shoulder and rubbed her sex along the hard shaft. I wanted inside right fucking now. This woman was perfect.

"Come here. Let me get you ready for me." I pulled her legs up as I slid down the bed. She rose to her knees, braced her hands on the headboard, and settled her center on my mouth. Since I knew what she liked, I did that, and she ground against me in a slow, relaxed rhythm. I loved it.

Her flavor was different this morning. Muskier but still sweet, and it made me fucking crazy. Occasionally, I met a guy who didn't like going down a woman. I felt sorry for those bastards. In the bedroom, there were few things I liked more than having my face between a woman's thighs, exploring that vulnerable side of her, tasting her, smelling her. Not perfume she chose in some pricey shop, but her. The real her. It was a goddamn privilege.

And when she came on my tongue, lost in pleasure, moaning gibberish until completely limp and satisfied, I knew *I* had done that with skill and perseverance. Damn, there was nothing better.

"Oh, your beard," she moaned.

"Too rough?" I held her immobile and firm.

"No, no, it's perfect like this. Not scratchy. It's a tease, not a scrape. It feels delicious." Delicious. My thoughts exactly.

Her body moved slowly above me. Her hands cupped her full tits, caressing the stiff tips. Somehow, I got harder. She was unapologetic about taking her pleasure, and hell if I wasn't here for it. Another privilege.

"Walker, I'm going to come."

"Yes, babe. Come on my mouth."

"No, no, I want you inside me."

Before I could stop her, she was off the bed, walking toward my suitcase in the dim morning light. "Where are they?"

I rose to my elbows. "Side pocket at the top."

"Got it." She held the packet high like a trophy before she climbed back on me. This time, her beautiful sex rested on my thighs. With her deft fingers, she opened the wrapper and, pinching the tip, rolled the condom on me to the base.

"Are you ready for this?" she asked, her eyes bright in the growing dawn.

Nope. No fucking way I was ready for this. I gripped her hips as she held me to her opening and took me inside her body. It was a miracle how we fit together.

"Don't move. Let *me* fuck you this time," she said, her voice dangerous and soft. "Let me torture you with my leisurely pace. Make you beg me to slam onto you, but I won't. I'll meander and tease until you can't hold back any longer and lose all that captivating control. I bet you'd make me come hard if I did that." Oh, hell. This woman. That was exactly what happened.

My phone rang later as we lay in the quiet after our breathing settled. Neither one of us was ready to let go.

"Walker dear!" The bright voice of my mother greeted me.

"Hi, Mom."

"Were you sleeping? What time is it there?"

"It's seven-thirty. In the morning. Where are you?" Nora shifted away, but I held her close against my side.

"We're still in Paris. So, we'll be later than we thought getting to the house. We won't miss the holiday, but if I remember correctly, you were planning to be there last night?"

"Yeah, that got delayed. Snowstorm here. I should be there tonight."

"Well, I'm sorry we won't be, but then you like your space after the season. This way, you'll have a few days to yourself. Carly and Nate will be there. So, if you need anything, they'll get it. Rest and relax. You had a rough year."

I sighed lightly at the mention of the season. "Thanks, Mom. Take your time." I kept my tone upbeat. "You're right. A few days to myself sounds good. I gotta go. Love you."

"Love you too, dear."

A few days to myself. What were the chances I could talk Nora into seeing me again? I could go to Bellingham. By the size of her suitcase, she was staying for more than a couple of days. The more I thought about seeing her again, the more I knew I had to try.

"Is everything okay? Your family?" She asked, her voice husky from sleep and moaning.

"Sure. No problem." I squeezed her close. "Breakfast?"

"Mmm. In bed?"

"You have the best ideas. Stay right there. In that shape. I'll be right back." I strode out to the sofa area and grabbed the leather-bound amenities menu.

Leaning against the headboard, I pulled the blankets up to cover my semi-hard dick. Nora was naked next to me. What did I expect? I opened the room service pages for us both to read. "What do you like?" I asked.

"Boy, that's a loaded question to ask me right now."

"What do you like for breakfast?" I smirked. Damn, I liked her.

"Most things. Carbs. Eggs. No meat, please. Not in the morning. Vegetables. Fruit. Let me buy breakfast. You paid for the room, rooms." Right. I hoped Mr. and Mrs. Williams had a good night.

"No, my treat." I placed the call for two veggie omelets, assorted scones, mixed fruit, and coffee. Lots of it. And two more huge bottles of water.

"Twenty minutes. I vote we stay here until then," I said.

"Now, who has the great ideas?" She wrapped an arm around me and pulled herself snugly to my side. I wasn't close to finished spending time with her. I would find a way to see her again.

"So, how long are you in Bellingham?" I tried to keep the question light as we sat in bed finishing breakfast. Me in my boxers, Nora in those lacy fucking panties and silky pink tank. The food came on a tray I brought into the bedroom and placed on the side of the bed where we could grab more coffee or butter for the scones. We each sat against the wood headboard and held our plated omelets in our lap, our shoulders bumping as we took bites.

"I'm not actually going to be in Bellingham. That's where I was flying. I'm staying in a town called Perry Harbor. It's on an island not far from there."

Fucking excellent luck. "I know where it is. It's where I'm going too."

She looked at me, her brow furrowed. "Is this where you get creepy?"

I laughed. "No, I'm serious. My parents' house is near there." I paused. "I'll be at the house through the holidays. A little over two weeks. What about you?"

"A week. Well, six days now. I'm working on that project and booked extra days, quiet time to write. No distractions. No groceries, no cleaning house, no parties or going out with friends. Only writing."

"I get it. Perry Harbor is nice. Beautiful all year."

"I believe it," she said. "It's so green here. Even this time of year. That's new to me. Minnesota is white in the winter. Nashville is brown. I landed in SeaTac yesterday as the snow was starting, and the trees were green everywhere. I felt like I could breathe better."

She stopped eating and sighed, reaching for another small scone, and spread a hunk of butter across the top. "If you get bored, maybe we could meet for dinner or coffee. If you want," she said, not looking at me.

"That call from my mom earlier. They'll be here later than planned. Turns out my calendar is a hundred percent free for the next few days, and I'd love to take you out. There's a great Italian place or this cool boat-themed bar. The food's good, and I think they may have entertainment. At least they do in the summer. How about tomorrow?"

Her expression brightened. "I'd like that. And not because, you know." She nodded to the bed.

"You mean the mind-blowing sex. You don't want more of that? I'm disappointed, but I'll take dinner if that's all that's on offer."

"Oh, I definitely want more mind-blowing sex. I didn't want to assume. But I was there last night *and* this morning. Damn, Walker. Are all ranchers as good as you?"

"I wouldn't know, but I doubt it." I grinned, though the secret I was keeping from her hung in the back of my mind. My time with Nora was feeling less and less like a distraction. I wanted to tell her the truth, but I also liked her being with me, the rancher, not the over-the-top Formula One driver.

Knowing I would see her again made packing marginally easier. And sharing a shower with her made the idea of having to wait a couple of days to have her curves in my hands again a lot more difficult.

She'd put her hair up for the shower, saying it was too thick to wash every day. Getting dressed, she brushed it out and braided it. She was beautiful no matter what, but I missed the soft curtain falling around her gorgeous face. Maybe I'd talk her into wearing it down for our dinner date.

Our one-forty-five flight out of SeaTac was still listed as on time, even though the snow continued lightly. We had a couple of hours to kill. So, after checkout, we left our bags with the hotel doorman and took a walk in the gray daylight. We stopped for coffee near Pike Place Market and walked the stalls now open on a snowy day. The newsstand where Nora had hung out last night while I bought the wine was busy. It seemed everyone had a coffee in hand as they read the headlines and searched for something interesting.

"What?" Nora gasped next to me, and I turned. "Walker. Isn't this the guy who took our picture last night?"

It had to be him. The photo even included the same man he was with. They were celebrating ten years of marriage, and the guy was Angus Hayes. World-renowned photographer for *Vogue* and *Time*, and others. He photographed rock stars and queens, and celebrities. And soon-to-be washed-up F1 drivers, it seemed.

"Did you say you saw Angus Hayes?" A tall woman on the other side of Nora leaned over. She was dressed in a long black sweater with ripped black jeans, and her deep purple hair was cut at sharp angles.

"I think so. He didn't tell us who he was," Nora said.

"Well, his husband is from here, and they recently opened a small gallery a couple blocks away, on Union." The woman nodded to the next street. "I read in *The Seattle Weekly* they're in town for the holidays." She bumped her shoulder like they shared a secret. "You're lucky. Hold on to those photos."

15

NORA

I felt like I was getting punked. Anyone else would've paid hundreds or thousands for something he so easily gave us for free. His work. But maybe taking photos on the street was what got him interested in photography. The same way bandaging a friend's hurt knee in middle school had set me on the path to becoming a doctor. That and my parents' unspoken but clear expectations.

"We have time. You want to walk past the gallery?" Walker asked.

"Sure."

I floated. What a trip this had been! The day with Walker. The museum, the hotel, the food, the sex, oh man, the sex, and now a brush with someone famous. I'm not sure what I did to deserve the last twenty-four hours, but I wish I knew so I could do it again.

The gallery wasn't far. It was smaller than I expected, with warm wood floors, steel structural beams to support the entire building crisscrossing the space in hulking angles, and crisp white walls peppered with photos. An impeccably styled woman approached from a small desk to the side.

She was in her late twenties, tops, with rich brown skin, dark eyes, and thick black hair that suggested her family was originally from India. She was beautiful and had the hair Walker seemed to like on me.

She glanced at him, then at our clasped hands. "Can I help you find something?" she asked Walker. Not us. Walker.

Did he notice her special attention? "We heard he opened a gallery here. My girl's always been an admirer of his. And I've always been an admirer of her. So, I told her to pick something out."

He squeezed my hand and shot me a little grin. I guess he had noticed. Man, I liked him.

"Babe, you spoil me," I said and gazed at him adoringly, uncertain about how much of it was my untapped acting skill and how much was actual adoration.

"We already own several originals. Let's add to our collection," he said.

Miss tall and stunning paused. "You own several originals?"

"We do. Recently acquired privately." He winked.

She smiled politely. "I'll leave you to look."

"Thank you," I said a bit sternly, and Walker coughed, his hand hiding a smile.

The photos were beautiful in a lot of different ways. Most were of people I didn't recognize and were breathtaking in their simplicity. They weren't models; that was obvious. They were just lovely. Inside and out, and it showed on their faces.

"Do you have small prints of those?" Walker asked the woman later while gesturing to the section of photos I'd been lost in. One of an elderly couple was particularly compelling. "We'd like to take a few home for further thought on the right full size for our collection."

"Of course. Let me see." She sifted through a bin under her desk and pulled out several choices, including that couple.

"Perfect." Walker made his choice after I chose the couple. He paid, and we left, his hand firmly clasping mine as my phone dinged with a text.

Dad: GDNL making headlines again. Check out the story. When you get to Africa with us in a couple of months, you'll be part of this. Finally, such a proud moment.

I didn't reply as a second text arrived with a link to a newspaper article. My eyes were still focused on the word *finally*. Were there no proud moments so far? I shoved my phone back into my pocket. I only had a few more hours with Walker, and I wasn't spoiling them with my petty thoughts. My parents were good people, and there would be plenty of time to discuss research and GDNL tomorrow.

We returned to the hotel and collected our bags. The plowed and sanded streets had traffic moving better, warming the roads and turning the bright snow to brown slush in places. The good thing about that was we could take an Uber to the light rail station instead of roll-dragging our bags like we did last night.

Securely on the train headed to SeaTac, together this time, we both received a ding in our airline app. Flight delayed. Pilot availability, the notice said. The storm had impacted several regional airports in the Pacific Northwest, and though the snow was slowing, it was still causing issues.

I squinted at the screen, worry forming in my brain. I couldn't miss this interview. People were counting on me. Not only the women expecting me but my peers and colleagues who would be part of this research. I couldn't let them down. I needed to take that meeting and finish the grant application.

Walker took in my anxious expression. "Since we're both going to Perry Harbor, and the roads are open again, why don't I rent a car at the airport and drive from here?"

"In this weather?"

"The snow is moving out, and I have a lot of experience driving in tough conditions." Walker stared at my face more intently. "Are you afraid of driving in the snow?"

"No, just not experienced with it, that's all."

"I thought you were from Minnesota," he said.

"I am, but I rarely drove in it, particularly on highways. I know how, but I don't like it."

The memory was fuzzy in parts and vibrant in others. A winter day in Minneapolis, and my dad driving me to dance class. I couldn't have been older than six or seven.

There was an accident ahead of us on I-94, and Dad ran to help. One victim was unconscious, and ultimately, Dad saved his life. Rescue breathing and compressions, instructing others to apply a tourniquet to his leg. The man had a wife and three baby boys in the car. I remember them crying and Dad saying that was likely a good sign as passers-by stopped to console and care for the other family members who didn't appear to have life-threatening injuries.

A few days later, the local news ran a story on Dad, the man who'd saved the father of triplets. I'd been in awe, but Dad said it was what he was supposed to do. He'd been a poor Midwestern farm boy growing up, and he'd been able to go to college, meet my mom, and make a good life. It was what he was meant to do, helping people, and that was *the most important thing*, he'd told me.

Dad received cards from that family every year on that father's birthday. They said Dad gave him those birthdays.

Saving lives, and giving people more birthdays, mattered more than anything else.

I closed my eyes to block the memories.

Walker pressed close and lowered his voice. "Last night, I said I wouldn't ever put you at risk, and I meant it. I can do this, Nora."

Thoughts of last night warmed my blood and settled my mind. I'd felt safe with Walker, and I believed he wouldn't suggest this if he wasn't sure. And people *were* counting on me. "Okay."

"ALL WE HAVE IS REAR-WHEEL DRIVE," said the lone woman at the rental counter. Her expression was bored or tired, or a combination of the two. "Not great for snow and these hills." So, that was why there was no line.

"What makes and models?" Walker asked.

She furrowed her brow at him. "You still want to rent one?"

"Probably, yes. Do you have something European-made?"

She raised her eyebrows and clicked her mouse, her eyes tracking the computer screen only she could see.

"In our luxury fleet, we have a Mercedes." Her expression was one of disdain. She likely thought Walker was an entitled asshole throwing money around. Walker had not acted that way once since I met him. I may have only known him for a day, but I knew he had money and was not an entitled asshole.

Walker frowned. "Anything else? A Jaguar? An XF Sedan, possibly?"

"Huh. We have three. Blue or white?"

"I'll take the one with the lowest mileage," he said.

"License, please."

Walker paused, reached for his wallet to pull out a Texas driver's license and his credit card, and finished the transaction, declining the insurance. If it had been me, I would've taken it.

The car was beautiful. "Walker. Are you sure you want to drive *this* car in the snow?"

"I've driven a lot of Jaguars. This sedan has a heavy engine, and I'm familiar with the suspension. With the mileage low, it'll be tight. Better for control. We'll be fine."

Walker loaded our suitcases, and I slid into leather seats that felt like a hug. Dr. Anders, the chair of the hospital board, drove a Jaguar. I always thought it was showy but damn. This one had me rethinking my stance on luxury cars.

16

WALKER

THE GENTLY FALLING SNOW REFLECTED IN MY HEADLIGHTS against the late-afternoon dark. I wasn't used to headlights. Race cars didn't have them, and I rarely drove anything else.

Nora sat quietly in the passenger seat as we made slow but steady progress north on I-5, and I did what I did best. I drove.

The four-cylinder turbocharged engine rumbled low. It wasn't the exact sound I was used to, but it was similar enough that my blood stirred with it. And with the woman sitting next to me.

Images of last night had played in my mind all day. I couldn't wait to hold her again. Could I bring her to my parents' island? She'd have space and quiet to work there. No cooking or cleaning required. And I didn't expect my family for a few more days. Visions of Nora in the hot tub, in the shower, and by the fire all had my dick stirring.

Fuck. I had to concentrate on driving. The car handled better than I'd expected. The weight heavy enough to provide traction with the right combination of acceleration and braking. It was a delicate balance and one I knew well.

Traffic moved in the two lanes with visible ruts. Other lanes were buried beneath several inches of solid white. That snow would hit a tire and pull a car sideways in seconds. I knew about suddenly being sideways in a car.

I watched the flow of traffic and Nora's body language.

"You okay over there?" I asked.

"Yes. I mean, I'll feel better when we get there. But I trust you." She paused. "You're impressive, actually. You haven't accidentally slipped or slid. When something happened, you told me before it did and how the car would react. You're like a car whisperer."

"Sometimes." I gave her my usual flirty smile when someone complimented my driving skills.

"You handle this thing as well as you handle me."

I glanced at her. "That's good to hear, but it's way too sexy for where my brain needs to be right now. Invite me up to your hotel room later and tell me again."

"Do you want to come up to my hotel room?"

"Absolutely. I can think of several things I'd still like to do with you."

Her eyes glittered, but the darkness inside the car hid the blush I knew was there.

I glanced in the mirror and saw headlights approaching on the outside, too fast. Not reckless, but we were on a bridge where the snowpack was more ice than slush.

As we approached the downward slope coming off the bridge, I noticed the brake lights ahead. With the line and the distance required for what looked like a massive SUV to slow ... there was no way.

"Nora, you're fine. But I need you to hang on."

"What?" was all she managed to say before the driver of the car now next to us hit the brakes too hard, swerved into the snow-piled lane, and slowly spun out past the bridge. That car was likely fine. It was the other cars I was worried about.

Reckless drivers put everyone in danger. Slowing the pace and changing technical plans to avoid a sudden obstacle on the track was one challenge we trained for. But as precise as you tried to be, crashes were a big unknown the instant they occurred. Surprises were never good when you were dancing on the line of out-of-control. It was you, the car, and your ability to make instinctual decisions that meant the difference between driving by or becoming part of the destruction.

The other drivers behind us panicked and slammed on their brakes. A delivery van rammed into the sedan in front of it, sending that car slamming into the concrete side of the bridge. The massive van needed more room to slow than the compact sedan. It'd been traveling too close. A miscalculation that people made every day.

I accelerated into the snow-piled lane, prepared for the pull on the tires. I kept the car steady, and once adjusted to the deeper snow, I turned hard to bring us to an abrupt stop.

I was out of my seat immediately. Nora followed a second later, her focus behind us on the bridge. She took a beat, then yelled, "Call 911," as she jogged along the snowy side of the road toward the wrecked cars.

"Nora! What are you doing?" I reached into the car for my coat.

"Walker. 911." Her powerful, confident voice was like a slap. I pulled out my phone before I knew what I was doing. I reported the accident and looked around for landmarks. As I spoke to the operator, I moved toward Nora. She was ... in command. That was the best word for it, and I stood staring for a moment.

"You! Do you have flares in your truck or anything reflective?" she called to a burly guy standing near an old pickup.

"I think so." He'd already turned toward his truck.

"Get them and grab a friend. Get the traffic moving safely in that far lane."

"Please stand to the side," she shouted to a group of approaching people. "Away from traffic." She pointed at a woman in a huge puffy coat that practically scraped the ground. "Tell the others to move to the deeper snow or get back in their cars. We need to secure this area for safety." The woman turned to the small group of bystanders and spoke with a voice I couldn't believe came from her tiny body. She had to be a mom. How did Nora know she could do that?

My instincts kicked in at the word safety. Gas leaks were a top concern in a crash. Rushing in to help an injured driver didn't work if the car exploded. That threat had to be neutralized first, with the fire-foam team leading any approach.

"Let me check the ground for gas leaks, Nora." I held up my palm to her as I moved closer to the car, thankful the snow had stopped and wouldn't hide any spills. Hitting the flashlight on my phone, I searched the area where the gas tank and pump would be. Nothing. I quickly checked the snow under the fuel lines and finally under the motor.

"No sign of leaks from the tank, fuel pump, fuel lines, or injectors." I rattled it off out of habit. "The hood is too damaged to check the intake manifold, but I think we're okay. I'm going to look at the other vehicle."

That driver was conscious and standing against the open door on the driver's side, his curtain airbag sagging. He said he was uninjured as I flashed him with my light. I walked around the van the same way I did the sedan, checking the snow for signs of a leak. This one was clear, too.

I returned to find Nora crouched below another sagging airbag, the passenger door now open.

"No, Kevin. Do not get out. Stay seated." Her voice was gentle but sure as she spoke to the driver. She had her phone's flashlight on, but it was pointed down, illuminating the passenger's lap as she removed the woman's seatbelt. I looked closer at the edge of the light. Below the knee, the passenger's foot wasn't turned in the right direction. Oh fuck. I glanced away for a breath.

"You are okay, Becky. EMTs are on the way. I know it hurts, but they'll be here soon. Try to stay calm."

"We should get out, babe," said the driver, a man in his thirties, I'd guess. He was a little dazed.

"No. We shouldn't move her. This car is the safest place for her right now."

That leg would not like being moved, that was for damn sure.

At that moment, the woman shifted and let out a scream. "Ahh! God, that hurt worse than childbirth."

Nora looked at me. "Walker, ask if someone has a clean rag or a first aid kit, something like that."

I took off as Nora again spoke in soothing tones to the woman. Someone with the pickup guy, maybe his teen son, found a kit and handed it to me. He followed close behind as I ran back to Nora.

The remaining people were comforting others who'd had minor collisions or helping to direct cars past the scene by the light of a few glowing flares at the edge of the road.

Nora assessed the red case in my hand. "Great." She opened it and took out clean gauze and some large bandages. She handed them to the kid next to me. "Becky, this is my friend Walker. He's going to talk to you while I check on your husband." Nora looked at me, and I nodded.

"Follow me," she said to the kid. I crouched down and asked Becky where they were going and what she wanted for Christmas, trying to make conversation. She moaned a godawful sound.

"Nora," I said.

"Deep, even breaths, Becky. Soothing tones, Walker," she said from the driver's side. I tried to focus on Becky, but half my attention was on Nora. What the fuck did she teach again?

"Hi, Kevin. I'm Nora. I want to look at your head. It's bleeding a little." Kevin lolled back against the headrest, and she flashed the light near his face. A little was not how I would have described that. The kid beside Nora looked away as she grabbed the gauze he held out for her.

Becky moaned again. "Motherfluffer."

Kevin leaned toward her. "Becks, you okay?"

"Look at me," Nora said, her voice confident and clear but kind. "How old are you, Kevin?"

"Thirty-six." He grimaced as she worked.

"And who's this with you?"

"My wife ... Becky."

"What day is it today?" The questions came clear but rapid fire as Nora mopped Kevin's forehead and pressed the gauze against a dark gash. When she was satisfied, she started through the standard concussion protocol. I'd been through it enough to know. She moved her fingers side to side and up and down, asking Kevin to follow it. She flashed a light in his eyes quickly. "Equal and reactive," I heard her mutter and knew that was a good thing.

"You have great eyes, Kevin. How do you feel? Sleepy? Nauseated?"

"No, I don't think so. Stunned is what I feel."

Nora grabbed more gauze from the kid, and Becky let out another wail followed by another colorful G-rated curse. She shivered, and her broken leg didn't like it. I took off my coat and laid it on her.

"Oh, that's nice," she said, a little loopy now.

"Can you hold this here, Kevin? On your forehead. Like this," Nora said.

"Sure." His voice was getting stronger.

She stood and looked out into the distance, probably searching for the red lights that meant help was here. She spun to the kid. "You got something like a stick the width of a broom handle or a couple of small boards, maybe?" She held her hands about a foot apart.

"I think so. My dad's got all kinds of sh—stuff in that truck. I think he has some garden stakes, a couple of inches wide."

"Get them, and some soft rope or a couple of belts from some of these people here would do, too." She strode back to Becky and knelt beside me. "I'm going to put a splint on your leg," she said, and Becky grimaced. "It will stabilize it and support it. It'll help with the pain while we wait for the EMTs. This snow may delay them a bit." Becky nodded. "Let's push your seat back some."

The kid returned with the items, and Nora went to work, gently but deftly placing the two thin pieces of wood on either side of Becky's leg.

"Look at Kevin, Becky. Tell me how he's doing. Does he have the gauze pressed to his head?"

I looked along with Becky, and Kevin smiled at his wife.

"He does ... Ahh," Becky moaned and grimaced again.

"That's the worst part." Nora secured two pieces of silky repelling rope, one low and one high, around the wood, now bracketing the leg. "I'm going to check your pulse in your foot. My hand will be cold." Nora slid two fingers next to Becky's ankle. "Strong distal pulse. That's a good sign." She smiled brightly, and Becky did too. "Can you wiggle your toes?"

"I think so." Becky braced but then relaxed. "I can. And it hurt, but not as bad as I thought it would."

"Good. That's fantastic." Eyeing the two empty car seats in the back, she said, "Tell me about your family." Becky started talking.

17

NORA

"Great job, Doc. You didn't have to get involved, but you did, and it made a difference."

"Thanks," I said. "Take care of her."

"We will." The EMT closed the door to the back just as they finished loading Becky and Kevin inside and then jogged to the front of the ambulance. The tow truck was ready to work on the car as soon as the scene was clear.

Several yards away, Walker stood beside the bright blue Jaguar that had been unscathed when the cars next to us crashed or skidded off the road. He drove like it was his job, and it prodded at the back of my mind.

Hunched by the car door wearing his coat, returned from Becky, and his baseball hat, he rubbed his left wrist absently, like a habit. I walked toward him, my pace slow. I had some explaining to do. But then, I think he did too.

"Hey," I said lamely.

"Hey. You okay?"

"Yeah. You?"

"Yeah," he said.

He moved to the driver's side, and I faced him over the

car. He wasn't angry, but his face wasn't the brilliant show of white teeth and sparkling eyes either. I opened the door and slid into the cushy leather seat, shaking as the last of the adrenaline eased.

I wasn't used to the field. I was a doctor, and the hospital was *my* turf. EMTs trained differently and learned different techniques. The field was their turf every time.

Plenty of doctors might see an accident and choose not to get involved. It was my license I was risking out there if it went bad. But not helping someone in need was something I couldn't do. It wasn't what my father did that day in the Minnesota wind and bitter cold.

My parents pledged their time, their lives, and their careers to people who needed help, and they expected the same from me. There was no way I could walk away.

Walker slid into the frigid interior of the car and started the engine, putting the heater on full blast.

"So … what is it you teach again?" he asked, his voice carrying a hint of a smile, I hoped.

I faced him. "I *am* a teacher. That wasn't a lie. And I do teach biology, of sorts … as well as emergency medicine to residents at Birch University Medical Center in Nashville."

"So, you're …" He squinted at me.

"An emergency physician."

Walker nodded and gazed out the windshield. The snow had tapered off, and the temperatures now hovered above freezing.

"I'm sorry I didn't tell the whole truth. Me being a doctor is sometimes weird for people, and dating—" I shook my head, "—I stopped trying. I don't have much experience with hot, normal guys talking to me. I enjoyed it and didn't want things to get weird."

Walker grinned. "I think you're hot too, a fucking

inferno." He winked. "And you were pretty spectacular to watch out there."

"Speaking of spectacular, you and driving? That move where you turned the car to stop it?" His face was barely lit by the glow from the dashboard lights, and he exhaled. "What's the story there?"

He sat back. "I can't fault you for not telling me the whole truth when I didn't tell you mine, either." He paused. "I am a rancher from Austin. ... About two months out of the year."

"What do you do the rest of the time?"

"Drive a race car in Formula One."

What? "Isn't Formula One all Europeans who own small countries?"

Walker tilted his head. "That's the team owners. I'm a lowly driver. And it's true most of us are not from the States. All but one." He pointed to himself.

"You're the only driver from the US?"

"Yep. There are others on the teams, but yeah, I'm the only driver right now."

"Wow." That was all I could say. I couldn't imagine being on my own and doing a job so far away from my home and everything I'd known. But then, that was exactly the world my parents lived in, the one they wanted me to join. I swallowed the thought.

"How did you get out of the car so fast?"

"Practice. I have to pass safety tests every season before I can race. One is getting out of a six-point harness and the cockpit in less than ten seconds," Walker said.

"So, you're in Europe most of the year?"

"Yeah. Though, we're scheduling more events in the States. I get a couple of months off each winter. That's when I come home and work the ranch."

I nodded, a little dazed by this news.

"I didn't tell you because ... well, similar to what you said. There are only twenty people in the world who have my job. I've been in and around F1 and F2 for almost two decades. People know me as that driver. Women like that driver. *You* liked the rancher. I didn't want that to change." He glanced down, rubbing his left wrist again.

"Did you hurt your wrist?"

He shrugged. "Four years ago. I had a wreck and broke it. It aches sometimes, but not too bad."

"You wrecked and survived?"

He nodded. "I've driven for years. Since I was a kid driving K1 karts. It came naturally to me. A lot of guys started in juniors when they were five or six. I was eleven and very late to the game. But I had a gift, or I wouldn't be racing now. There are too many others gunning for the job."

"You race around a track at like two hundred miles an hour. You crash, and there'd be no need for me. Humans can't survive that."

"I guess I better not crash in the straightaway," he teased, then sobered. "It's something I do well, and I like it." He stared out the windshield again.

"Walker ... I ..." What? What did I think? I had nothing. Making decisions quickly, if not instantly, and taking the next step was my job. And now, after the last thirty-six hours and discovering that this man was probably famous, rich as fuck, and a revelation between my thighs, I wasn't sure what to do.

"It's not saving lives, like you, but I am good at it. Or I was." Something flickered in his eyes. "Might as well put it all out there." In the same voice from last night, he mumbled the words low to himself. My nipples hardened. And not from the cold.

"The season recently ended. I'm taking some time to

consider if I want to go back next year. Being the rancher with you was like trying on a new suit, I guess." He smoothed his hand over his mouth and scruff, resigned. "I'm thirty-four. Practically elderly in my world."

"Thirty-four is barely out of diapers in my world. With school and residency, I didn't get my first actual job until I was thirty-three. Friends from undergrad were getting jobs, buying houses, and taking trips to the Bahamas while I was still logging student loans in medical school. I feel old and yet younger than them sometimes." He looked at me with a silent question. "I'm thirty-five," I said.

"Most of the guys comin' up in F1 are nineteen or twenty," he said. "I worked with this one kid this year. Fucking phenom is what he is. Better than I was at his age. He belongs in the seat. I couldn't even negotiate a crack between people on a crowded platform to make it on the train yesterday."

He sifted his fingers through his hair, the silver at the edges glinting in the low light as melting snow dripped down the windshield outside. The air was thick with thoughts, and his eyes suddenly sparkled.

"Listen, now that we've revealed all of our secrets, I have an idea," he said. "I know you're in Perry Harbor to work, to write. But I'd like it if you stayed with me at the house. I have some things to do, some thinking. Being with you clears my mind in a way nothing else has lately. You're easy to talk to. And one more night with *you* won't be enough." His grin promised pleasure, and my core clenched as a thrill surged through me.

I inhaled deeply. "Really?"

"And I think you could use an escape or could continue the one you're on." His eyes held mine.

I nodded. He was right. I needed an escape. From my demanding job, my parents' expectations, and the rising sense of dread I had about GDNL. I needed to focus on the grant application. It was a life preserver. That grant would buy me more time to either get good with joining GDNL or get good with disappointing my parents on a colossal scale.

"Let me be that escape for you, Nora." His expression was warm as he whispered close.

"Is there room?"

"It's a big house. Great satellite internet. Quiet. Fireplaces. An indoor lap pool steps away. A running loop through the woods, if you're into that. We'd be alone there except for Carly and Nate sometimes. They're the property managers and caretakers. They don't stay on the island but live in Perry Harbor."

"Isn't Perry Harbor on the island?"

"No, I meant they don't stay on my parents' island, where the house is."

Yep, rich as fuck. "Your parents *own* an island?" I tried not to let my confused surprise show too much.

His grin was sheepish, and I was glad the vibe had lightened. "They aren't the only ones. I think Oprah has one, and Bill Gates, possibly. A bunch of people. I don't really know, but you'd have plenty of space and quiet. And I'll take care of the food. Remember, I like to cook. Let me cook for you, Nora."

What sort of alternate universe had I landed in?

"Let me get this straight. You, super-hot guy and the source of multiple orgasms, would like me to come and stay with you, *alone*, at your parents' big house on a private *island* where I can work in quiet, there's an indoor lap pool, and you'll do all the cooking?"

"Yes. Well, Mom hired a chef to bring in prepped stuff for some days, but I'll have to cook those meals and most of the others we want."

This was not real. "I have a meeting tomorrow morning in Perry Harbor, then I'm attending a seminar in the afternoon. Would you bring me back for that?"

"Sure. The island is twenty minutes by boat."

Was I seriously thinking about doing this? Was I seriously thinking about *not* doing this? Could I trust a man this much when I'd known him for less than forty-eight hours? Even if he knew my body better than I did, and his eyes promised more nights like the last one?

It was illogical. It was impulsive. But Walker was a unicorn in the sports world and in other more personal places, and *I liked him*. I didn't want it to end yet. It would soon enough, but not right now.

"Is there a washer and dryer where I can wash these clothes?" My favorite leggings were dirty with salt and muck from the slushy road. No way I'd get another day's wear out of them without washing them first.

His lips curved on one side. "I think there is."

I hoped I hadn't lost my motherfluffin' mind.

"Okay."

18

WALKER

Relief. That's the best way to describe it.

The rest of the drive to Perry Harbor was uneventful. The weather report said most of the remaining snow was falling south of the convergence zone, wherever that was. I was pretty sure we were north of it, though, because the roads were less snowy here, and the clouds were thin enough in spots to see moonlight.

Nora called to cancel her hotel reservation since she would be staying with me. A thought that pleased me more as we drove. I liked her, and not just for the mind-blowing sex but for the conversation and those mysterious smiles. And now that I knew more about her big brain and her job, she was even more enticing. And definitely too good for me.

She was a doctor who helped people. I drove a car around a racetrack. I was a player. Women used me, and I used them back, most of the time. I didn't belong with an exceptional woman like Nora.

"Do you need anything from town? Little Debbie Swiss

Rolls?" I teased when we stopped at a light near the marina.

She yawned and covered her mouth. "Excuse me. Someone kept me awake most of the night." And I planned to do it again, more than once, but not tonight. We both needed sleep after traveling what probably felt like days to her and actually had been days for me.

She shook her head. "I'll be back tomorrow if I do. All I need right now is food and a bed and … a warm sleeping partner?"

"Say the word gorgeous. I want you in my bed. If you want separate rooms, I can do that, but I can't say I won't try diligently to convince you otherwise."

We crossed the high bridge from the mainland to Perry Harbor with no problem. It had been cleared and sanded. After pulling into the Harbor Marina, I found my family's designated parking spaces, and chose the first spot.

"Okay. We'll leave the car here. Hewitt Island, we call it, is only accessible by boat or helicopter."

We climbed out into the chilly, damp air scented with briny seawater. "Helicopter? Tell me you don't have one of those," she said as she reached for her bag in the trunk.

"Let me." I snagged the handle and pulled it out for her. It wasn't heavy. I'd known women who were a bit much with clothes or shoes or makeup. Not Nora, and I liked it. "No helicopter." My father, though …

I locked the car, and we headed toward the docks. "It looks like low tide," I said. "Be careful on the gangway. The pitch is steep at this water level."

Again, I reached for her hand, and again she placed hers in mine. Hands that did great things. Healing things.

Our boat slips were close, under the covered part of the dock. I grabbed the keys I'd brought and helped Nora aboard. My family had two boats here, each a Nimbus 405

Flybridge, for ferrying people to and from Perry Harbor or Bellingham. They were nice, and they were fast but not too attention-grabbing.

The big yacht with the dark glass windows, staterooms, crew berths, and the equipment for open ocean travel was currently docked off the coast of Greece. This island, this area, was about retreat in the beauty of nature and something *closer* to a normal life. We didn't want flash and attention here.

Dad hadn't grown up a billionaire. Not even close. Neither Mom nor Dad was raised in a world with anything close to this level of wealth, one where they could learn the rules of having money from a young age. Instead, they'd had to find their way, and it hadn't always been easy, with plenty of people eager for a piece.

It was more than either of them had ever imagined, and it didn't fit. They'd been working on a plan to give most of it away for the last few years. The extravagant life of the super-wealthy was losing its sparkle for all of us.

I helped Nora board at the stern, then lifted our suitcases aboard. I unlocked the sliding door past the outdoor table for four back here and flipped on the lights as she stepped inside the brightly lit salon. There was a long thin table and banquette for seating to the left, and the galley sink, counter, cabinets, and small appliances were on the right. I dropped my bag behind the elevated cockpit beyond the galley.

Nora was by the doorway where I'd left her. Her hand gripping the handle of her suitcase.

"Everything okay?"

"Is this a yacht?" Her eyes looked concerned.

"I think yachts have a crew. Does it matter?"

"No." She shook her head slightly, and her regular bright expression returned.

"I'll drive from here." I nodded to the cockpit. "There's a seat next to me." I waved her closer. "Down there is the head, bathroom," I gestured to the stairs leading under the bow at the front of the boat, "and beyond it are a couple of sleeping berths. The trip isn't long, but if you want to take a nap, you can."

"And miss this?" She looked around. "No thanks."

I chuckled. "It's better in the daytime. Tonight will be dark, with only the lights of a few tanker ships. When we're on the other side of Anna Island, we'll be able to see the lights of Bellingham in the distance if the clouds aren't too low. Hang on a sec. I'll undo the lines and be right back."

Nora nodded, taking the seat on the port side opposite the cockpit and looking around as if she were cataloging everything in sight. Out on the dock, I moved quickly around the boat, casting the lines on board that had secured it to the dock. Back inside, I flipped the switch for the heater, took off my coat, and stepped up behind the wheel. I glanced at Nora, still wide-eyed, as I started the motor.

"Hey." I leaned in and stole a quick kiss before returning to the business of navigating the marina in the dark. I confirmed my lights were on, my charts were up on the screen showing me the buoys signaling our path, and my VHF-FM radio was tuned to the correct channel for the Vessel Tracking System used by the Coast Guard in the nearby shipping lanes. Commercial ships, particularly those tankers being towed in by tugs, always had the right of way and required a huge perimeter for safety.

Boating at night was not ideal, but this close to the winter solstice and this far north meant the days were short. It was early evening, but it was dark like midnight.

Once we cleared the marina's no-wake zone, I pushed

the boat faster, and Nora jolted at the acceleration. I barely noticed. Formula One drivers dealt with forces as high as four Gs coming out of a turn or into one from a long straightaway. A few knots increase in speed wasn't even a blip for me.

"You're quiet," I said.

"Sorry. I'm ... I've never ... Minnesota is the land of ten thousand lakes, and I've been on a speedboat, but never anything like this."

I nodded, hesitating.

"Nora, I need to tell you something, and I'm afraid it will change the way you see me. But ... I hope you'll understand why I didn't say anything earlier." I glanced over. Her face bore an uneasiness similar to what I felt. "My father is Preston Hewitt of Hewitt Computer Company."

She squinted at me. "What?"

I held my breath, letting her process.

"Your father started ... the international one?"

I nodded.

"O-kay. So, your parents have more money than God." A beat of silence passed, and then she shook her head as if deciding. "Well, I don't. And something tells me I'm about to be wide-eyed again with the *island* like I was with this non-yacht."

I chuckled. "Noted." I stared out at the darkness. "You understand why I didn't tell you earlier?"

Nora swiveled to face me, or my profile, as I kept my focus all around us. I probably should have waited until I wasn't driving a boat at night to have this conversation, but that genie wasn't going back into the bottle.

"I think so. People may treat you differently when they find out what your family does or has, and you want to be treated like you."

"That's it. A hundred percent. Everyone I've met since I was a teenager, every woman, they've all known I was a driver and who my dad was."

"And it's tough to trust that they see you and not the dollar signs or fame or whatever else you have around you," she said, naming the vulnerability better than I could.

"Does it change the way you see me?"

She leaned in as if studying me. "Nope. I can see you just fine."

I grinned. "You know what I mean."

"I do. I live in Nashville. I'm used to the talented and famous, just trying to live a normal life. And, on a much smaller scale, I get it personally. People discover I'm a doctor and superimpose my face on whatever assumption or preconceived notion they have about doctors. Or they ask me for medical advice." She shook her head, and a private little smile graced her lips. "Like I said, dating is a challenge, and I'm not always sure I want them to know what I do on the first date. I don't want to give up hope, but it's hard." If she married me, she'd never have to date again.

Wait. I'd known the woman for two days. I'd been engaged. The idea of marriage didn't scare me. It agreed with my brothers and even my parents, though some of their peers were divorcing in scandal. But marrying someone like Nora?

I shouldn't be surprised. I always went big, so thinking about an incredible woman like Nora choosing *me* after knowing each other for two days was actually about par for me.

19

NORA

Once we crossed what Walker said was the shipping lane, he relaxed. The boat was beautiful. Sleek and clean in muted tones of gray and milk-chocolate brown set off by dark wood cabinets and accents. The kitchen, or galley, was possibly nicer than the one in my Chicago apartment in med school.

This was definitely an alternate universe.

Walker slowed as we approached what appeared to be the darkness of a landmass. Closer, I saw a string of lights glittering from the railing of a long, slim, and mostly covered dock nestled in a cove. We reached it, and he cut the engine.

"Help me," he said, and I followed him out the sliding glass door. He grabbed a rope and jumped onto the dock, quickly looping it over a giant boat cleat bolted there. "Can you throw me the rope by that rubber bumper at the front?"

I was already walking and spotting it; I tossed it to him. He pulled the boat's bow closer, and I pictured the roll and bulge of the arm muscles I'd caressed last night.

"Now toss those other bumpers over the edge there, and that should do it." A few beats later, he looked at me with excitement as he hopped back aboard. "Let's grab our things. We're here."

I zipped my coat and put my knit cap on again. The wind off the water had a bite like the wind in Chicago, colder than I expected. Walker powered off everything in the boat and set both suitcases on the dock before holding a hand out for me. In the distance, I saw four buildings with lights on. Two were close to the shore, and two were farther up the low hillside.

Walker gripped my hand as we walked toward a snowy stone path leading to the first building.

"This is my middle brother Canyon's house. He and his wife Emme stay here. The Gators are in the shed behind it." He continued around the drive to the back.

"Gators?" I asked.

"Utility vehicle, the size of a golf cart. We use them to haul stuff from the dock."

Once we were settled in one, we drove the snow-covered pavement that circled the slope and entered the trees.

"Over there is the lap pool. We can check that out another day." He pointed to my right before turning sharply to the left and pulling in front of a long, beautiful home.

Clad in gray plank siding with thick cedar beams, the Craftsman-style house glowed with warm lights shining out from the covered porch and several windows. Deep evergreen bushes and old-growth trees were nestled into the landscaping, so naturally, it was as if the house had sprouted and grown here along with them.

Walker stopped the golf cart on steroids and hopped out. I followed quickly, eager to get to the warmth within.

It was really effing cold. The damp chill had seeped into my bones. Silently, Walker grabbed both of our bags, and we shuffled inside, stomping off the snow. The heavy wood door closed behind us with a thud, and the heat and comfort of the space enveloped me. I sighed before I could stop myself.

"Let me get a fire going, then I'll give you a tour," he offered as he walked deeper into the space and took off his coat. Tentatively, I stepped out of the entryway and the dark slate flooring there. The house appeared to be one level, though it flowed with the land, and I noticed a few stairs leading down to more rooms on one side and a few stairs leading up to others on the opposite side. The walls were white with cedar-cased windows, doors, and high transom windows that probably flooded the area with light in the daytime.

The main room in the center was an open-concept rectangle with vaulted ceilings and massive exposed rafters and beams. The kitchen was to the right, at one end, then a long farm table was straight ahead in front of three sets of double doors out to a stone patio facing the water beyond. To the left were a sofa area and an enormous river rock fireplace.

Walker sat on the hearth, stacking logs and kindling. A real, wood-burning fireplace. Not gas or something modern. The space was rustic and luxurious at the same time. Cozy and inviting as the fire caught and began to snap and pop.

"Let me show you around." He grabbed our bags and led me off to the left side, the air scented with lemon cleaner. "Here is the den, and the study is there. There's a desk there if you want to use it. Back this way is a TV room and the loft bedrooms. My parents are eager to be grandparents." Walker chuckled. "They built the house about five years ago, and Mom was very clear that there were to be kid-friendly spaces."

"And here is my bedroom. Ours." He grinned and rolled our bags inside. I stepped into the space located in the back, opposite the TV room in front. Another stone fireplace filled most of the far wall. A doorway on the same wall led into the ensuite and a closet. A king-sized bed faced a set of double doors and more floor-to-ceiling wood-cased windows. The moon was visible now, and its reflection off the snow left the land and water beyond cast in shades of blue and silver. It was like something out of a magazine.

He turned and sauntered back toward the main room along the rough wood floors covered with plush-looking area rugs in muted patterns. He walked past the kitchen and gestured to the side. "Here is the laundry and another bathroom." He pointed toward the steps beyond. "And there's another bedroom and ensuite that way. Basically, a mirror of mine. Usually, my parents stay in there."

We walked back to the main room. "That's pretty much it," he said.

"Walker. This is amazing. I can't believe I'm here." I knew my eyes were huge, but I'd never seen anything like this in real life. Not even the homes of my parents' doctor friends.

"I'll tell my folks you think so. It's their house, not mine." His expression shuttered.

"Hey." I grabbed his hand. "I like you. *You*. I'm a bit overwhelmed right now by all of this, but the reason I'm here and the reason I want to crawl into that bed is because you're here. *You*." I cradled his face in my palm, his original scruff softening after another day.

"Nora." He pulled me into his arms and brushed a sweet kiss across my lips as I melted into him. His tongue delved deeper, warming my blood, and I shivered with the sensation.

"Let's get you some food, a drink, a bath if you want, before that warm bed."

Carly and Nate, who I learned also served as housekeepers and pantry packers, had left the fridge and kitchen fully stocked.

"Margherita pizza and Caesar salad sound good?" He asked, staring into the double sub-zero refrigerator.

"Sure. Can I help?"

"Nah, make yourself comfortable. I won't be long. The dough is pre-made, and I'll cook it quick out there." He pointed to the back patio and a gleaming stainless grill.

"First, red wine, or do you want something warm? Herbal tea or decaf coffee?"

"Wine. Definitely."

I texted Jamar a quick *proof-of-life* text and let him know where I was, then looked around the large main living space. A console table against the front wall held a series of photos, and I moved closer. "The one with the horse, that's Canyon's high school picture," Walker called from the kitchen. "The one by the truck and the lake, that's Vince. He's the youngest."

"This one of you and ... is that a go-kart?"

"Yeah, that's what they look like in European karting," he said.

"All those sponsor stickers and the suit you're wearing. That is not the skateboard attached to a lawnmower motor I expected."

Walker laughed. "No, it's not."

I studied the other photos. Weddings of both Walker's brothers and his parents, along with what looked like ranch action shots with sunsets and gently rolling land stretching to the horizon. Canyon had sandy brown hair cut short and soft eyes as he gazed at his new wife, a striking blonde whose face held the same look of love. Vince had a smirk exactly like Walker's, but Vince's dark hair was shaggy, even in his wedding photo. He and his wife were caught mid-laugh with her deep red hair flowing in long soft waves as he appeared to be lifting her in his arms.

They all seemed ... normal. There was even a picture of the three boys when they were young, sporting matching western shirts, similar hazel-green eyes, big smiles with missing teeth, and what anyone would describe as bowl-style haircuts. I chuckled.

Raising my gaze to take in the other pictures on the wall, I landed on one in the center. A painting of a simple gray vase on a table against a plain, muted green background, tall, deeply colored red flowers overflowed the top. The strokes, the contrast of color and light. I wasn't familiar with the specific piece, but I'd bet my life I knew the artist. I stood staring at an original Van Gogh.

"It's part of the series with the sunflowers, I think." Walker stood behind me with a glass of wine stretched out to me.

"Did you already know all that stuff I told you at the exhibit?" I took the glass and eyed him.

"No. Mom likes art. I never paid enough attention, honestly. But after seeing it through your eyes, I will from now on."

A light dawned. "You didn't talk us into that exhibit. They let us in. Hewitt Family Foundation." I recalled the logo of the signature sponsor listed on the banner that hung outside the Seattle Art Museum. It didn't even register at the time that this man, this Hewitt, could have been one of *those* Hewitts.

Walker rubbed his hand against the back of his neck as I faced him. "Are you mad?" he asked.

"I'm ... stunned. I'm ... Are there any others?" I asked, possibly much too eagerly.

He chuckled. "Not here."

"Not here?" I snapped, my disbelief making the words come quickly.

"There's too much natural light. It's not good for the paintings. They practically had to design the house around having this one here. No natural light hits it directly. And this place could probably crumble, and that painting would stay right where it is and be fine. There's more security surrounding that thing than anywhere else here." He laughed. "There's another at my parents' apartment in Austin where it's less challenging to control the environment. I think it's one of the Paris park scenes. Bright blue sky, tall fall-colored trees."

I knew the series.

"Oh, my God. This is nuts, Walker." I shook my head. "I've never ... I don't know. This is nuts." I held my face in my palms, the shock of it all likely clear in my wide eyes.

"You know, that's not my painting. It's my mom's."

The statement brought me up short. There was a wound there. Someone he loved had only loved him for what he could give them.

I set the glass on the console table before I put my arms around him. "I won't lie. This is ... a lot. But I want to be clear. I'm here because I wanted to spend more time with you. I believe I was told to expect days of quiet and writing and no cooking. Oh, and more smokin' hot sex. That's a pretty sweet deal. Van Gogh or not."

Walker grinned, the smile finally hitting his eyes.

"And I'm here a week," I said, telegraphing my sincerity. "Not enough time to take advantage, even if I wanted to. Let me help with dinner. I want to hang with you."

He squeezed me close, but the earlier frown hadn't

completely disappeared. I'd work on that. "It's almost ready," he said. "Sit at the counter. Let me look at your pretty face while I finish the salad. The pizza will be quick once the grill's hot."

WE ATE at the kitchen island, sitting next to each other in the tall chairs. This was fast becoming my favorite seating arrangement.

The food was perfect. It was simple, and the slices of fresh mozzarella on the pizza were uneven. One of the basil leaves was trimmed, likely of a brown spot. And more than one piece of lettuce in the Caesar salad had been too big for me to chew with any manners. Like I said, perfect.

We laughed and talked about his family. His brother Canyon and his wife, Emme, were expecting their first child, and Walker and his other brother Vince, were taking every opportunity to harass their sibling as much as possible.

"Do I need to sign some sort of non-disclosure agreement or something?"

Walker smirked, then took a sip of wine. "Probably, but I don't carry those things in my back pocket. Not anymore, anyway."

"Oh, I see," I said, dripping innuendo.

"Wild past, Sweetheart. Not such a wild present."

My heart did a tiny flip. I had a week with Walker's wild all to myself. I clenched my thighs together on a surge of sensation at that thought. "I don't know. You brought a woman you've known for two days to your family's holiday hideaway. That seems at least a little wild or at least reckless."

Walker laughed. "Are you going to tell some tabloid about our week, this place, my favorite positions?" His voice grew low and growly, and wet heat pooled as he leaned closer. If he kept this up, my panties would be toast.

"No." My words were breathy again. "A doctor who couldn't maintain privacy wouldn't be a doctor for very long."

"I didn't think so. Plus, lawyers." He patted my thigh at his tease before sobering. "You said you trusted me in the car, driving in the snow. You trusted me with your life, in a way. So, I'm trusting you with mine."

WHEN WE WERE BOTH FULL, we worked together to clean up the kitchen, then Walker led me to the sofa by the fire with our topped-off wineglasses.

"What do you need now, Sweetheart? Hot tub, a bed, an orgasm?" He quirked his eyebrow.

"There's a hot tub?"

Walker nodded toward the patio.

"I don't have a bathing suit," I said.

"I don't mind." He grinned. "We're the only ones for miles, and this house is secure. Anyone approaches, we'll see them long before they see us."

"Hmm, in that case," I said in my best 1950s Hollywood starlet voice, "can't I have it all?"

He stood and, once again, reached for my hand.

20

WALKER

I shrugged on one of the thick robes I kept in the closet of my bedroom, *our* bedroom, at least for the next five days. I'd never had an *our bedroom* in this house, and I imagined it as I looked at Nora's things and mine, hanging together or folded on top of the center storage drawers. Claire had never made the trip, and I was glad Nora was the first person here with me. Even if it was only for a week.

I returned with the other robe to find Nora staring out the wall of windows across from the bed.

"Get those clothes off, woman. It's hot tub time."

She turned. "So, you get me up here with no one for miles and go all caveman," she said, a smile in her voice.

"Anxious. That's all." I moved closer, encircling her in my arms from behind. "It feels like days since I touched your skin and heard those sexy sounds you make when you come."

"I think I like the caveman," she said, glancing back with one raised eyebrow. I got hard, about to get harder.

She stepped away and held my gaze as she pushed her tight black leggings down and off.

"Oh my God, it's cold," Nora said, hopping toward me across the stone patio barefoot. With the snow shovel Nate left by the back door, I'd scraped a thin walkway earlier.

She tiptoed to the edge of the hot tub, set into the ground like a swimming pool, and surrounded with the same slate. This stone was warmer, and she could stand without the little hop that made her tits jiggle and my blood pulse. She hesitated.

"Never been skinny-dipping?" I asked.

"Does it show?"

I reached for her hand and pulled her closer. "We don't have to do this if you don't want to. But if you're worried, I promise we're alone. I've seen your gorgeous body in the water, and I'd love to touch you this time. But it's your call."

She bit her plump bottom lip. "Say the word?"

"That's right."

She loosened the belt of her robe, letting it open and fall away before she tossed it into the portable towel warmer I'd pulled nearby. I'd left the patio and hot tub lights off, hoping she'd feel less exposed. In the moonlight reflected off the snow, her pale skin glowed. Taking my hand again, she stepped in and sank lower onto the ledge seat. I hit the switch, and the jets started rumbling. The water roiled and fizzed.

She peered up at me as I tossed my robe into the warmer and closed the lid. Her eyes roamed my chest and tracked to my stiff shaft.

"You're hard already?" I could both see and hear her smile.

"Something about your sweet tits bouncing as you hopped. It's a condition. Do you know any doctors that can take a look?"

She smirked at me. "It's not my specialty."

"You're wrong, Sweetheart. It's absolutely your specialty."

She chuckled. "You realize that's the oldest line in the *how to seduce a doctor* playbook?"

"There's a playbook? Sweet! That'll cut down on some time."

She splashed me with water, then snuggled close. I wrapped my arm loosely around her back as she placed her hand on my thigh and teased her fingertips across my skin.

"You know, that won't improve my condition? How good are you at this doctor thing?"

"I'm an excellent physician." Her tone was teasing with a slight undercurrent of defensiveness.

I squeezed her shoulders and laughed. "Babe, I saw you. I know you're great at what you do."

"Tell me about your job," she said.

"What do you want to know?"

"What do you like about it?"

I thought for a moment. "The challenge. Being successful at something not everyone can do and making my parents proud feels good. They liked to brag about my wins to their friends, to people they were trying to impress. I enjoy being impressive." I scrubbed a hand over my face, hoping it didn't sound too cocky. Nora's gaze was distant for a beat before returning to mine.

"I became obsessed with winning. It was all I cared about. Every loss was a reason to push harder. Then I had that crash and broke my wrist. The disappointment from the people around me was like a second hit to the wall.

When I returned the next season, I wanted to prove to them I was still in it. I won the championship a second time that year."

"Wow, twice. That's a big deal, right?"

"I'm not Lewis Hamilton, but it is a big deal."

"Who's Lewis Hamilton?" she asked.

"British. Drives for Mercedes. First Black driver to win the World Driver's Championship, and he's done it seven times and counting. He's tied for the record with Michael Schumacher. They're both all-time greats."

"Is that why you didn't want to rent the Mercedes earlier today?" Her brows lifted, and her lips curved.

"I would have rented the Mercedes, but they had a Jaguar. Far superior machine." I furrowed my brow in mock seriousness and took the conversation away from the weighty topic of my past performance, the keyword being *past*.

"Let me guess, you drive for Jaguar."

"Yep." I gave her a sly grin.

"What do you like about ranching?"

I sighed. "The fresh air, the horses, the sunrises, the quiet." The chance to meet someone like Nora and build a life together. I thought about the ranch more often these days. "It's tiring work, but lately, it's like my skin fits better when I'm there. Does that make sense?"

"It does," she said.

"The break-up I mentioned—" Nora stilled, "—I told you she left because I wasn't winning."

"I guess you weren't talking about ranching, after all." She'd remembered my slip and how I tried to cover for it yesterday in the bar.

"We met the year I won the championship that second time. I assumed we were good," I shrugged, "though we didn't see each other much that season." The memory of being her fool had stayed vivid.

"After that winning year, something changed with my racing. It was like I didn't have any more gas in the tank. I was inconsistent and only won a handful of races the next season. I thought she was trying to encourage me and be supportive when she pushed me to not accept defeat but to win and go out on a high that could lead to other positions with the team. I mistook her admiration for real feelings, and we got engaged."

I laid my head back on the cold stone edge and gazed at the stars. "A few months later, I told her I didn't want to stay in F1 after I retired. I didn't want to be a team principal, the person who calls all the shots, the boss. When I finished racing, I wanted to be finished. I wanted to be a rancher. It was where I belonged in the long run, and we'd have a good life in Texas. We'd be together."

I sighed. "We fought, and I saw a side of her I had tried not to see. She said she would never be a rancher's wife, no matter who my father was. And she left."

"Oh, Walker." Nora spun in my arms, bringing her knees to the ledge and bracketing my hips as she faced me. "She sounds awful. I'm sorry you were hurt, but she didn't deserve you."

I chuckled. "Yeah, she was pretty awful. When she was gone, I wasn't even heartbroken. I was embarrassed about being played." I turned my tone to teasing. "I'm a professional race car driver. I'm supposed to be the big player." I winked, hoping to lighten the mood.

"She's the one who used you. A wise person once told me that people like that aren't really a *prize*, anyway." Her luscious lips curved as she referenced what I'd said to her yesterday about that prick who'd hurt her.

Damn, I liked her. I leaned in and placed a sweet kiss on her tempting mouth. "I like the quiet here and the softness of your skin," I whispered against her neck before inhaling her coconut scent. "I like you relaxed. Are you relaxed, Sweetheart?" I smoothed my hands up her sides, following the curve to those full tits. The tail of her braid rested along one swell, and I wanted to see her hair loose again.

"Too relaxed." She rested her forehead on mine.

Gently, I turned her back to my front and pulled her head to rest on my shoulder so she floated above me with her face to the stars. The angle made her body more buoyant, and her deep pink nipples broke the water's surface. I couldn't look away as my fingers roamed.

"Relaxed is a good place to start," I said.

As the water swirled, I caressed her hips. Her arms were weightless, stretched out to her sides. All that held her to me was her head on my shoulder and my hands on her curves.

"Tell me how to make you feel good, Sweetheart?" I brushed a kiss along her temple. "What do you like?"

Nora was quiet. I couldn't see her face, and I wasn't sure what the silence meant.

"Nora?"

"I …" her chest rose and fell as her breathing deepened.

"Don't be shy, babe. It's just me. What do you want?"

She paused. "I … I don't know."

I stopped for a beat at the sad tone in her voice. A woman like Nora, confident, beautiful, and perceptive, and she didn't know how she wanted to be touched by a man? I sensed her unease at the confession.

"Has no one ever asked you?"

"No," she said, her voice barely above a whisper. "I've had it fast. I've had it long and tender, but my partner always decided. I enjoyed it. But I was never asked that question, never had to think about it. I focused on my partner."

She floated above me, a goddess in the moonlight, as my hands glided over the smooth dips and valleys of her.

I had an idea. "Has anyone ever tied you up?"

"Um, no. Have you tied someone up?"

"I have. She asked me to. But it wasn't what I expected. I thought it would be me doing what I wanted and her taking it. I was young and stupid." I grinned at what an arrogant idiot I'd been, and my cheek brushed her jaw.

"Instead, she told me how to touch her and please her. Being bound, she couldn't get distracted trying to reciprocate, and I didn't expect her to. All she could think about was what she wanted and tell me to do it. Honestly, it rocked me. I learned that giving pleasure is something I really fucking enjoy, and she was free to just experience it." I paused. "If you could only enjoy it, what would you want me to do first?"

Charged silence stretched between us like she was concentrating.

"Touching me is good," she whispered. I dropped my hands. No cheating and going along with what I was already doing.

"Where do you want me to touch you?"

She inhaled a deep breath, and something shifted as her breathing returned to a slow even rhythm. Relaxed.

"Touch me on my stomach, my thighs, my breasts ... but not my nipples or my sex. I want to imagine you there first," she said like it wasn't the hottest fucking thing I'd ever heard.

"You want me to tease you, Sweetheart?"

"I want you to take your time."

Yes, ma'am. I wanted that too.

Her eyes closed, and we sat in the quiet like that. Her breathing was deep and even as I returned my fingers to trace every gorgeous curve while I memorized the images before me.

The jets turned off automatically, indicating it was time for a break. I slid from beneath her and held her head in my hand before I pressed a kiss to her forehead. She sighed, a soft moan that made my dick twitch again.

"Let's go in, Sweetheart."

She nodded, then moved slowly, even in the cold. Wrapped in our warm robes, she helped me replace the padded cover on the tub, then I led her inside and back to the bedroom.

"We can wash off the salt water from the tub," I said and pulled her into the ensuite. I started the shower, and the steam swirled above us.

Nora appeared dazed and sedate, with her pale skin flushed. The sound of the water broke the silence as I washed her, taking my time here and kissing her gently. She did the same to me. Her fingers explored every muscle along my arms, then my abs, and down my thighs, but she didn't touch my straining dick.

When she finished, she stepped out and grabbed a towel. Her expression was now one of confidence. Like she was certain I would do anything she asked me to. Damn right.

I shut off the water and snatched a towel for myself from the fluffy pile. I found Nora turning down the sheets in the dimly lit bedroom.

"So how does this work, tying me up?" she asked. "The headboard is solid padding."

"Get comfortable. I'm going to light the fire."

Nora removed her towel and climbed onto the bed. She lay on her stomach with her arms tucked under her and one knee bent, giving me a teasing peek at her center. She gazed over from the pillow. "Hurry, or I may have to touch myself."

"This isn't about me denying you or controlling you, Nora. If you want to touch yourself, go ahead. You decide what you want."

I stacked the logs in the fireplace, barely glancing at them. Nora was the single point in my vision as one of her hands slid lower, and she held my gaze. I couldn't see, exactly, and I wanted to. Another time. This wasn't about what I wanted.

When the kindling caught, I stood and moved the screen into place. Stepping back into the bathroom, I grabbed an extra roll of toilet paper.

"What's that for?" Nora asked and rose on her elbows, a question in her eyes.

"To tie you up. I'll wrap it tight, so you feel held, but you and I both know you can get out of it at any time. I'm not trying to actually hold you down. I want to make you feel secure."

Nora swallowed and nodded as she rolled onto her back. Carefully, I wrapped her hands together in the fragile paper. When I finished, I placed a pillow under her head, pulled her bound wrists above it, and instructed her to grip the edge of the mattress. I rested a couple of pillows on her lower arms, adding the pressure and security of weight.

"Stay there like that and tell me what you want."

21

NORA

Walker removed the towel at his waist and knelt on the bed between my legs. It was a strange feeling, being bound. And I did feel bound, gripping the mattress above me, the weight of the pillows adding to the sensation. Even though I knew I could easily get out of the restraint, I relished the idea that I couldn't. I could only tell Walker what I wanted him to do.

What *I* wanted.

The realization that no one had ever asked me what I wanted hit me harder than I expected. But what I wanted in most cases didn't matter. It was what I could do for others. I'd let that idea from work into my personal life. Into my bedroom.

Not with Walker. I would make the most of my time in this alternate universe. "I want you to massage my feet." The words *I want* sound breathy and foreign.

Walker smiled and lifted a foot. First, he rubbed the ball with both thumbs and moved to my heel. Gently, he caressed between my toes, testing to see if I was ticklish. I wasn't, and he did the same thing with my other foot. It was sensual. Decadent. My blood hummed, and I grew bolder.

"I like your hands. I want them on my thighs along with your lips."

Those magical hands moved higher, and with a sexy smirk that did things to my belly, he kissed and nipped up one leg, then the other, like he did last night. My core sizzled as he hovered close to my sex. I let my eyes drift closed as I soaked in the gentleness of his kisses and the soft scrape of his growing scruff.

He inhaled at my apex. "You smell so fucking good, babe."

I met his questioning eyes. "Not yet. I want your mouth on my breasts, my nipples."

Slowly, Walker kissed my stomach, then stroked the undersides of each heavy globe before following his fingers with tender bites and wet licks. We both moaned, and my back arched. The vision of his sexy smirk and naked body waiting for my next request drove me higher. My sex was drenched, and I squirmed against him, losing control.

"My neck." I panted. "I want you to kiss me, suck me there. Mark me." My words came fast.

In one movement, Walker latched on to that place where my neck met my shoulder. He sucked and bit before he let out a low growl that went straight to my core.

I got wetter. I was slick, almost dripping, as his warm mouth pulled at my skin, making it tingle. Damn, when was the last time I had a hickey? I didn't remember it feeling this good.

My breath heaved. "Suck my clit. I want to come." My newfound boldness consumed me.

Another growl rumbled in my ears, and I reveled in the scratchy scrape of his chin sliding between my breasts as he moved lower again.

Quickly, he licked a broad stroke along my pulsing sex, and I bucked.

"Eating you makes me so hard. I can't get enough." He moved to his side by my legs, and resting one cheek next to my thigh, he pulled my other leg over him as he lay on his back. He placed that knee on the other side of his face, twisting my lower body, so my sex rested right over his mouth. With my bent leg holding me at an angle over him, I had purchase to grind against his lips as he kissed and licked and sucked in a constant rhythm. I moaned, or was it a cry?

"There's no rush. Fuck my mouth as long as you want."

Oh. God. I clung to the bed and rolled more to grind down harder. His arms wrapped around my thighs, holding me secure, and bringing my legs closer together, deepening the sensation of contact with his tongue.

My breath heaved, and my head spun as fire filled me. All there was in this world was his mouth on me. One hand spread across my ass, caressing and teasing. It felt so, so good. He snuck his other hand under me and inserted first a single finger, then a second, into my slick channel, curling them to press against my inner wall. His fingers stroked against me from the inside while he licked and pressed his lips against my clit. I rocked my hips, the pleasure mounting. It was like nothing before, and it quickly consumed me until I exploded with a cry.

Walker released my pulsing center and lapped sweetly all around before dipping his tongue inside.

"Condom?" I asked between shattered, panting breaths.

He lifted my leg and shifted out from under me, leaving me twisted. I certainly couldn't move on my own. With a grin, he wiped his hand down his nose, cheeks, and chin, now slick with my wetness. "Stay like that," he said.

I struggled to catch my breath, rolling my forehead against the cool sheets between my arms, stretched to the upper edge of the bed as if it would hold me to earth.

A moment later, Walker's hands were at my hips, pulling me and turning my face to the mattress. I was on my knees, ass in the air.

"Is this okay?" He rested his tip near my opening, pulsing with aftershocks from the best damn orgasm I ever had.

"Yes." It was a bit of a squeak, but I was wrung out.

I rose to my elbows, my head hanging between my arms. He didn't move. His stiff shaft nestled against my wet folds as his hands caressed my hips and back with light pressure.

He shifted, and with a groan, he surged inside. I gasped at the fullness and stretch. It was electric.

"Can you come again like this?" he asked.

"I think so. You're hitting that spot perfectly."

"Like I was made for you. Like you were made for me. Give it to me again, Sweetheart."

His voice was so rough, and his hands gripped me tighter. My hard nipples scraped against the smooth sheets, and every time he thrust against that special spot, my sex rippled around him.

"More, Walker. I *want* you deeper."

"Oh, fuck," he said gruffly and plunged into my body. My back arched and flexed as I pushed against each thrust.

The sensations mounted as our bodies made complete contact, and Walker added a rocking motion against my fevered flesh as he secured me to him after each thrust. Could I come this way without touching my clit? That would be a first. One more surge and rock motion, and I tensed, unleashing the pleasure. It was unbelievable.

He held my hips, and we both lingered, with the tremors moving through me. Then, after a few more slow, deep thrusts, he stilled and groaned his own release before we crashed into the mattress together. Him on top of me, inside me, his front to my back in stopped time.

"Nora. Hell. That was ... so fucking good. You're incredible."

I couldn't stop the lazy grin. No one had ever said that to me before. I satisfied my lovers. But maybe never quite like this.

"Same goes, Walker."

"Women are truly blessed. I love how you can come again and again with barely any break. It's so damn hot."

He lifted and grabbed the edge of the condom as he left my body.

I stretched on my stomach and unwrapped my bound hands. I'd never heard of this use for TP. Wasn't there some old commercial about a brand so strong it could hold a quarter? This would certainly make a compelling advertisement for the strength of the stuff. I snickered as I imagined that million-dollar spot airing during the Super Bowl.

After disposing of the condom, Walker brought a warm, wet cloth and rolled me onto my back. "In case I was too rough," he said and slid next to me, caressing the velvety material against my folds.

"You weren't rough," I said. "You were perfect. Thank you for giving me what I *wanted*." I sang the word a little.

"My pleasure." His grin was sly.

He returned the cloth to the bathroom at record speed. After pulling me to drape halfway across his muscled chest and covering us in warm blankets, he removed the elastic from my braid, now a wreck probably, and tenderly loosened the woven pattern, stroking his fingers through the strands as they fell away.

THE ALARM on my watch buzzed, and the light filtering through the edges of the blinds was bright as I rolled against the solid, heavy body at my back. But wait, was that someone's voice I heard? My sex and sleep-addled mind did the math. If the man was here with me, who was out there?

"Go back to sleep, babe. Not ready to let you out of bed."

"Walker, is your family here?" Oh shit. Did he want his family to meet me? Did I want to meet them?

"It's Carly or Nate or both."

"We should get up." I nudged him.

"We don't have to. They know we're here. We know they're here."

"Walker. Aren't we being rude?"

He chuckled. "Carly and Nate know what they're doing. They don't need us."

"Walker."

He checked the clock and groaned. "Okay. We'll get up. What time is your meeting?"

"Ten."

"Alright, sexy. You can have the bathroom. I'll go check in out there. See what they have planned for today and let them know what we're doing. Do you still want to go to dinner tonight, or would you rather eat here?"

"Whatever you want."

"Nora." His low voice was like a warning and brought me up short. *What I want.* The words bounced in my brain along with images of last night.

"I want to go out. Take me out. Then we can come back and play *What Does Walker Want* this time."

"Babe, you're reading my mind."

He took a deep breath and rolled out of bed. I watched his magnificently naked backside stroll into the closet off the bathroom.

22

WALKER

Carly stood at the stove with her back to me. She and Nate were in their late forties with twin girls about to graduate from Perry Harbor High School.

"Hey, Carly. Where's Nate?"

"Hey, stranger." She opened an arm, inviting me in for a side hug. "Nate's checking on the other cabins. Making sure the heat's on, appliances working. Everyone should be here by the weekend, if not sooner. Nate and I are picking up the decorator in about an hour. He's coming to set up all the Christmas trees today. Will that work for you?"

"Sure. We're heading to Perry Harbor. My ... Nora has a meeting there." I thumbed back toward the bedroom.

"Your ... Nora?" Her brow quirked. I'd forgotten to tell anyone I was bringing someone with me. I needed to fix that. If any of my family arrived before Nora had to leave, I didn't want them, or her feeling ambushed.

"Well, I don't *own* her."

Carly laughed and returned to the egg casserole she

was making. "I wasn't told you were dating. You brought a woman home for Christmas?"

"Not exactly." But I couldn't say I didn't like the idea of Nora here with me for the holiday. Emme, Canyon's wife, would probably ask her a million questions about pregnancy and childbirth. Vince and his wife, Michelle, would take it easier on her. It was anyone's guess what Mom and Dad would say. I'd never brought a woman to any family holiday. At first, because I was too busy playing *racing Casanova*. Then more recently, because I was too busy recovering from a grueling season. Claire had been the first person I'd imagined here, but somehow, that image hadn't felt as right as the one I pictured now with Nora.

Carly set a package of sausage links on the counter.

"Are you and Nate eating, too? Otherwise, you don't have to cook the sausage. Nora doesn't eat meat for breakfast," I said, and Carly raised her brow. "Better to save it for when everyone else is here." She smirked at me and returned the package to the fridge.

"I hope you're planning to say more about *your Nora* before she gets out here, and I have to admit I've never heard of her."

"She won't expect you to have. I picked her up at the airport." I rubbed my hand on the back of my neck. That hadn't sounded good.

"You what? Walker. What are you doing? Who is she? Did she recognize you?"

"She's not a spy, Carly. She's a doctor."

Carly stirred the casserole ingredients. "A doctor? Well, that's new."

"Hey, what's that supposed to mean?" I moved to the coffeemaker to start the Swiss-made machine grinding the beans for a full cup.

"Walker, really. I can access the internet. And I know what your driver name is, *Hugh*," she teased and emphasized the name I used in the circuit, Hugh Walker. Walker Hewitt was my real name and not that difficult to discover, so Dad's security team had staged like fifty social media accounts to throw folks off. It wasn't foolproof, but it helped maintain some search engine privacy. Most of the crazy stuff went to the Hugh Walker account, which someone else managed.

"I've seen the super-models and heiresses," Carly continued. "I've not seen a doctor."

"How do you know one of *them* wasn't a doctor?" I leaned against the counter and crossed my ankles.

"Walker." She sounded more like my mom by the second.

"Fine. Yeah, it's a first. She's ... different. It was supposed to be one night, but then it became two, so I talked her into coming here with me."

"For the holidays? Is that smart? She's going to get attached."

"Maybe I want her to get attached." I paused at the truth in those words and ran my hand through my hair as the machine finished with the crema layer on top of the dark liquid I loved. "Look, she's here. I want her here. And we're going to Perry Harbor for the day."

"Alright. Well, do you know if she wants white or wheat toast?"

"Give me a sec. I'll find out." I gave Carly a gentle hip check as I passed her.

I set down my cup and strode to the bedroom, replaying the conversation. Nora getting attached would be nice. That thought surprised me. But how would that work? She was in Nashville. Even if I didn't go back to racing, I'd be in Texas. Shit. I was going too fast. We were on day three of knowing the other existed. I needed to relax and enjoy the ride for a while.

Nora charmed Carly and Nate almost as effortlessly as she'd done to me. Sincerity, kindness, humor, smarts. She had it all. And I really liked her boobs. Something I assumed hadn't been a factor for them. Comparing her to past girlfriends was no contest. She was definitely exceptional and far too good for me, F1 driver or not.

Gorgeous in fitted black jeans, a black cashmere sweater, and a long, brown wool coat with brown boots, she was professional and tough. Alluring and feminine. The style fit her perfectly. I needed to up my game for this date.

After breakfast, I took a quick shower and shaved the scruff that had become a bit itchy while Nora reviewed her notes and prepped for the interview. Attending Europe's Fashion Week on the arm of some celebrity every year, usually arranged by the team's publicist, wasn't totally wasted on me. I wore a casual gray sweater with black accents on the collar and the sleeves, a white button-down, dark wash jeans, a charcoal wool blazer, and light gray suede oxfords.

With a thanks and a wave to Carly and Nate, we bundled in coats, scarves, and hats and headed to the dock. Sunlight glinted off the snow bright enough to require sunglasses, and I wished mine had the thick rims Nora liked instead of my wire Cartier Aviators.

"The sun is so warm," she said, smoothing a hand along her braid. "It's beautiful, the way the water shines and glitters." The rows of solar panels on top of each building that provided most of the energy we consumed on the island would certainly get a workout today.

Nora took my offered hand as she stepped onto the stern of the boat.

The ride to Perry Harbor was bright and beautiful. With a little imagination, you could believe it was summer with all that sunshine. Would Nora wear a bikini and sunbathe on the deck if we stopped in a private cove? Would she let me go down on her out in the open? Shit. Now I was half hard.

"You could pick up a bathing suit for the hot tub in town. My brothers may arrive soon, which will put a damper on our skinny-dipping."

"Your brothers?" She bit her lip. "Should I go somewhere else? You don't want me here when your family comes."

I chuckled. "No, you shouldn't go somewhere else. Not unless you want to. You're not a dirty little secret, Nora. We're friends. My family would be happy to meet a friend of mine."

She turned and peered out at the glistening water speeding by.

"You're thinking pretty loudly. What's up?" I asked.

"It's none of my business."

"Nora, the way you let me *into your business* last night, I think we're beyond being polite."

She blushed. "Fine. I was wondering how many *friends* of yours they'd welcomed in the past."

I glanced over. "None. You're the first. I didn't say anything because I didn't want you to worry, but my family may be a little surprised."

Another conversation that would have been better when I wasn't driving a boat. What the hell was wrong with me these last few days? I was usually smoother than this.

"What about your fiancée?"

"My family met her, of course, but she hadn't yet traveled with me for the holidays and definitely not here. ... But look, nothing's changed," I said, and it felt like a lie. I coughed to regroup. "I want you here. I hope you'll stay until the weekend like we planned, regardless of when my family arrives. There will still be plenty of space and time for you to write."

She was quiet for a beat. "It's probably not a good idea, but damn it, Walker, I don't *want* to leave early. And now that you've gotten me voicing what I *want* all the time, I can't seem to stop." She grinned and made a face at me.

Good. "What you really *want* is my tongue, isn't it?" I teased.

She laughed. "Among other things."

WE GRABBED the Jaguar at the marina and parked closer to town, uncertain if the meeting spot and the presentation location this afternoon were close enough to walk. "This is where they said to meet you?" I asked as Nora stopped in front of the *Nip & Purl*. I wasn't sure if it was a bar or a yarn shop. And *nip* and *purl*? Was I the only one who thought that was a sexy play on words for a couple of my favorite female body parts?

I held the door open then followed her inside. A tree decorated in red and green sat to the side of one front window, and white lights hung above the small bar area. A couple of shelves held whiskey bottles, and a coffee machine hissed at the other end. What sounded like Sinatra or Tony Bennet versions of holiday classics played low and pleasant in the background while the scent of cinnamon and coffee floated in the air.

"Hi, I'm meeting Ms. Edwards and Ms. Miller. Do you

know if they're here yet?" Nora asked the man behind the bar with silver hair and a burly build. Another man a couple seats away checked her out. I caught his eye and moved in closer. This guy was older, too, pushing seventy, but that didn't seem to interfere with my instinct to let him know she was with me. He grinned knowingly and turned away.

"Sure," the bartender said and nodded to a corner near a tall wooden bookcase filled with every color of yarn where two ladies, probably in their sixties or seventies, sat at a table, knitting. These were the teachers? The sex educators Nora told me she was coming to meet? I didn't know what I expected, but it wasn't this. But then, not much had been what I expected since I met Nora.

Other groups, mostly older women, clustered in cushy chairs or sofas, knitting and talking.

"You do your thing, babe. I'll stay here." I brushed a kiss to her temple and glanced at an empty bar stool.

"You don't have to wait," Nora said. "I can meet you somewhere if you'd rather."

"You think I want to be somewhere other than with you?" I winked, and she grinned before turning back toward the ladies.

"What can I get you?" the bartender asked, his booming voice pulling my attention from Nora's rounded ass.

"What do you have?" I asked.

"Coffee. Tea. Water. Wine. Whiskey."

"Got it. I'll take a coffee, black."

"Comin' up." He glanced at the other man as he walked away.

"I wasn't checking out your girl. Not in the way you think," the man down the bar said and stretched out his hand. "Jacob Landers. You're not from Perry Harbor."

We shook. "Walker Hewitt. No, my girl's in town to meet with those ladies."

Mr. Landers nodded. "One woman she's with, the one in the purple shirt, she's my girl."

I turned to see a lady with a bright smile talking animatedly with Nora. Her hair was shoulder length and silver as it reflected the light above the table. She was thin, with rosy cheeks and a sweet expression. I turned back to the man in a thick wool sweater that had to be straight out of some fisherman's catalog.

"She's lovely. How long have you been married?" I asked.

"Not married. Yet." The bartender making my coffee at the other end coughed.

"Watch it, Jimmy, or I'll tell Mary about your big Christmas surprise." Mr. Landers didn't look away from me. He just smiled as Jimmy sighed.

"Never should have told you about that," Jimmy said as he brought my coffee.

"He's not wrong," Mr. Landers said to me. "So, your girl's the doctor who came to meet with my Natalie and her friend Nell?"

23

NORA

Ms. Edwards and Ms. Miller had been incredibly easy to talk to. Even with the distraction of knowing that Walker was close, I relaxed into the conversation about their backgrounds and how they became the well-respected educators and bloggers they were.

Ms. Edwards, Miss Nell, she told me to call her, had been an advertising exec in Dallas. Ms. Miller, or Miss Natalie, had been a high school biology teacher. A fact that made me smile.

They'd been friends for decades and, long ago, had plans to travel together with their husbands after retirement, enjoying those promised golden years. Instead, they were both widowed in the same year.

Grief and loss had put them both on a path to reinvention much sooner than expected. I'd say they could check that box. Finding what they described as a shocking lack of common knowledge and products related to sexual health and dating later in life, they set out to rectify the situation as much as possible.

They started a popular blog for women about sex toys

and techniques for masturbation that took into consideration hormonal and physical changes in our bodies as we aged. They'd read articles, asked questions, and connected with doctors and experts with the help of Natalie's son, a family therapist in Bellevue, near Seattle.

Soon they were doing more. Writing for popular magazines and speaking to a growing number of groups each year. They received hundreds of items and products from manufacturers worldwide to review and comment on. They'd become influencers before it was a thing.

A healthy sex life for seniors was their professional passion, and it showed with every word.

"Thank you both for meeting with me. You've given me several resources, and I think I have enough to finish my writing. Vulvodynia and how it limits women sexually, young and old, is a problem we should solve."

"Well, I won't disagree with you," Miss Nell said. "Imagine if a man developed pain in his penis with no known cause, and his doctor told him to *apply this cream to dull all the sensation so you can have intercourse. It won't feel bad, but it won't feel good either.*" Miss Nell eyed me over her funky-framed glasses. She didn't have to say more.

"Some men would do it for the joy of pleasing a lover, especially an older man," Miss Natalie said with a demure glance toward the bar.

"You got me there, Nat." Miss Nell nodded emphatically. "Older couples are finding many ways to enjoy sex and experience sexual pleasure. I doubt a numb penis would be much more than a speed bump to some men our age."

I stood with a grin and shook both ladies' hands. "I hope to do good in the world like I believe you're both doing."

"Oh, my dear, I have every confidence you will. You're

still planning to attend the University Square talk this afternoon?" Miss Nell asked.

"Yes, and I was hoping to bring a guest. I know I only RSVP'd for one." I nodded toward the bar and Walker.

"Not a problem, dear." Miss Natalie said.

"Unless Jimmy and Jacob have talked him into fishing instead with the clear weather," Miss Nell said.

With plans to meet later today, I packed up my notes and laptop before heading back to Walker.

"How'd it go?" he asked.

"Great. I think I'm ready to finish my writing. I want this grant, and this interview will help seal the deal. I really think I can get this one."

"I'm sure you can." Walker shifted in his seat. "This is Mr. Landers, Jacob. He's with Ms. Miller," he said.

"Oh yes. She mentioned you." I reached to shake his hand as the man sat taller in his chair.

"When are you gonna stop preening, you jackass?" the burly bartender said to Jacob. "Dating a sex educator may just mean she thinks you need a lot of education on the subject," he added as he walked away, and Walker and I both chuckled.

THE TALK WAS SCHEDULED for four o'clock, and it was barely noon, so we had time to explore. Jacob had given Walker some suggestions of breweries, bakeries, and local restaurants to try. We grabbed a couple of sandwiches from a coffee shop and café, Shakey Grounds, and took the boat out in the mid-day sunshine before the clouds returned tomorrow.

The light danced on the water, and the sky was a deep blue, clear and bright, as Walker navigated through the channels and around the islands. We passed a giant oil tanker anchored near the refinery and a rustic resort on the water's edge of another island. A nearby state park boasted a high bridge, and the narrow waterway below it churned with swirling currents. I was grateful for the powerful boat we were in.

As the sky darkened with the coming afternoon sunset, we headed back to the marina, then drove the few blocks to University Square, an independent living facility for older adults. Walker and I greeted Miss Natalie and Miss Nell, then took our seats.

The room was busy with people who appeared to be both in couples or attending as singles. All were casually talking while sampling the coffee and cake set out by the facility's staff. The vibe was one of energy and vitality despite several walkers with tennis balls attached and wooden canes stained dark or natural.

"This gives me hope," Walker said, looking around.

"What do you mean?"

"I intend to be having sex, making my partner feel good, for as long as possible, just like these guys." He nodded to the men in the room, from those with thinning hair and paunchy stomachs to others with broad shoulders and pressed khakis.

My heart stuttered. I envied that woman he'd be loving into her eighties or nineties. She was going to have a very happy life.

The talk was a success. Questions were asked and answered as the awkward laughter at first morphed into genuine vulnerability and interest.

Miss Nell approached as Walker went to help Jacob and a few others put away tables and folding chairs.

"Thank you for letting me observe," I said.

"We're glad you came. Spread the word. Sex doesn't end at forty or fifty or even sixty."

"I will."

"Your man was paying close attention," she said.

"He's not *my* man. We're, well actually, we were supposed to be a hookup, a one-night-stand, but it became a seven-night-stand."

Miss Nell shifted. "Well, I'm not usually the romantic. That's Nat. But that man, the way he listened and smiled and looked at you. I'd wager if you wanted more than seven nights, he wouldn't complain."

Did I want more with Walker? Sure, if there were no other circumstances. But there were. His job was in Europe. I was going to be doing research in Nashville or in an African village or some other place equally distant from the life of a professional Formula One driver.

WE PARKED NOT FAR off Commerce, the main road in Perry Harbor, and walked through town a bit before dinner. The streetlight poles were wrapped in white lights, and several colorful banners celebrating Christmas, Hanukkah, and Kwanza hung on the sides. Holiday-themed displays decorated the windows of every store lining the street as shoppers shuffled along with bags and steaming cups of something warm. It was bright and festive.

"Oh, I should look for that bathing suit," I said as we passed a small boutique attached to The Elliot Hotel, a majestic four-story building with tall windows and creamy plantation shutters.

"Let's do it." Walker headed toward the heavy double doors at the entrance. Inside were muted yellow walls, plush fabrics in greens and browns, with sparkling holiday wreaths and pink poinsettias scattered throughout. It was what I imagined a nice hotel in Europe would be like.

Quaint, luxurious, and calm, mixed with a dash of elegant Noel.

The small boutique sat off to the side of the cozy lobby.

"Champagne or spiced cider?" A stylish saleswoman approached, beaming. "Holiday shopping is always better with refreshments." She winked.

"Champagne would be great," I said and glanced at Walker, who nodded. "Thank you."

At a table beside the counter, the saleswoman poured two glasses. "Are you looking for something in particular?" She handed me a delicate flute of golden bubbles.

Walker was already shuffling through a stack of soft cashmere sweaters in all colors.

"A bathing suit," I said as she handed a flute to Walker.

"Wonderful. Winters here are the perfect time to take a trip somewhere warm and sunny." She grinned.

I smiled, unwilling to share that I needed one because I would no longer be skinny-dipping with my sinfully hot shopping partner.

"You're a size ten?" she asked, and I nodded. "Right this way," she said.

Walker's head snapped up, and he followed us toward the back of the store. I glanced at him with my brow furrowed.

"What?" he asked, keeping his voice low. "I thought today was about a little game called W*hat Does Walker Want.* And Walker wants to help you pick it out."

"Fine." I wanted to huff, but I was too busy smiling.

I tried all the options in my size. The last one was a red bikini. The bottoms covered my ass well enough, but the top was likely illegal, with my breasts popping out on all sides.

"That's it, babe."

"No, Walker. You want your brothers and their wives, your parents, to see me in this? I'm not sure it paints the image I'm going for."

"Oh, right. How about that brown one with the band thing for a top?" He motioned across his chest, and I chuckled as the saleswoman held it up for another look.

The price was higher for the brown one, but it had more fabric to cover the girls. "I'll take it," I said and slipped back into the dressing room.

As I turned, I noticed a stack of lacy undies and bras tucked into discreet bins on a side wall near the single-curtained space at the back of the boutique. I'd worn my sexiest pair already. Five more days with Walker required more options. Would he want to pick some out for me?

"Hey, babe," I called after him, and he spun smoothly, without breaking his stride, to walk back toward me.

I fingered the delicate fabric, drawing his attention before I lowered my hand. "I need a few new sets. These two bins are my size. Would you pick something out for me?" I tried to sound innocent, but the fire in Walker's eyes would have melted steel. I heard the saleswoman greet another customer, so I delivered a heated gaze of my own before I pulled the curtain closed on the dressing room.

24

WALKER

Damn. She was smokin' hot in that red bikini. No way I wanted anyone else to see her in that thing. And then she asked me to pick out new underwear for her. Fuck, I barely held it together, examining the options and imagining them on Nora. I wanted to see her in all of them, but I narrowed it down to a handful, including a pale pink set that was sweet and erotic at the same time, like something the dream girl next door would wear. The images in my mind made all my blood head south.

"Is there a set you want to see me in first?" she asked, her voice innocent as hell.

"This one." The words caught as I shoved the pale pink set through the curtain's opening.

"Oh pretty," Nora said in a breathy voice that again, would not help my dick situation. "Pick three or four more and take them to the counter for me along with the brown bathing suit?" she asked.

"Yes, ma'am."

I handed the saleswoman my card as Nora approached, back in her black jeans and turtleneck sweater. I took the fuck-hot red bikini she'd just changed out of and added it to the pile on the counter.

"I got this," I said to her questioning look.

"You don't have to do that," she replied.

I glanced at the pile of lace in bright and muted colors, the tags from the pink set she was wearing, and the two swimsuits.

I leaned in, not entirely out of hearing range of the saleswoman, but not making an announcement. "Are you going to wear those things for me this week?"

Nora held my gaze as usual, but I saw the blush rise on her cheeks. "Absolutely."

"Then I'm buying, Sweetheart."

WE MADE our way across the street to The Boathouse restaurant and bar with a small brown bag of even smaller clothing. My brothers and I had come here occasionally in recent years to play pool or have a beer when we were all in town. The summers were especially beautiful, and taking a mid-racing-season vacation here, usually in early August, meant simple peace and calm that I couldn't often find in the luxury resorts of Europe. And it was much cooler here than in Texas in the summer.

Inside, the large open room was warm, with exposed brick walls, dark wood tables, and a couple of small boats decorated with colorful lights hanging from the high rafters. It was busy but not crowded, and the vibe was welcoming and familiar like everyone knew each other.

We found seats at the bar, stashed our coats, and ordered drinks. The bartender brought us printed menus. No QR codes here, and I winked at Nora, who grinned as she accepted hers.

"Who's the America's cup fan?" I asked, nodding

toward a large poster hanging on the wall above as I pushed up the sleeves of my sweater and rolled the white cotton shirt along with it.

"Me, mostly," the bartender said. "I used to race. That's my old team."

"Oh, are you in the picture?" Nora asked and sat taller. If she liked racers, she already had one. I made a mental note to send her a poster from this past season.

"I am," he said and pointed to a guy about halfway back on one side of the huge catamaran. "That's me. I'm Jake." He shook our hands. "I was a grinder. We turned the winches that controlled the sails. Tough work. And not nearly as fun as owning a bar with your brother. What can I bring you?"

"So, the day was successful?" I asked Nora as we finished our dinner of salmon and herb-roasted potatoes. The food was great, but eating drew my attention to Nora's mouth and that damn little freckle on her lower lip that I thought about biting almost to the point of obsession. She wore all black without the brown coat and capped with her dark, thick braid, her face glowed in the low lights, her blue eyes shining. She was vibrant and compelling, like one of Angus Hayes's photos.

To make matters worse, I kept imagining her in that pale pink lace throughout our dinner conversation. I wanted this date. I wanted to talk with her, and we needed to eat, but as the night continued, my hands itched at the thought of getting her back to the house and unwrapping her.

I willed myself to relax. Slow, deep breaths.

"Those ladies know their stuff," she said. "And they were certainly approachable no matter what the topic."

"They must have folks asking them for advice all the time."

"Well, I don't think so. Miss Nell joked that most people here aren't aware of what they do, and rumors abound. I think she gets a little kick out of being a mystery. They'd vacationed here with their husbands many times, sailing, and loved the area. When they were planning to move here several years ago to be closer to family, they both fell in love with the house and decided living together beat living alone in a new town. Gossips decided they were lovers, CIA agents, or part of a cult. Miss Nell said the theories were pretty entertaining."

She squirmed in her seat, adjusting her sweater, drawing my eye to her full breasts that I knew would smell and taste sweet. "Everyone at Nip & Purl knows what they do. That place is sort of like a secret club the seniors are keeping from the younger generations. They talk about sex toys while quietly knitting on the sofa or telling big-fish stories at the bar. It's actually genius. Sexual expertise hiding in plain sight because our culture doesn't think older people have anything to teach us in that department."

"And you disagree," I said.

"Absolutely. Miss Natalie and Miss Nell had some great recommendations for products and techniques that enhance sexual pleasure for both partners when penetration isn't possible."

I blinked. "And that's part of your research?"

Nora took a breath. "My proposal centers on conditions attributed to anxiety in women without a clear cause. One condition I'll be researching causes unexplained pain around the vulva, drastically impacting women's sex lives and relationships. One treatment is to numb the area with topical cream. Numb it!" Her voice rose in emphasis or outrage. "If the condition *is* related to anxiety, treatment options could include techniques and products that make sex pleasurable without penetration, which may help to alleviate some of the anxiety. We need to find clear reasons for conditions and better treatment options, and I want to include that aspect in the project too."

She brushed some lint from her black jeans and crossed her legs to angle toward me. "A lot of people think that sex is all about the vagina for us. It isn't. Most of the sensation for many women comes from the lower part of the vaginal opening and the surrounding outer area, including the clitoris, but not only there. The mons, the labia, all contain hundreds of nerve endings. Much more than inside the vaginal canal. Numbing that area sort of negates the whole deal for some women."

I blinked, not quite sure how to respond but very aware of my dick and all the smart, sexy things coming out of her mouth.

"Sorry. I'm doing it again," she said, her expression wary. "Did I make you uncomfortable?" She glanced around to see if she'd attracted any attention. Hell, if I cared. She was dazzling when she talked about her research. Truly dazzling.

"No. I'm not uncomfortable. I love your passion. It's hot as fuck." She bit her lip and grinned. "You going to do that someday? Be a sex educator?" I asked.

"Nah," she lowered her gaze. "Emergency Medicine is where I belong. Saving lives, bringing order to the chaos." Her voice quieted. "Researching women's health is more like a dream, a hobby, or something on the side."

"Racing is the same. The charge of being on the cusp of chaos and keeping it under control is practically addicting. But … the endurance, strength, and reflexes required aren't as easy for me as they once were."

I inhaled deeply. "Racing is all I've ever known, other than ranching. For as long as I can remember, it's been my life. I don't know how to step away from my life."

"But you want to." It was a statement, not a question.

I nodded. "I think so."

She hesitated, then held my gaze with intensity.

"I think I'd like to do research full-time. There's a huge gap between what we know about men's health and women's. In recent years, the NIH has funded more projects with specific efforts to have clinical trials on both men and women, which had been considered too expensive and complicated in the past. It's becoming a priority. The time for this work is now."

"So, you get this grant, and you get another and another."

Her gaze dropped again.

"Nora?"

"My parents want me to join GDNL, practice medicine alongside them, and save lives around the world like they do."

I understood the weight of parents' expectations all too well. "Do *you want* to do that?"

"Sure, I have a responsibility. I can be the difference between someone living and dying, having more birthdays with their families or not. There's nothing more important than that. Self-sacrifice is usually necessary to do the right thing. It doesn't matter what I want."

"Nora, it always matters what you want. If research is your dream, then you should do it. It may not be saving lives directly, but it could make life worth living for those who are still here. That's important too."

She shook her head, her eyes fixed on something above the bar that I doubted she was actually seeing.

Sensing the need to change the subject, I went back to

talking about the presentation. "It surprised me about all the safe sex stuff. I mean, I learned all that when I was younger. I didn't really think about it for the older generation."

Nora's shoulders relaxed. "Yeah, it's a big issue. Since they're past childbearing age, many don't even think about it. It sounds strange, but senior living facilities can be an epicenter for STIs. So, it's good to get the word out about safe sex practices like mutual masturbation and getting tested often."

Overall, this was going down as one of the strangest conversations I'd had in a while, but I couldn't have enjoyed it more. Being with Nora was surprising and fun, and comfortable.

A small band had set up in the corner by the window and drew our attention as they tuned their instruments.

Another bartender slid onto a stool and rested his guitar on his leg. "Hey, guys. Thanks for coming out tonight. That's Doug on drums, Slade on bass, and I'm Rhys."

They were good. Country, rock, and scaled-back arrangements of some alternative and grunge classics from Nirvana, Pearl Jam, and Thirdy Dogs. After another drink and three games of table shuffleboard, where Nora legitimately beat me two to one, I was more eager than ever to see her new lace.

25

NORA

"This one goes out to Jo from Lucas," the lead singer said, and a large group by the pool tables in the back raised their beers with shouts and laughter.

"Dance with me," Walker reached out his hand as the band started a new song. His voice was deep and less playful than earlier in our shuffleboard games. I pictured his muscular arms holding me. I slipped my palm against his as naturally as breathing.

I'd heard the song before. "Body Like a Backroad" by Sam Hunt. Another influence of Amber from work. She and some friends went to see him play a big club on the river in downtown Nashville last year, and she hummed the chorus for days after.

Walker held me close, dancing in a quick beat, probably some sort of two-step with turns and spins, his confident arms leading me. After I missed a few steps, I finally picked it up, mostly. Hoots and shouts, a couple swaying in the back, and the crowd singing along with the background rhythmic "hey, hey, hey," had me smiling. Walker singing about knowing curves and taking it slow made my heartbeat thrum.

As the song ended, he dropped a gentle kiss below my ear, his tongue coming out to taste the spot hidden by my thick braid. My nipples peaked, and heat rushed to my core.

He pressed closer, his hardness against the softness of my belly, and I wished my boots had a higher heel, so I could feel him at my center, where I needed him most. A low moan escaped my throat as Walker nipped and kissed behind my ear again.

"That moan is making me hard, honey."

"That hardness is making me wet, honey."

I felt more than heard his chuckle because of the blood rushing in my ears and the growing crowd of dancers to the next song.

"Let's get outta here," he said.

Back at the bar, I grabbed the brown bag and slipped into my coat and scarf as Walker left a cash tip with a wave to a tatted-up Jake, the bartender. He waved back and leaned over to kiss a woman seated at the bar with rich brown skin and a smile only for him.

Walker took my hand as we stepped out into the chilly air. The sky remained mostly clear, but I could make out some clouds scattered about in the bright moonlight as we walked down the sidewalk toward the car. I'd bet the stars here were endless on a dark, new moon night.

Across the corner from where I expected us to turn in the direction of the luxurious blue Jag, there was a broad, brick wine shop. Neon signs burned in the windows, including one that said *open*.

Walker checked his watch. "Let's stop in there. Jacob made his own recommendation this morning about a particular selection." His warm caramel eyes flashed.

"Oh, really. What's so special about it?"

"It pairs well with ... a woman, let's say," and he licked his lips as that little glint in his eyes flashed brighter.

I stopped in my tracks. "You're kidding me?"

He shook his head. "Nope."

"He came right out and said drink this wine when going down on a woman?"

Walker's smile grew impossibly bigger. "Not really, but he said enough. He didn't have to draw me a picture." Walker moved to fully face me and pulled me close with one hand while the other brushed against my center, hidden by the drape of my coat.

"Did you know the acid and alkaline balance of a woman's pussy is similar to that of some wines?" His voice was soft and teasing, but his eyes glittered with mischief.

The tingles and rush of wetness in my panties caused by the caress of his fingers made my head spin. I vaguely remembered the information from a chemistry or anatomy class and some jerk making a joke while grabbing himself.

"Yes, I knew that." My voice was breathy because, oh, those fingers.

"Certain wines pair better than others," he said. "A particular Beaujolais was mentioned."

"I can't believe you had that conversation." I shook my head and tried not to rock against his touch.

"Why, Sweetheart? How else am I supposed to learn if not from my elders?"

His tease broke the spell, and I chuckled. "Fuck, Walker. Just get the damn wine." I pushed his hand away from my apex before I came right there on the sidewalk.

He grinned. "You can fuck Walker later. Let's get some wine now."

We entered the shop and found what we were looking for. Walker grabbed three bottles, and I raised my brow.

"You think we need more?" His tone was all play.

"Three is a lot," I said.

"If we don't like it, I'll give the others away."

"Oh, you'll love it," a middle-aged woman across the aisle said, and I startled, my cheeks flaming. I bit my lip, trying to hold back a little-girl style giggle.

We paid as quickly as possible, and I bolted out of the shop. "You almost got us busted," Walker said once we were outside. "The manager probably thought we were stealing something. You looked so guilty."

"I'm sorry, but when the woman said we'd love it, and her wife nodded behind her, I could swear they knew what we were doing. This town is … unexpected."

Walker stopped and pulled me to him near the car. "Maybe they've found the fountain of youth."

We parked at the marina and walked down the gangplank. The tide was higher, and the slope wasn't as severe as it had been yesterday. A few boats docked close together were lit with colorful lights along the masts and rails. A small group sat on the one in the center, bundled in blankets and hats by a heater. Low music played, and they raised their glasses with a "Happy Holidays" as we passed.

After we cleared the marina and the shipping lane, Walker pulled me next to him as he drove, and I snuggled on the edge of the seat, enjoying his spicy scent and warmth.

"Did you have a good day?" he asked while scanning 180 degrees in front of the boat.

"A great day. Thank you for coming with me. And for dinner, dancing."

"Don't forget the table shuffleboard."

I grinned. "Right. It was a wonderful date. The best one I've had in … a long time." Or ever.

"Me too," he said.

The rest of the trip was quiet, with the shining lights of other boats across the water and Walker's thumb and forefinger rubbing the skin at my nape above the neck of my sweater. I kept stealing glances at his profile, imagining my lips there while I inhaled his clean, spicy scent.

I'd never experienced this kind of connection with someone. Walker was thoughtful and generous. Funny and easygoing. He made me feel not only sexy but enticing and worth the effort. He made me *want* things, and I wasn't used to *wanting*. Not things like this. Not something for me.

It would be my secret, taking this time to indulge in food and wine and sex with the hottest man I'd ever met. It wasn't forever. I'd go back to the long hours and important work soon enough. But this night, and the rest of this week, was about doing something for me, and I inhaled deeply with the decadent thought.

Walker pulled into the cove like he'd done last night, and this time, he didn't have to ask for my help. I followed him out of the back slider, threw him the line, and kicked the big rubber bumpers to hang off the boat's side. Images of Walker naked and tempting started to invade my mind, and my pulse picked up.

I grabbed my backpack with my computer, notes, and the brown paper bag from the seat and jogged off the boat to meet Walker, who carried the wine. We'd left the Gator parked at the dock, and it was a quick ride to the glowing house. From the drive, I saw a majestic Christmas tree twinkling in the windows, adding to the warm light streaming into the brisk night.

"Is someone here?" I asked, hoping to keep the disappointment out of my voice at the possibility of not being alone with Walker and this fire in my belly.

"No. Carly left the lights on for us and lit a small fire in the fireplace. They left ten minutes ago once they knew we were close." He held up his phone to show that's how he knew.

"Oh, thank God." I couldn't hold back the relief.

Walker chuckled. "Same page, babe. We're alone. And if we weren't, I'd have kicked everyone out. Family or not. Canyon and Vince have their own houses here."

With hurried and jerky movements, he parked, cut the engine, grabbed the wine, and then jumped out to open the heavy wooden door for me. I trotted inside the house, removed my boots like Walker did, and stopped short as we entered the main room. The tree had to be at least twelve feet tall, and it glowed with brilliant silver, gold, and white.

The mantel above a small fire was draped in real evergreen boughs and perfect pomegranates that had to be fake. On the opposite side of the main room, the thick, square wooden posts near the kitchen that framed the barlike seating area of the island and supported a cross beam for a pot rack also held more evergreens and pomegranates. Hints of cinnamon and orange filled the air along with the scent of cedar.

"Walker ... this ... is beautiful."

"It is," he said as he pulled off his jacket and strode over to add more wood to the fire. "Now, come here and show me what you're wearing."

I glanced around. "You're sure we're alone?"

"Hal, who's here?" He shouted toward the ceiling, and a disembodied voice said, *Walker and guest.* "See, just us."

What the hell? "Who is Hal?"

"The computer in that old space movie. That's who he's named after. He's the security system."

"Can *he*, or someone, see us?" I asked, suddenly panicked about the skinny-dipping last night.

"No, heat sensors and biometric data on me. That's all.

This house is secure like I said yesterday. You're safe here. Now get over here, or I'm coming for you."

My head snapped to him, and the command in his voice had me forgetting about Hal and thinking about my new lacy panties going up in flames.

"We'll save the wine for later when I can savor. I want you fast this time." He vibrated like a man possessed.

"Ohh. Is that *what Walker wants?*" I teased and shrugged out of my coat.

"I swear to all that is holy, Nora." He rushed at me, and my blood surged as he crushed his lips to mine in a bruising kiss. Our tongues tangled along with our arms and hands. He grabbed my ass and lifted me. I wrapped my legs around him as he carried me closer to the fire and laid me down on the plush rug.

He pulled back and bunched the edges of my sweater, lifting it.

"Yes," I said and rose enough for him to pull it off.

"Oh fuck. That's better than I imagined." His greedy eyes took in my half-naked form and the pale pink bra.

He shifted and worked the button on my jeans. I stretched to do the same for him, then pulled his shirt loose from the waist.

Walker paused and reached to the back of his neck. He yanked his sweater over his head like men do in one swift move while I concentrated on the crisp white button-down. Our mouths fused, and he groaned.

Finally, the fabric opened, and his broad chest hovered above me, my hands roaming and caressing the warm skin and soft hair there.

"God, Nora. I want you." He rose above me and released the buttons at his cuffs before the garment went flying. He rolled off me, and I lifted to push my jeans off. He grabbed the waist and dragged them down, turning them inside out as they came off, and took my thick socks with them.

Sitting back on his knees, he gazed at me. "So, fucking beautiful."

Slowly, his finger traced a path up my thigh, over my mound and stomach.

"Walker, please." My breath panted.

He stood and slipped off his socks, followed by his jeans and boxer briefs, before coming down over me again, his face buried between my breasts.

"I want to fuck your tits." His words were harsh and every muscle in his body tensed. This wasn't the Walker I'd known so far. This one was impossibly hotter with his gruff voice and dirty requests. I wanted him like air.

I met his hungry gaze, pushing my breasts together and offering them to him. "Then do it," I said, breathless that I'd made him lose control. He made a feral sound as he crawled up my body and took his pleasure.

Later, after he stripped me of the lace he loved and gave me a mind-blowing orgasm with his tongue, then another with his cock, he lay holding me against him under a fluffy blanket as the fire crackled.

My eyes glazed, blurring the vision of the fire and the shining tree. Wrapped in Walker and his delicious scent, I felt singular, cherished. "You make me feel like I'm the only woman in the world."

He paused. "Nora, you *are* the only woman in the world." My stupid heart skipped.

26

WALKER

How she'd met me passion for passion was incredible. She was incredible. She wasn't shy or hesitant but gave and took it all. And I was in too fucking deep.

Everything about her overwhelmed me. Her smarts and her smiles. The jokes, the togetherness, the conversations, and this session of fuck-hot sex that had been unlike anything I'd ever experienced. My absolute need to touch her and feel her respond had rocked me to the core.

"You were phenomenal, babe," I said, holding her close.

"You too." She wiggled against me, the move making my flaccid cock imagine one more time with her.

"It was my miraculous tongue, right?" I repeated my tease from earlier today.

"Well, you know what Miss Nell said, something she read somewhere."

No doubt this was going to be good.

"She said no man should ever worry about his dick as long as his tongue works. I like your dick. But that seems about right to me."

"The tongue for the win!" I said and pulled her tighter.

"I think we all win." She laughed.

The fire died back, and I wanted to wrap myself around Nora in a warm bed for the next ten hours. As we entered the bedroom clutching our discarded clothing, she turned to me, her expression soft. "I'm going to wash my hair tonight. Do you *want* to help?"

"Yes," I said simply, privately. The dark moonlight outside added to the sensation that we were the only people in the world.

In the bathroom, I reached to undo her braid, letting the thick mass slide between my fingers as I worked it loose. "Will you wear your hair down for a few days?" I asked. The idea of seeing her across the room, the dark tresses dusting the tops of her gorgeous breasts, or her slim fingers running through it as she read or worked did something to my heart. I figured it was probably dangerous, but I wanted to see her here like that. I couldn't let her leave without witnessing that casual intimate side of her.

MY PHONE CHIMED, and I moved to silence it on the bedside table before Nora woke. Glancing at the caller ID, I sighed. It was the team principal, the leader of the racing team, and the person who ultimately decided who was in the driver's seat.

"Mick. Hang on." I slipped out of bed and crept into the nearby TV room. "What's up?"

"Did I wake you? What time is it there, mate?" His thick British accent echoed through the phone.

"Seven-thirty in the morning."

"Oh hey, sorry. I thought it was more like ten," he said.

"It's ten-thirty in New York. I'm on the West Coast three hours earlier."

"Ah, right, mate, that's it." He paused. "No sense beating about the bush. I wanted to check in. See where your head's at."

I furrowed my brow. "I thought I had more time."

"You do. But knowing your plans sooner would be better than later."

Reality sank in as he went on to highlight the new kid, Messina, and his progress due to my recent work with him. Mick didn't come out and say the kid should have the seat, but that was out of respect for my two championship wins. If that hadn't been my history, he would have already released me.

Privately, I'd hinted at retirement all season, and I told him I was seriously considering it now. He didn't try to talk me out of it, which said enough. I agreed to let him know before New Year's, and he ended the call with holiday wishes to my parents and the rest of my family.

Could I really leave racing? Did I have a choice? What would my parents say after all they'd invested in their *winning son*? I didn't relish the idea of disappointing them. But then, I'd have the ranch and my brothers and be in the same country as Nora.

I looked toward the bedroom where the best woman I'd ever known lay sleeping. She'd said she liked me for me. She slept with me when she believed I was a smooth-talking rancher and not much more. Would she ever consider staying for real with the real me, whoever that was?

I stood and headed into the bedroom for my running gear. I'd slacked off these last few days, and my thoughts were all messed up. Running was an outlet and a time to clear my head. I needed a run.

"Hey." Her sleepy voice broke the silence as I knelt beside the bed and stroked her silky hair.

"Hey, beautiful. Go back to sleep. I'm going for a run, and I'll be back in an hour."

"Where?"

"There's a mile loop through the woods. I'll do a few laps and make breakfast when I get back."

Her smile was lazy and wanton and sweet. God, I loved her smiles. "That sounds perfect," she said.

The air was frosty, and my lungs burned at first, but as my legs and body slipped into the routine, my mind wandered and processed all that had happened in recent weeks. Thoughts about racing and Nora played like the loop I was running. After the sixth mile, I'd made my decision about Formula One. But I wasn't much clearer in my thoughts about Nora.

I liked her, liked being with her, and it was so good between us. In bed, it was hot and good. Out of bed, it was easy and good. She made me feel grounded, like I could be still, and it would be okay. Like I could stop pushing and striving for tiny fractions of *more*.

I was falling for her, and she was leaving in four days. My feet pounded the ground as I increased my pace, trying to run away from that truth.

Toward the end of the eighth mile, I slowed to a jog and heaved my breath. I did the stretches that were part of my cool-down routine before jogging the last hundred yards.

At the top of the trail, I saw the front door open, and Nora came out in her coat and boots, her dark hair wild around her shoulders. Her legs were bare, and an image of her naked under that coat woke up my dick.

Then it wasn't my imagination. She opened her coat to flash me all her creamy skin and lush curves. I tripped, and she laughed.

"What are you doing, babe?" I asked as I approached.

"*I wanted* to see if you were ready to come in. Thought maybe I'd try to convince you." She stepped backward, teasing me with more little peeks of her. I lunged and grabbed her, holding her close while our tongues tangled, and we stumbled the rest of the way to the front door. Fuck, I liked her.

"You know, studies show that some men feel most sexually potent after vigorous exercise. Do you feel that way?" she asked, her breaths heaving. I loved her fun little sex facts. They got me hard.

"Yes, I do. Now, get in the house and take off that coat."

She laughed. "What about my boots?"

"I don't fucking care about the boots. They aren't covering any places where I'm going to put my mouth."

She screamed a laugh and ran inside. I was right behind her and slammed the door as I snagged her coat. She slipped out of it with another scream, and I caught her again, pulling her bare back to my front and my sweaty shirt.

"Ahhh, you're cold and wet," she said, squirming and trying not to giggle.

"Yes, but what about you?" My chilled fingers explored her velvety folds. Damn, she was practically dripping. Already? Her laughter became a moan.

"What did you do in here while I was running? Did you touch yourself, my naughty Nora?" I growled into her neck. "Did you imagine it was me?"

"Yes," she hissed, her arms reaching back over her shoulders to grasp my hair. The move arched her back, and I needed my mouth on her right fucking now.

We stumbled to the rug where we'd been last night, and I pulled her down under me. The room was chilly in the morning with no fire. But she had to know how I would react to her coming outside like that. She was a fantasy come to life. I couldn't take the time to get to the bedroom, so I'd just have to keep her warm another way. I stripped off my wet shirt, and she sighed

"I won't be gentle, Nora. Are you with me?"

"Yes," she panted.

"How close did you bring yourself?"

"Right to the edge, but I didn't want to come without you."

I groaned. "You're so fucking perfect." I trailed kisses along her neck and the sweet valley between her tits. I covered one tight point with my mouth and bit lightly while plucking the other with my fingers. Nora moaned loudly.

"Yeah, babe. Make noise," I said. She moaned again and bucked toward me. "You're greedy this morning."

"I am," she said. "You started it. All that focus on what I *want*. I know what I want."

I kept kissing and sliding lower. "And what is that, Sweetheart?"

"Your mouth. My fingers don't even compare."

"My mouth where?" I nuzzled her skin with more light brushes of my lips and strokes of my tongue.

"On me," she groaned.

"My mouth is on you," I teased.

"Walker, my clit. Your tongue. Now."

"Yes, ma'am."

"Screw your cowboy sweet talk and give me what I want," she demanded. So, I did.

Nora writhed and clawed and moaned my name as a chime rang in the distance. I checked my watch.

"What? What is it?" she asked breathlessly, looking down at me.

"We have company." I returned to her glistening pink

center. She was hotter this morning than ever before, and I loved it. I was going to shoot in my shorts like a damn teenager, I was so turned on.

"What?" She struggled to sit up as I continued to work her.

"It's Carly. She's on her way. You want me to stop, or do you want me to make you come right now? We have a little time if you can be quick."

"Walker!" Her frustration showed on her face.

"Tell me what you want, babe. It's up to you," I said between soft kisses to her hot center.

Her breath heaved. "Yes, make me come. I don't want to stop, but … oh God. What if? Oh … no, do it. Please do it now."

I pulled the skin around her clit tight with one hand, exposing the swollen nub, and I sucked it like I did that first night while I curled two fingers inside her, pressing against that same area from underneath. She screamed, and then she was coming, gripping me in powerful waves.

"Yes, fuck, I love it when you come." I licked the flood of her wetness as she struggled to breathe.

After a beat, I stood, grabbed my shirt then scooped her up to carry her back to the bedroom. I kicked the door closed, and we both landed in a heap across the bottom of the bed.

Nora swatted at me. "Oh, my God. She might've walked in. I can't believe I did that. You make me do crazy things."

I laughed. "She wouldn't have walked in. The chime meant they were nearing the island. I knew it would be at least ten minutes before they even got off the dock. And you were about to come. You didn't have ten more minutes."

"What?" she yelped.

"I'm sorry. Except, not really. It was exciting, right? Thinking we might get caught. You came hard when you let go." I softened my teasing tone. "Plus, I told you I never want you to feel uncomfortable, and I meant it. I'd never put you in that position if I thought someone could really catch us. I know that's not you, but it was fun to think about, right?"

"You shit," she said and laughed as she swatted my shoulder.

"Was I bad? Should I be punished?" I waggled my eyebrows at her.

"Yes, you were very, *very* bad. I sentence you to *torture* by blowjob. I won't be gentle, either. Get in the shower."

I pushed up and off the bed. "Yes, ma'am."

"Walker, I swear," she snapped, but I still heard her smile.

"I'm going." I checked the bedroom door was locked, not that it would matter, and glanced back at Nora. She was still stretched across the bed, wearing her boots and nothing else.

27

NORA

Shower sex had never been *that* exciting. Whether it was Walker or me, I wasn't sure. But the combination of us and sex was mind-melting no matter where we were. I barely recognized myself as I took him to the edge with my mouth before backing him off again and again in tantalizing torture that had him begging for mercy.

When *I* decided he'd had enough, he pulled me to him and rolled on the condom he'd stashed on the shower ledge. He entered me against the wall as the steam rose and encircled us. He was fantastic and brought out something in me that hadn't been there before. Going outside in only my coat and boots? Old Nora would never have done that.

No, wait. I hadn't changed. This was just fun. An out-of-the-norm experience. A respite from the usual grind, like a spa weekend. In a few short days, I'd revert to my real life. I'd be home soon and have a little time to get myself together before my next shift at the hospital on New Year's Eve. I was still *Original Nora,* and I belonged somewhere else.

Walker strolled out of the bathroom in a towel again, and my reaction was the same as that first night. My belly fluttered.

"Babe, that was ... I'm not sure how to describe it," he said and leaned down to place a gentle kiss on my lips as I sat on the bed, already dressed and brushing my hair. His distinctive aftershave surrounded me, and I inhaled, memorizing the scent and how he made me feel.

He stroked a lock between his thumb and forefinger. "You have beautiful hair. You're beautiful everywhere, but your hair, it's distracting." He looked dazed.

"Well, you can be distracted. I need to write." I stood and gave him a pointed look and a wink.

"Fine. After this morning, I think I can keep my hands off you for a few hours." He strolled back into the closet to dress. His smile was bright and big.

So far, the day had been productive. Carly arrived sometime while we were showering, made a pot of soup, and stashed a platter of sandwich makings in the large fridge. Walker had briefly been in her way preparing spinach and cheese omelets with sliced fruit for our breakfast.

With my belly full and my sex drive quiet for the moment, I'd parked myself at the desk in the study and made real progress on plans for the research project and writing my grant proposal.

The cozy study was a nook off the den with two walls of bookcases and two walls of windows that looked out onto the lawn and the melting snow. It was a peaceful place to write, and I hoped I could someday have something similar. Not the big house. That was way out of reach but a calm space close to nature. The words came readily for me here, the thoughts and theories clearer.

With the late breakfast, it was almost one o'clock when my stomach reminded me I was hungry. I had a quick text exchange with Jamar about some work he needed my help with for a hospital committee he served on, then walked through the warm den with its small fireplace and overstuffed club chairs.

Walker sat, dressed in his pajama pants, a Henley, wool socks, and those sexy AF glasses. The fire crackled, and he held a thick book in his lap. He was so freaking hot.

I moved closer, and my stomach let out a growl. Walker smiled before looking up at me, and I bent down to wrap my arms around his neck, placing a tender kiss on those lips that drove me to distraction.

"Mmm, what was that for?" he asked, glancing at my hair. I'd left it loose for him and felt desired under his gaze as he fingered the ends lightly.

"No reason. You look sexy and tempting, and I wanted a piece." I shrugged.

"You can have a piece anytime, Sweetheart. Say the word." He closed his book and pulled me onto his lap. "But food first."

My stomach growled again, and we both chuckled.

Another ping sounded from somewhere, and Walker checked his watch again.

"More company?" I asked with my eyebrow raised in playful question.

He grinned. "Yep. Looks like my brother Canyon is here just in time for that lunch Carly made."

My heartbeat thrummed. "Who will you say I am?" I wasn't fishing for a title, but girlfriend wasn't right. Hookup? Booty call? He would never refer to me that way.

"I'll tell them you're my friend. Which you are. Relax. I texted him yesterday and told him I had someone with me. They'll be curious, but I'm not embarrassed that I brought you here or that we haven't known each other long. It'll be fine. You'll see."

He was right. All the worry that I'd built up about the possibility of meeting his family was completely unnecessary. Canyon and his wife Emme were kind, down-to-earth people who'd met in college. We ate lunch and chatted like any other two couples. Canyon and Walker were in the kitchen ribbing each other good-naturedly now while Emme sat quietly, watching the fray.

"If I wasn't twelve months pregnant, I'd probably jump in and take a side, but I don't have it in me right now," Emme said.

I grinned across the sofa at her, where we both sat mesmerized as the afternoon light faded and the lavish tree twinkled brighter. The fireplace crackled nearby, and I wanted nothing more than to sit here for the rest of the day. "How far along are you?" I asked.

"Almost eight months. Doing fine, so my doctor okayed me to fly."

"Yeah, with most healthy pregnancies, you can fly until thirty-six weeks."

"Canyon's dad sent a private jet for us. That helped make the trip easier." She sighed. "So, you're a doctor?"

"I am. Emergency Medicine."

"So, if I went into labor or had some sort of issue on the island, you could help me."

"Most likely, yes." I reached out to take her hand. "You won't need me. You are doing this all on your own, and you're doing great. This is natural and normal, and everything's going to be fine."

"Thanks, Nora."

I stood and stretched. "Speaking of doctoring, I should get back to work. I'm writing a grant proposal, and it's due soon." I headed to the study, and Emme headed to the sofa in the TV room for a quiet nap. There was no telling what Canyon and Walker were doing puttering in the kitchen after cleaning the lunch dishes.

Hours later, I followed my nose and the scent of warm sugar out to the main room.

"What are you making?" I asked.

"My specialty," Walker said. "Brownies."

"A double batch," Canyon said. "We want to have plenty for the solstice on Saturday."

"What happens on the solstice?" I asked.

"Nothing," Emme said, now perched on a bar chair and looking brighter after her nap. "When we're here, absolutely nothing. We stay in bed. Eat, watch movies, read. There are less than eight hours of gray daylight. It's a skip day, and ranchers don't get a lot of those."

"That sounds ... wonderful." I looked at the warm brownies cooling on the stove.

Walker winked at me. "Are you getting hungry again, babe?" His voice was low as he came closer, and I wasn't entirely sure he was talking about food. I caught the stare from his brother out of the corner of my eye.

"Sorry. Just weird. I'm not used to seeing him with someone, and I have no idea how he won over a woman as smart as you," Canyon said with a big grin.

Walker rubbed his hand over his face. "How about some wine? I could use some." He strolled away and punched his brother in the arm on his way to the pantry.

Dinner was one of the chef-made dishes, beef stroganoff, rustic bread from a bakery in Perry Harbor, and a field greens salad with pickled beets and goat cheese. I patted my stomach, and he poured the last of the wine into my glass.

"When do you head back to Nashville?" Emme asked.

"Sunday."

"Oh, you won't be here for Christmas?" Emme looked at Walker then at me. "I guess you have family expecting you."

Walker said nothing, sitting there with a little smile on his gorgeous face.

"Not really. I'm an only child, and my parents are in Guatemala. They're physicians as well. They work for Global Doctors No Limits."

"Oh, is that who you work for, too?"

"No, not yet. I work at a university medical center."

"And you have to get back to work?"

"Are you a professional interrogator?" I chuckled as I glanced at Walker, still silent and gorgeous. Emme didn't answer, keeping her eyes locked on me.

"Actually, my next shift isn't until New Year's Eve," I said.

"Oh, okay. Well, why don't you stay?" she asked.

I looked at Walker again, a bit thrown. "Yeah, Nora, why don't you stay?" he said, and a light dawned.

"Was this an ambush?" I asked and grinned at Emme, who was now blushing.

"Okay, he put me up to it. I'm sorry. I want you to stay. Canyon and I both do. Walker likes you, but I think we would feel better about being so remote with a doctor here." Emme raised her hand. "Walker gave it the green light. I would never ask if he hadn't wanted it too." Her grin grew.

"I'd have to change my flight."

"That can be done," Walker said.

"Okay, you're bringing Canyon and Emme in on this.

Let's bring them all the way in. You *want* to share the holidays, this family tradition-filled time, with a woman you just met and barely know?"

"First, yes, I do. Second, I don't barely know you. I know you well. I know how you like your eggs and how you take your coffee. I know who your favorite painter is and why. I know what you do for a living and that you're very good at it. I know you don't like to cook, but you need to eat. I know you can't dance, but you try hard."

"Walker!"

He laughed and dodged my punch. "And I know other things, too." He waggled his brows.

I saw Canyon cover a smile with his napkin as Emme slapped his leg under the table.

"You don't have to answer right now. But you are welcome here for as long as you want. Emme mentioned being happy that you were here since this is the end of the earth, and I said I wasn't sure you'd be staying. Think about it. If you *want* to stay, I can easily make that happen."

"We'll talk about it later." I gave him a side eye, and he knew he had me. I'd stay. Even though it wasn't smart and would only make leaving more difficult. I'd stay.

I insisted on cleaning up after dinner since Walker and Canyon cooked all afternoon, and Emme was making a human. It wasn't much, anyway, and I enjoyed watching the brothers sit across from each other at the long table and talk about the ranch.

It was what I always thought family would be like. Walker's eyes lit up as they talked about the herd and breeding and the expected calving numbers this year. He loved it. I wondered if he truly realized how much.

Canyon and Emme said their goodbyes and loaded

into the Gator they'd brought from their cabin near the water.

Walker closed the door behind them with a snick and turned to face me, a slight curve on his lips. Silently, he crossed the room, turned out the lights, and started the dishwasher.

"They're nice," I said.

"Yep. She's good for him. Canyon was always slightly wide-eyed with life. Not the daredevil like Vince and me. Too trusting, probably. Emme is sweet, but she has the heart of a warrior. He never had a chance."

He headed into the pantry and returned with a bottle of the Beaujolais we bought last night, then placed it on the counter to open it. He snagged two clean wineglasses from the shelf and walked past me. "Time for bed. We can talk about you staying if you want to, but I have other plans for my mouth and this wine."

I grinned and followed as if I could resist.

In the bedroom, he set the bottle and glasses down, then went to the fireplace and grabbed logs and kindling to start a fire.

"Walker, are you sure?"

His gaze held mine. "Yes, Nora. I don't want you to leave yet."

"And I don't want to. But, I'll have to, eventually."

"I know." He stood and walked to me. "But if we have a little more time, let's take it."

"Do you think that's smart?" I bit my lip, hesitating.

He shrugged. "Probably not. But I can't help myself with you." He wrapped me in his arms and pulled me to his chest. "Stay a little longer. Stay until you have to go back. We both *want* it."

I stared into his warm, melted caramel eyes and nodded.

His hand came up to caress my cheek, and his lips pressed against mine in a kiss that stole my breath. This time, he moved against me slowly as we undressed each other between gentle, caressing kisses, and I feared my heart would not recover from the sweet and sensual loving he promised with those eyes.

28

WALKER

MORE DAYS WITH NORA. I DIDN'T WANT TO THINK ABOUT the relief that filled my chest when she agreed to stay. It took no convincing when Emme asked if she could talk to Nora about staying. She said pregnancy was sometimes scary, and having Nora close reassured her. Whatever made Emme feel better made Canyon feel better, so he was on board. And God knows, I wanted her with me for as long as possible.

The next day passed with calm and ease. Canyon and Emme spent most of it at their cabin. The trip had worn Emme out more than they expected, and she was taking some time to rest before Vince and Michelle arrived.

They were skiing in Vale and would probably blow in like a tornado of energy tomorrow. They were both athletic and daring. The day he introduced me to Michelle, they'd been skydiving. She was exhilarated, and Vince was a little green. I knew he'd met his match, and he never looked back.

I guessed that's how we Hewitt men did it. Once we found the right woman, we didn't look back. An image of

Nora flashed through my mind. I shook it off. I had to. She *would* leave. She never promised to stay, which meant she couldn't be my *right woman*.

And now wasn't the time to ask her to be. I had to tell my parents I was leaving racing. There would be a disappointing conversation, prodding and pushing, and possibly shouting. This was not the time to try and romance someone into choosing me, even if I wanted to.

Carly and Nate had stopped by earlier while I was out for a run, and now there was more firewood stacked on the back patio and more groceries in the fridge, likely to prepare for Vince and Michelle's arrival.

Nora spent most of the day writing again, and I spent it watching race film in the TV room, making notes and plans for Messina's driver training that would begin in a couple of months. My number two, Marc Garza, would move to lead driver, and Lorenzo would take the number two spot. It would be his first year in the seat, and I'd remembered all the things I wished someone would have told me in the beginning so many years ago. I hoped he and the team would see some benefit from this old ex-driver's advice.

She emerged from the study for a dinner of burgers on the grill with asparagus and roasted potatoes. Canyon and Emme had stopped at the lap pool for a swim before joining us and headed back to their cabin shortly after the meal while Nora slipped back to her grant proposal.

"Come to bed, babe. It's late." After a long day of working, I'd found her hunched over the desk. I rubbed her shoulders, enjoying the brush of her silky hair on my fingers. She moaned and leaned into the massage. My dick twitched at the sound and the sight of her closed eyes and relaxed features. But tonight, I wanted to hold her, bury my nose in her neck and pull her curvy body close to mine under the weight of heavy blankets as the rain fell outside.

"It's almost eleven. Come on. Let's get some sleep."

I WOKE ALONE for the first time since meeting Nora. I didn't like it. I needed a run, so I dressed and headed to the study, where I knew I'd find her.

"Hey, you want coffee?" I asked from the doorway.

"Hey." She was bright and energized, and gorgeous. "I'm good." She nodded to her cup on the desk.

"You're up early," I said.

"I want to finish today. I'm close enough that if I push, I can submit it and be done." She shook her head. "I have to say, I was worried I'd gotten so distracted by," she glanced at my crotch and licked her lips before returning her gaze to mine, "someone that I might miss the deadline. It will feel so good hitting that send button."

I grinned and stepped closer. "I'd like to make you feel good hitting your button."

She laughed and said, "Go away," as she pushed me, but I caught her eye, and she winked. "Until later."

"Count on it, babe." I placed a quick peck on her cheek and left.

After my run, I brought her a warmed muffin, and fresh coffee, then headed to a shower and those racing videos. I still needed to do a few things before I called Mick to make it official. Now that I'd decided, I wanted to finish my notes for the transition and take the next step. Finish my work so I'd have no distractions. Tomorrow was the solstice, and I planned to stay in bed and worship soft curves all day if she'd let me.

She missed lunch, so I brought her a slice of quiche, and a Cobb salad, one of the pre-prepped meals the chef mom hired had made. I found Nora staring out the window, her hands in her lap, gripping her phone.

"You okay, babe?"

She looked up. "Oh, yeah. Sure."

Something wasn't right. I said nothing and waited.

"I need to get back to work." She set her phone on the desk. "My mom texted me a few minutes ago. She wanted me to know about her conversation with a regional director at GDNL. No big deal."

Something about that GDNL was a big deal. I'd stepped on it at the bar the other night. Thankfully, when she turned fully toward me, her bright eyes and smile were back.

"I'm going to the Bellingham Harbor to get Vince and Michelle. Both boats are here, so someone needs to go, and Canyon wants to stay with Emme. You okay here?"

"Is it okay if I'm here alone?"

"Sure. I'll be gone about an hour. How much more do you have?"

She glanced at her laptop. "Probably another two or three hours." She glanced at her laptop and back at me, biting her lip.

"Take your time. Vince and Michelle will get settled in the other cabin near the water, and I'll grill steaks here for dinner about seven. Join us when you can."

"Thanks, Walker. Really. Your support, it … it means a lot." A sadness flashed behind her eyes before the light returned.

"Of course." I hesitated, wanting to make sure the sadness was gone. "If you need something, help yourself. Then get back to work, and I'll see you soon." I kissed her quickly to avoid getting sucked into the feel of her that would make me want to be less supportive of her writing and more supportive of her orgasms.

...

"So, bro, a woman? Where is she?" Vince looked around. This was my youngest brother's greeting as he and Michelle walked down the dock at the marina.

"I've been great, Vince. How 'bout you?"

Michelle smacked his arm playfully before stepping aboard the boat and reaching up for a hug. She was small, but she was fierce. "How are you, Walker?"

I smiled at my sister-in-law. "How were the slopes?" I asked.

"Awesome," Vince said. "But I'm glad we left before the weekend crowd pushed in. It's good to see you, man." He gave me a one-armed-back-slap hug.

They stowed their luggage, and I eased the boat out of the marina. Michelle went straight to the fridge and grabbed two beers.

"Rough trip?" I asked, eyeing them.

"Not really. Celebrating being here. The ranch is home. Vale was fun. But here, it's just … nice. Calm. Care-free. No early mornings. And tomorrow is the solstice." She snuck a side glance at Vince who didn't miss a beat pulling her onto his lap in the seat opposite me in the cockpit.

"Speaking of the solstice," Vince said. "You brought a woman to family Christmas? At least you won't have to jerk it alone all day while the rest of us enjoy the real thing?"

Michelle rose from his lap with that comment. "Are you twelve? Did you hit your head on the slope? This is not how you ask your brother about the woman in his life. What is wrong with you? You have to butter him up. Ask him about new recipes or what's for dinner. How the race season was. Start with stuff like that."

"So, you're an expert on human relations?" I asked.

"No, I'm a human. Something I wonder about you guys when you're together." She bumped Vince with her hip, silently telling him to scoot aside and make room for her.

"Her name is Nora. She's an emergency medicine physician from Nashville." Two sets of eyebrows rose. "Yeah, not my norm."

"How'd you meet her?"

"Well, that's the thing. I sort of met her in a bar at SeaTac airport when our flight was delayed the other day."

Vince laughed out loud, bold and sure, like always. "You picked her up in a bar? A doctor? And you talked her into coming here with you?"

I nodded.

"Damn man, that is all kinds of smooth. I have to say, I'm impressed."

That made me laugh. Though he was my youngest brother, Vince was not easily impressed by me or anyone other than his wife.

"I like her. Probably more than I should since she's leaving on the twenty-ninth. I booked her ticket this morning. She was going to leave Sunday but decided to stay longer."

"Wait, hold up. Look at your face," Vince said. "You *like* her? Damn, man, you look like you love her. After a week? Dude, you've always liked to go fast, but this is next level, even for you."

Yeah. Like I didn't already know how crazy this was.

ON THE WAY to Vince and Michelle's cabin, we met Emme and Canyon, their hands filled with plates of cheese, olives, nuts, and other stuff.

"We brought snacks to welcome you," Emme said, placing a cheek kiss on Michelle and then Vince.

"Where's Nora?" Canyon asked. "She didn't leave, did she?"

"No," I said, trying to keep my voice light since Canyon was just giving me shit. But I didn't want to think about her leaving me. "She's working on her proposal. She'll probably join us for dinner." I nodded to the brightly lit house up the drive.

She wanted that grant. I'd told her I'd give her space to work, and I kept my promises. Even though that work was from a life I wasn't part of. A life she would go back to without me in nine short days. I ran my hand through my hair and looked out across the water to get myself under control.

The afternoon sun through gray clouds was all but gone as we ate and drank and caught up. It had been several months since I'd been in the same room with my brothers. We talked on the phone regularly, mostly about the ranch, but the time difference between me in Europe and them in Texas made it tough. It was good to actually hang out a while.

Seeing my brothers with their wives, I realized I wanted Nora with me. Not just to have someone but for a million other reasons that were unique to her. Because her smile lit up the room, and her laughter both calmed me and stirred my blood. No one else had ever had that effect on me.

"So, you decided about racing?" Vince asked as we walked from the sofa to the kitchen for another beer.

"Yep. I'm retiring from it all. Not staying to train the new guy or gun for a team principal position with another team. My racing career is done."

Vince's broad smile split his face. "Would I be a shit brother if I said I was glad?"

I chuckled. "No, man. You can be a little shit, but you're not a shit brother." I took a pull from my new beer.

"Canyon, man. Come here," he shouted. Canyon unwedged himself from his wife with some effort and a frown before walking over.

"What?" he growled.

"Our boy's coming home," Vince said and fist-bumped my shoulder. "He's leaving F1."

"Oh, hey, man. That's good. We could use you on the ranch full-time." He paused and lowered his voice. "Are you happy about it? You look … well, is this someone else's decision, or is this what you want?"

What I want. The words hit my brain with small thuds. What I wanted were the ranch and Nora and to not let my parents down. I could expect to get one out of three, and that sucked.

"It was my choice. Mick wouldn't have released me, not with my record, but they would have nudged me more toward training the new guys, getting them ready. My reflexes aren't the same." I rubbed at my wrist and noticed the ache again. "It's time."

"Then let's celebrate. This is good news, right?" Vince asked.

"Let's do it before Mom and Dad get here on Sunday. You know how they are about my racing. I'm not sure how they're gonna take this."

Years ago, I'd asked my brothers how they felt about Mom and Dad spending so much time with me in Europe. We'd had it out, you could say. Aired all the hurt and jealousy of our childhoods. My time with our parents, racing, and the attention. Their time on the ranch, normal high school, and avoiding the weight of scrutiny and expectations.

We each envied something the others had. But after that discussion, we'd let it go. *Time to put away childish things*, Miss Del had advised as she cooked something delicious at the ranch that day. Mom and Dad had been on another business trip.

"Look, we all know you're the *golden boy winning driver* and all that shit that matters to their friends, but recently," Vince shrugged, "I think Mom and Dad are changing. They're getting older. Maybe becoming grandparents soon did it. They parked the yacht in Greece four months ago. Haven't been out on it since. They've come back to Austin more, even missed most of your late-season races to do it."

They had. It hadn't registered at the time.

"Mom's doing something with the symphony in the city." He gave his head a little shake. "I can't put my finger on it, but they may not need you to impress those so-called friends of theirs anymore."

29

NORA

I hit send and two emotions slammed into me at the same time: relief and panic. Relief to be finished. Panic that I'd missed some typo or detail. Relief that I could focus on Walker for the rest of my time here. Panic at how much I liked that idea.

The text from my mother earlier had been a distraction I didn't need. As usual, it was all about GDNL. She didn't ask about me. She unloaded info on their work and how one of the regional directors was looking forward to my application. Everything was riding on me. All I could muster in reply was a thumbs-up emoji.

A hot bath and a glass of wine, plus an orgasm compliments of Walker, would clear my head. Ideas of what I wanted were coming all too easily lately. I needed to get a grip. Getting what I wanted wasn't how the real world worked. And soon, I'd be back in the real world.

Walker texted earlier that he would hang out at Vince and Michelle's cabin with Canyon and Emme for the afternoon, giving me some space to finish writing. I appreciated it, but a part of me wanted to be there with him, included in the family. Too many years of being on my own, or with friends or colleagues for every holiday since undergrad, made me wish for that kind of family time.

In the kitchen, I poured a glass of chilled chardonnay and returned to the study to select a book for the bath. Walker's parents had an eclectic collection from political commentaries to biographies to historical romance novels, which I assumed were his mom's, but men his father's age had surprised me lately. I probably shouldn't assume anything.

I selected one about a highlander and the fierce warrior woman who stole his heart and headed to the bath. The room was mostly square as it jutted out from the side of the house, with a claw-foot tub in a nook at the end surrounded on three sides by windows from floor to ceiling. Across the tub was a sort of table that held a place for a wineglass, a bookstand with a clip-light, a loofa, and a couple of jars of bath salts I hadn't noticed before.

These rooms had to be for guests as well as Walker. It was hard to imagine him with a glass of wine and bath salts. But then again, I shouldn't assume. I'd have to ask him about it. Ask him to join me one evening.

Smiling at that image, I started the water, added some of the honeysuckle salts, and slipped into the closet to strip out of my sweatpants and fleece pullover, replacing them with a robe. For a moment, I considered the wisdom of getting naked in a room of windows, but the darkness of the land and the sea beyond seemed vast and solitary. Like I was the only person for miles.

I swept my hair into a loose bun at the top of my head, lowered the lights, then quickly dropped my robe and slid into the steaming warmth. With another sip of wine, I clicked on the tiny light, opened my highlander book, and got lost.

"You look beautiful." Walker's deep voice washed over me from the doorway, and I startled.

"I didn't hear you come in. How did you know where I was?"

He nodded to the window and came closer. "I saw the light from the driveway." His voice was low and seductive. "I might have slowed a bit at the sight of you. You finished your proposal?"

"I did, and I feel good about it. I think I have a real shot. So, I treated myself to a romance novel and a bath." My belly flipped at the electric desire coiled between us.

He raised his eyebrows. "Romance, huh? Learning anything good?"

"I'm learning that Scottish highlanders in their kilts were a lot sexier than I first thought."

Walker's smile was wicked. "I don't have a kilt. Role-playing that one would take a few days to prep."

"I don't need to role-play. The real Walker Hewitt is more than enough for me."

Walker's expression softened, and he knelt next to the tub.

"What do you need, Sweetheart?" He brushed back a lock of my hair that had escaped the knot.

You, I wanted to say. I need you, but my heart stuttered. I couldn't need him.

"I'm good. What do you need?" I swallowed, my voice sounding distant even to me.

He paused, and something passed behind his eyes. "I'm good too." He leaned in, placing the softest kiss on my lips. "Finish your bath. I'm going to make dinner. Canyon and Vince will come up that drive in about fifteen minutes, so I'm closing the blinds on that side." He went to the windows, and with a soft thwack, he lowered the wooden slats.

"You don't want your brothers to see me in the tub?" I teased.

"No. You're mine." He turned to me. "It may only be for one more week, but for those days, Nora, you *are* mine. And I take care of what's mine."

My breath caught. Oh, that sounded perfect. Maybe it was the romance novel, but the idea of being Walker's was lighting those now familiar sparks in all my places. I was a capable, independent, smart woman. I never thought I'd like someone calling me *his*. But oh, my good goddamn, I liked it.

"Does that idea excite you, my naughty Nora?" His smile curved lazily, and he licked his lips. He already knew the answer. Everything about him excited me. "I should go make dinner before I decide to eat you instead," he said, that wicked gleam back in his eye.

I exhaled. The movement swirled the water at my breasts, drawing Walker's gaze. "But tomorrow, I plan to be starving," he said.

My thoughts exactly. This family's winter solstice tradition of spending the day in bed sounded better by the minute.

EMME AND CANYON arrived for dinner first, and Emme pulled two low chairs closer to the bar. One for her and one to prop her feet on. "How's it going?" I asked, pausing by her chair.

"Tired. Baby kicked me most of the night." She sighed.

"That's a good sign. It's getting cramped in there. The kicking will continue for a while until it gets too tight to even kick, but remember, it means she's growing stronger."

"Thanks, Nora." The creases in her brow relaxed as well as on Canyon's.

"Can I check your ankles?"

She pulled up the legs of her jeans, and I pushed on the skin. She was a tad swollen, but nothing I was too worried about.

"Looks fine, but let's get you some water. Try to drink a lot throughout the day. It will help with swelling. It'll seem like you have to pee constantly, but it really is a good thing to do along with elevating your feet like that."

She and Canyon both nodded.

Vince and Michelle arrived, and Walker introduced us before stepping outside to grill the steaks and potatoes for dinner. Michelle and I made a garden salad with pre-chopped vegetables from the fridge and what had to be homemade rustic croutons.

His youngest brother and his wife were in their late twenties and had been married for just over a year. She was a CPA and had taken on the management of the ranch's books when she started as an associate at her father's accounting firm after college. She knew who Vince was and who his father was before she ever met him.

"I tried to get him to stop pursuing me. It was like I had a target on my back, visible to all the mean girls in the state of Texas. And there are a few, let me tell you. If I had a nickel for every gold-digger jab I heard." She rolled her eyes. "But he refused to give up."

"That's right, baby, and I never will. I don't care if you married me for my family's money as long as I get to be with you." He grinned at his wife, who obviously loved him and would have married him, money or not.

The evening was relaxed, without too many questions about how Walker and I met and our night in Seattle. I may have only known him a week, but it felt like I'd lived a whole lifetime in those days.

We said our goodbyes, and once again, Walker closed the door behind them and walked the house, turning off lights.

"Let's leave the Beaujolais for tomorrow," I said and headed toward our bedroom. "If I'm going to be yours for the rest of the week, then tonight, you're mine to take care of."

Without a word, he clicked off the last light and followed me. I started the shower heating in the bathroom and pulled his sweater off before I removed my own.

Once we were both undressed, I pulled him into the steam and guided him under the water. First, I washed his hair and slowly massaged his scalp and neck. Then, with a soapy washcloth that smelled clean and spicy like him, I scrubbed the hard planes and lines of his body. I especially took my time with his hips and between his legs. Gently, I soaped and caressed and rinsed him from head to toe. My hands smoothed up his thighs and under his balls.

I tapped two fingers on his perineum, and he jolted lightly with each tap. "Does that feel good?" I asked. Silently he nodded, his eyes never leaving me except to close softly on a sigh before opening again to connect with mine.

Quickly, I washed, then stepped out of the shower to greet him with a plush towel. I took my time drying every ridge and slope before I quickly dried myself, slipped on a robe, and re-tied my hair that had gotten damp in the steam.

"Do you want a fire?" he asked, and I nodded before turning down the sheets and fluffing the pillows against the headboard.

The logs snapped and popped as the light caught, and

I removed the towel from his waist, letting it puddle at our feet beside the bed.

"Lie on the bed. I'll be right back." I knew coconut oil would suffice in the absence of massage oil, and I'd spotted some in the kitchen earlier. I returned to find Walker relaxing in the soft sheets, his shaft not yet at full attention. Good. This wasn't about thrusting and release. This was about relaxation and enjoyment.

"Turn over," I said, dropping my robe and keeping my voice low and silky instead of demanding. His gaze scanned my naked body before I added some oil to my hands, straddled his legs, then massaged his back and shoulders. He groaned at the pressure, and I moved lower to the firm muscles of his very fine ass.

"Relax, Walker," I cooed in his ear as I shifted to scrape my peaked nipples across his warm skin.

"Damn, Nora. That's good."

I smiled at his praise and my plans to make it even better. I nudged him to roll and began the same routine of stroking and massaging with the oil to smooth my way across the ridges of his abdomen and chest.

"I love to touch your body. You are so sexy, you make *me* feel sexy."

He exhaled a deep sigh. "Damn, babe. You are so fucking perfect," he said and twitched against my center.

"There's no rush." I shifted lower and slipped between his legs, opening them a bit wider as my hands slid to massage his hips and pelvis.

"Relax, I'll go slow. You can trust me."

He gazed at me from the pillows, and I met his eyes as I lowered my mouth to kiss him right below his hip bone. I did the same on the other side and nudged his legs to open more as my hands continued to massage closer to his now fully stiff cock.

I nuzzled close to his center, nipping and kissing with light sucks and licks. I teased my fingers through the coarse hair there and dipped lower to kiss and lick around his balls.

"Oh, babe. What are you doing?" His voice was low and heavy.

"What you've done to me ten times in the past week. I'm worshipping you. Nothing for you to do but enjoy."

His face appeared pained for a moment before another exhale.

I moved to his other side and continued the slow, sweet routine of kisses and nips and licks, moving ever closer to the center of him, but not all the way. His cock twitched next to my cheek. I shifted to massage his hips and slipped my thumbs under his balls, again teasing that tender spot filled with nerve endings.

Walker moaned a sweet sound, and I got wet. His hips bucked slightly.

"Relax, Walker. Nothing for you to do. I'm in control, and I want this. *I want to taste you.*" Another groan escaped his throat, and his head slammed back onto the pillow.

With a few last teases along the loose skin of his balls, another place filled with sensitive nerve endings, I grasped his hardness and licked the swollen crown. Gently, using only my tongue, I let him feel the warmth of my mouth on him and the promise of more.

30

WALKER

Oh fuck, her mouth. And the sensation of floating and needing to take charge at the same time. I wanted to thrust into her warm body, but she held me back, making me lose control in the most incredible way. I'd never experienced anything close to this blowjob.

"I love tasting you, teasing you. It gets me so hot, Walker." Fuck, had a woman ever said that to me?

"Same, babe." I had no more words as she licked the head of my dick in a leisurely rhythm that changed as soon as the intensity started building. She was doing it on purpose. I thrust my hips, and she backed off her grip and returned to the teasing nips and sucks that drove me out of my mind.

"Slow deep breaths," she said. My words to her coming back to me. Is this what that felt like? The utter inability to relax mixed with the intense desire to do it merely because she asked? I'd do anything she asked me to. I tried to release some of the muscle tension in my legs and torso, but it didn't work.

Her breasts rubbed along my thighs, the stiff points

grazing my skin. I imagined holding them, licking them, burying myself in them. I wanted to push deep into her, explode, and watch her do the same. I was losing my grip on reality.

"Nora, honey." I didn't know what I begged for, but I begged.

"I've got you, Walker. You don't have to do anything. You don't have to be in control or perform in any way."

She shifted and brought her center to rest on mine. "Thank fuck," I said and thrust up.

"Ah, no. Not yet. I want you to feel how wet I am." She lowered more, pressing her warmth along the underside of my dick, and I almost came. Holding me there, she brought her legs together, and her folds wrapped more tightly around my shaft. "Don't move, Walker. Feel. You did this to me. You made me so hot, so needy for you. Think about how good it will feel for both of us when I bring you inside."

Oh, fuck fuck fuck! It was torture I never wanted to end.

She slid lower again and resumed her licks and nips at my tip, now coated with her wetness. Every muscle in me tensed. My dick was rock hard and leaking.

"Nora, honey, please let me inside you."

She met my request by taking me in her warm mouth, not deep, only the crown, but that was the most sensitive part of me, and damn, it was good. Two fingers lightly caressed and teased my balls and the skin behind them. Every time she stroked me there, electric bolts hit my spine.

"Babe, I'm gonna come."

Without changing her rhythm, she grasped my shaft tight near the base and pumped her mouth over the head. No deep throat, but steady, sweet suction and constant licks on that perfect spot below the crown. My blood was on fire. My whole body tensed, and then I was coming, hot and explosive, and she swallowed me down with each shudder. Fuck, I was dizzy with the intensity of it all.

After, I lay on my back with Nora tucked into my side. She had one leg hiked over mine. Slowly, I teased the skin of her thigh with my thumb. I had to take a minute to regroup after that orgasm. The best of my life. No competition.

"I hope Carly doesn't need that coconut oil to cook with. It's not leaving this room," I said when I'd regained the power of speech. She giggled and snuggled closer to me, but I meant every word.

"How did you get this scar?" she asked, stroking the raised skin along my jaw and chin.

"Wreck. Karting. Stupid mistake and I didn't have my helmet secure like I should have. Pieces of the other guy's kart hit mine, my helmet, and my face. It could have been worse, but you better believe my helmet has been secure for every race and practice since."

"Walker." She sighed, and I heard the worry in her voice.

"It was a long time ago, babe. It never happened again. I can learn from my mistakes." I chuckled and stared at her mouth. "Have you always had this freckle here?" I caressed her bottom lip with the tip of my thumb.

"No, I had a bad sunburn once when I was little, then a big blister, and it turned into the freckle."

I nipped at her lip then kissed her.

"Now," I said, pulling her tighter to my body as I rested my head on the pillow. "Give me a minute for my dick to return, and I'll fuck you so hard we break this bed."

"Your dick. Really?" Her tone was listless, and my eyes popped open.

"I thought you liked my dick."

Her eyes held a wicked gleam. "Oh, I do. But your tongue means no waiting."

THE SOLSTICE WAS PERFECT. The gray light never brightened more than a twilight due to the heavy clouds that had blown in from the north, and Nora and I barely left the bed. We touched and teased and came. We ate and napped and read.

Finally, we dressed in sweats when Canyon and Emme, along with Vince and Michelle, joined us for dinner. We watched a movie in the TV room. Something the girls picked. I barely noticed. Nora was all I saw.

The next day dawned brighter, and Carly and Nate arrived early.

"Another laundry day, and your folks will be here this afternoon," she said.

"Want to take a swim or walk the loop?" I asked Nora when she strolled into the main room dressed in yoga pants and another fleece pullover.

"Sure, but I should probably wash some things since I'm staying longer than planned."

"I'll do it," Carly said. "Set it in the basket in the laundry room. No problem. You too, Walker."

"We could go into Perry Harbor. Do some more shopping." I waggled my eyebrows, remembering all the hot lingerie we'd bought, and I'd enjoyed seeing on and off her.

Her eyes grew wide. "Gifts. I have no presents for anyone."

"We don't really do presents anymore," I said. "Once we outgrew toys, we picked themes each year like food and books, and we all had a package to open, but there wasn't this pressure to get the perfect thing."

"We can't always be together, so presents became more of a hassle," I continued. "Emme and Canyon will exchange along with Vince and Michelle. Mom and Dad will probably bring something for each of us. But don't feel like you have to buy anyone a present."

"What about you and me?"

"You want to buy me a present, Sweetheart?" I lowered my voice and waited for Carly to enter the laundry room. "Because you've already given me the best present." I winked. That blowjob the other night will live in infamy.

"Yeah, I do." She smiled. "Nothing fancy, but something to open might be fun."

"Okay. Should we see if the others want to join us?"

THE DAY WAS overcast but not rainy. The water of the Salish Sea reflected the darkness of the sky, with the green islands and a couple blue-hulled tanker ships breaking up the gray.

At the marina, Canyon grabbed his car for Emme, who'd popped into the restroom at the top of the gangway, but the rest of us walked the short blocks into town to meet at The Boathouse for lunch. The dinner I had with Nora there and the day we spent together were memories I wanted to hold on to.

The temperature hovered in the low 40s, but the dampness of the air made it seem colder. Nora pulled her coat tight and snuggled into my side as we walked. Her loose hair peeked out from under her knit hat and occasionally hit my chin with the wind, making me think of coconuts and a tropical island with her and that red bikini.

On the way to the restaurant, we passed a gigantic Christmas tree consisting of painted wire cages with a garland made of different colored floats like the ones you saw in chain seafood restaurants going for a beachy vibe. The tree had to be thirty feet high. We stopped for a photo, and I remembered the night at Pike Place Market with Nora. Photo evidence of this time with her. Would the pictures make it easier or harder when she left?

We passed The Elliot Hotel and the little boutique. I squeezed Nora's hand, and she blushed, temporarily turning her face into my shoulder.

Inside The Boathouse, the air was warm, and I spotted Canyon and Emme at the bar. Emme's round belly nestled under the bar top, and Canyon's arm rested on her chair, claiming her like I wanted to claim Nora.

"Did you put our name in?" I asked Canyon, and he nodded.

"Did you guys see the tree?" Nora asked. "The one that was in front of that old courthouse-looking building?" She took out her phone to show the pictures.

"That's so cool. What are those?" Emme asked.

"Illegal crab pots, believe it or not." A bartender appeared. It was the guy who'd played the guitar the night Nora and I danced here. Well, I danced, and Nora tried.

"We take crabbing seriously. A lot of people make their living from the water. Assholes who come here thinking they can crab anytime they want, anywhere they want, and without a license." He shook his head. "The Harbor Patrol enjoys taking up those pots. Each year, they make a tree from the ones they've confiscated as a friendly reminder for us all." He nodded. "What can I get you? We have special holiday cocktails, and Chuckanut Brewery has a couple special taps." He pointed to a chalkboard sign next to the liquor shelves on the wall.

"We're waiting for a table," I said, nodding at Canyon and taking in the moderately crowded space. At least the music in here was pretty good. Holiday classics like Bruce Springsteen and others.

"How 'bout some drinks while you wait?" he asked.

We gave him our orders then Michelle said, "Let's split up to shop. Girls against boys. We'll take one side of the street, and you take the other."

"What if all the good stores are on our side, and you guys can't find dick?" Vince asked.

"Excuse me," Michelle waved down the other bartender, the sailor one. "Can you give us some advice on the best places here for holiday shopping?"

He chuckled. "I might not be your go-to resource for that advice." He looked away. "Hey Tess, come here a sec."

The person working the hostess stand came closer. She was pretty. Tall, with startling blue eyes and brown hair styled away from her face that carried an expression of *I mean business*.

"What's up, Jake?" she asked.

"These folks need some shopping advice, and Emily isn't here. You're the next best thing."

"Aw, Jake. You do care." Her voice was sing-song and teasing.

"Just help the people, Tess, and quit being a pain in my ass."

"Oh, so me helping when the regular Sunday brunch hostess called in sick, that's me being a pain. Noted."

The bartender didn't respond as he walked away.

"Brother?" Emme asked.

The girl, Tess, shook her head. "I have two brothers who are more than enough most days." She nodded toward the pool tables. "But their friends like to join in too, including Jake and Rhys there at the end of the bar. I usually feel like I have ten big brothers in here. How can I help?"

She listed off places, the bookstore, the upscale kitchen store, several gift shops, and clothing shops.

"The Spa at the Elliot offers gift cards and has great products. When I'm looking for gifts, I always go there. The lavender lotion is to die for."

"Oh, a spa." Emme sighed.

"How about another pregnancy massage?" Canyon asked her.

"My brother's fiancée works there," Tess said. "She's great. She was saying they weren't too booked this weekend with the holidays so close. I bet they have openings if you call ahead. Ask for Emily."

Tess glanced around the room. "Looks like we have a six-top leaving. Let me get it cleaned off, and we'll get you seated."

Lunch was warm and filling. Nora and I had the clam chowder, and it was some of the best I'd had. Full of clams. The fresh seafood here all year must blow the mind.

Being here with Nora was kinda blowing my mind too. How she fit with my family. My sisters-in-law clearly liked her. They'd never included Claire like they were Nora. I know that was Claire's fault, but the difference was difficult to ignore. I had to remind myself almost hourly that this wasn't real. She wasn't my wife or my girlfriend, and I'd known her for barely a week. Because this felt real. It felt like forever.

Bellies full, we proceeded out to the sidewalk with a nod to Tess.

"I see you looking, Vince," Michelle said teasingly as the door closed behind us.

"What? I wasn't." Vince was so busted. He only had eyes for Michelle, but he still had eyes.

Michelle smiled. "It's fine. Someone that beautiful, I think you'd have to look."

Vince landed a smacking kiss on her lips. "You're the only one for me, babe."

"I wonder what skin products she uses. Her complexion is flawless, gorgeous," Emme said, and Nora nodded.

I grabbed Nora from behind and whispered in her ear. "So, you know, she's pretty, but not like you, babe. You in my bed all day yesterday, that was the most beautiful thing I've ever seen."

Nora turned and kissed me. Quick lips and a soft hmmm, but I still felt it in my dick, like always. "Sweet words," she said.

"They're true."

Her expression was full joy now. "Let's do the gift theme," Nora said. "Food, books. Sound good?"

I wanted to get more lace from that boutique, but maybe not to be opened in front of my entire family. Books and food would have to do. "Sounds good."

31

WALKER

I RECOGNIZED MY FATHER'S HELICOPTER FLYING LOW AS WE returned to the island from the day in Perry Harbor. Carly and Nate were there to help them unload and get settled. Which would provide some buffer. In my experience, Preston and Margo Hewitt were easier in smaller doses.

"Was that Dad?" Vince asked.

"Yeah." I glanced at Nora.

"Was that your father where?" she asked, sitting taller in her seat.

"In the chopper ahead of us now," Vince said.

Nora's gaze snapped to me. "You said you didn't have a helicopter."

"I don't. My father does."

She turned her body fully toward me. "Technicality, Walker and you know it."

"Not really. I told you, this is all my parents', not mine. And there is no guarantee I'll ever have any of it myself."

"Fine." Nora sent a teasing glare but didn't ask questions about the money or even make light of it, saying *sure you will*. It was like I'd told her we were having chicken for dinner when we were really having steak or something equally uneventful. Fuck, I liked her.

In the house, my mom greeted each of us with a hug.

"You must be Nora," Dad said before I could introduce her and held out his hand. His salt and pepper hair had recently been cut, and he was more casually dressed than usual in a Jaguar Formula One sweatshirt and jeans. He looked good, relaxed, and fit as ever.

"Yes. It's a pleasure to meet you. Thank you for having me."

"We're happy you're here," Mom said. Her light brown hair dusted over slim shoulders, and her cheeks were rosy. The large diamond still glittered from her left hand, but her dress was casual too. A long sleeve T-shirt and athleisure pants that fit well. She'd put on a little weight recently, which was good. In my opinion, she'd been too thin for too long, like so many of the other women in their circle.

Nate made another run to the Gator to collect their remaining luggage, and Carly appeared with two cocktails, handing one to each of my parents. "Can I get the rest of you anything?" she asked. "Dinner will be ready soon."

We all sat near the blazing fire with our cocktails and beers, talking about Mom and Dad's travels since leaving me in Monaco several weeks ago. Mom mentioned the symphony in Austin and her participation on the board. My parents shared a quick smile that looked like it held a secret.

Nora tucked into my side like it was natural. She said little but listened and leaned into me like a shield. I hoped her being here for a few more days would delay the pending waterfall of disappointment when my parents learned I was no longer going to be their exceptional racer, their exceptional son.

Mom and Dad asked about Emme's pregnancy while hovering close by. The baby began a kicking fit, Emme said, and Mom and Dad both smiled like kids as they tentatively placed a hand on her belly, feeling their first grandchild for the first time. Mom's eyes were unmistakably teary, and Dad's glistened a bit more than usual. I hadn't seen that before.

They asked about the ranch and Nora's work and showed genuine interest.

It was all unexpected. Usually, they regaled anyone new with stories of their wealthy lifestyle or my winning record. I saw the same thing in their peers, and it annoyed me. Whether people were bragging or acting cold and aloof, it was all just billionaires trying to impress. I heaved a sigh.

Carly and Nate were making drinks, cooking dinner, and tending to the fireplace. The glow of the enormous Christmas tree and images of possibly having Nora here for more holidays lulled me into a daze.

"Come with me, Nora. You must see Walker's trophies."

What? I'd missed some conversation. "Mom, no," I said, my voice coming sharper than intended, and Nora's head snapped to mine in question. But they were already walking back to the large office I intentionally hadn't shown Nora. The one tucked behind my parents' bedroom, like the TV room was tucked behind mine on the other side of the house.

Nora gaped at the walls of shelves filled with trophies and plaques, ribbons, and crystal bowls. "I don't know why you didn't show her, Walker," Mom said. "Your father and I love this room." She leaned toward Nora. "We had these units designed specifically to store everything."

Shit. Shit. Shit. My blood pulsed. I hated this room

and what it represented. It looked like a fucking shrine, not to my career, but to them. Photos of us with celebrities and world leaders. Photos of me accepting a trophy, them on each side. Like I was the Derby-winning horse, and they were the trainers. That's certainly what it had felt like for a long time.

This room and those pictures were part of their sanctuary here, they'd said, my success validating *them* in some fucked-up way. I'd done the work and didn't want to do it anymore.

This little show from my parents. The phone call with Mick and the decision I'd made. The support from my brothers when I told them I was quitting. Hell, even Nora's interest in me when she thought I was that rancher. My feelings about all of it and my frustration at being seen as a disappointment, a quitter, in my father's eyes after literally years of winning, simmered under the surface. Why couldn't my own parents just support *me* no matter what? Why did I have to keep pushing to be more? Too many months of unsaid things boiled over.

"Here, Nora, look around," I said, my voice harsh. "It's a bunch of stuff I won. This proves I'm a winner. They're winners. We're exceptional. But check the dates. Not many since the championship two years ago. Maybe not so exceptional anymore."

Nora's eyes grew wide.

"Now Walker," my father said, his expression soft. "Next year, we'll get it done. I bet you come back for a third championship win. You'll see. Hamilton's older than you, and he's still doing it." He lowered his voice like I was a toddler. I hated it when he did that. It was so patronizing. "I'll reach out to Mick," he said. "I've got a few ideas. We'll get you back on track."

"No. I'm done," I said with conviction. "Mick called

and asked for my decision about next season by New Year's. I've decided. I'm retiring. I want to work the ranch."

"Walker." The dreaded disappointment colored his tone before he regrouped. "Well, okay. You'll train the next guys," Dad said. "You're a two-time champion. One of maybe forty people who've ever won the championship since it began. You still have more wins ahead of you."

"No. As usual, you're not hearing me. I don't want this anymore." I waved my hand around the room, the shelves glittering with reminders of my former life. "And I'm definitely not training the next guy. I won't push a kid to make sacrifices just to win. I won't teach him winning is what matters or makes him matter. You say Hewitts don't quit, but this one is."

32

NORA

Walker vibrated beside me. I slid my palm against his. He gripped it, and the sensation caused my arm muscles to tense in solidarity. He needed me, not the doctor, but me.

"I don't want to race anymore. It wasn't supposed to go on this long, anyway. You remember after that first championship? The ranch has always been in the back of my mind." Walker brushed his other hand through his hair.

"How long have you felt this way?" his father asked, confusion etching his face.

"A while."

Mrs. Hewitt's voice was low. "Does this have anything to do with Claire?" She glanced at me.

"No," Walker snapped. "Claire was a wake-up call. Nothing more. I'm not your winner or hers."

"Our winner?" she asked.

"You like me winning with all your friends there to watch. But I won't do it anymore."

Silence stretched, then Mr. Hewitt huffed quietly, and his shoulders relaxed, understanding dawning on his face.

"I never intended to disappoint you," Walker said, looking away.

"Hold up. Disappointed?" his dad asked. "Son, we're not disappointed with any of you." He looked at Vince and Canyon standing inside the doorway, flanked by their wives. Not unlike the way I flanked Walker.

I wanted this. A family who was in it enough to show up for each other. People who supported and needed support.

"I'm sorry," Walker's mom said, her tone soft but audible in the quiet. "I'm sorry we made you think you had to win for us." She shook her head. "At first, we were just so proud of you and what you were doing. You were talented, inspiring. People noticed you and us. Sure, we were wealthy and successful in business. So was everyone else. But *we* were just a little bit more because *we raised such an impressive son too*." She heaved a sigh. "I see that now."

She moved to the overstuffed leather sofa and sat. "I told myself it was for you, the pushing. We wanted you to have the best opportunities, the life we never had when we were younger. And when you won, I thought I'd been right to push, like I'd had something to do with your success. Everyone around us was envious." She lifted one shoulder and let it drop. "And I liked that."

His dad brushed a hand over his face and glanced away before he met Walker's gaze. "We did that, didn't we? Made you feel you had to win so we'd look good."

Walker looked away, saying nothing.

"Damn it. I'm sorry. Come in, everyone, take a seat," his dad said.

We all shuffled forward to find seats, and his dad reached for Emme, making sure she found the right spot in a soft leather chair near the sofa. Even while arguing, this family still took care of each other.

"Your mom and I need to talk to all of you. Now's as good a time as any."

"Maybe, I—" I suddenly felt out of place. This wasn't my family. But Walker's hand moved to grasp my thigh, holding me in my seat next to him.

"I want you here," he said, his voice low, but everyone heard.

All eyes shifted to Mr. Hewitt. "It's been a tough time. A couple of scandals, high profile divorces. Your mom and I watched as the people in our social circle showed their true colors. I'm not sure why this year was the first we admitted we'd noticed, but it was, and we decided to make some changes. We've been seeing a therapist in Austin."

Walker's mom moved to stand next to her husband. She wrapped her arm around his waist, letting him feel her support.

"We realized some things we'd been missing." He smiled at his wife, and she returned it. "You know we planned to give most of the money away someday." Everyone nodded.

"Well, that day is here. We've spent the last month meeting with our attorneys and talking to the board of the family foundation. By the end of next year, 97 percent of all our investments will be under the foundation's control, not us. No more *billionaire*." He nodded his head to his smiling wife as if it were a decree.

"With the rest, we'll set up funds for the ranch and any lean years. We'll create funds for each of you and any kids you may have. We'll decide as a family what properties to sell, how much more to donate, and where. Your mom and I will travel, but not as often and mostly to places we've never been." He squeezed her shoulders, and she blushed.

"There's a new baby on the way, and we can't miss that." He looked at Emme as she rubbed her hand over her swollen belly. "Too many people we associated with let the money run their lives and change their priorities. They lost their families. We don't want that to be us. We'll usually split our time between the apartment in Austin and here. So, I think you could say we're quitting too."

His parents were ... incredible. After hugs for everyone, even me, Walker and his father went to the wine room off the pantry. They returned with bottles of chilled champagne, and we toasted new beginnings. Emme had a sip in solidarity.

"That was intense tonight. Are you okay?" I asked Walker as we undressed later that evening.

"I am. I'm surprised ... and relieved. A little stunned that they were seeing a therapist, but I'm glad. They seem happier."

"Your parents are amazing." The awe I felt was evident in my voice. "I wish mine were more like them." I looked away. The words felt disloyal, but they were true.

Walker brushed a piece of my loose hair behind my ear. "They weren't always like that. But I've always known they loved me underneath the pressure. And yours love you. How could they not?" He grinned.

"You haven't met Drs. Kenneth and Elise Reynolds." I knew my parents loved me but doing what I wanted instead of following their plan would be selfish, and that had never been an option for me. Butterflies hit my stomach. I needed to get that grant, and the time it would buy me to figure my shit out. I would get it. I would.

"Are *you* okay, Nora?" Walker's hand was gentle as he cupped my cheek.

"I'm tired. Writing, meeting your family, traveling. It's all so different from my usual routine."

Gently, he held my face and kissed my cheeks and then

my lips with so much tenderness. No one had ever done that the way he did. God, I would miss him.

Dressed in our pajamas, Walker led me into the bedroom. He opened all the blinds on the wall of windows across from the bed, then pulled me under the covers with him. Without a word, he cradled my back to his front and kissed my hair before nuzzling into it with me in his arms.

Snuggled together under a sea of blankets, we stared out the wood-cased glass to the lights of an anchored ship glittering in the distance on the blue-black dark of the water.

FOR THE NEXT couple of days, we swam in the lap pool, walked the wooded loop after Walker had run it, and ate too many good meals. We took the boat out in the afternoon with his brothers. We made cookies, and Carly dropped off everything imaginable to decorate them. Some weren't half-bad, and Walker baked his blue ribbon-winning biscuits for breakfast. They were the best I'd ever tasted, and I lived in Nashville. So, that was saying something.

The sex was different now. When he was over me, he held my gaze until I had to turn away with the heaviness of it. That look in his eyes felt real, and I wanted it forever.

We had fun sex, too, teasing and laughing, but the gentleness of his touch held something more even then.

His family was warm and wonderful, exactly like him. My heart ached, and I hadn't even left yet.

33

NORA

"It's Christmas. Kiss me." Walker held a sprig of laurel above my head as I finished getting dressed. A drop of rain that had fallen on the bush outside the bedroom's French doors dripped from the newly cut branch in his hand.

"Is that mistletoe?" I eyed the wet twig.

"Sure." He winked, and I kissed him. Fake mistletoe or not.

We'd slept in, like usual, taking our time with each other's bodies. My orgasm count for these last ten days was likely higher than the entire year before. Walker knew my body, and I knew his.

"Let's go. We always open presents before breakfast," he said.

Holding hands, we joined his family in the large main room. Everyone was sitting on sofas or chairs with cups of hot coffee and sleepy smiles. I felt lazy being the last one here when I slept steps away, and a woman eight months pregnant walked here from a cabin down the hill.

Walker pulled me onto his lap in an overstuffed chair. I

shifted to move off, but his hand clasped my thigh like it did the other night. "I want you here."

I relaxed back into his hold. Once everyone gathered, we each grabbed packages to share. Walker handed me two gifts wrapped in beautiful paper. "The blue matches your eyes," he said with a grin. "Merry Christmas, Nora. Thanks for staying. Open the big one first."

It was a book about Van Gogh. "Do you have that one?" he asked, his voice uncertain.

I shook my head. "No, no, I don't have any books about him."

His eyebrows furrowed. "Why not?"

"I never bought one. I guess there was always something else to do with my money. Thank you."

His grin grew. "Now, the other one. I think you're really gonna like it."

I gave him a questioning expression as I pulled the paper back. It was a box of Little Debbie Swiss Rolls. I laughed, and I loved it.

"My favorite." I leaned in to give him a family-friendly peck, but he took it deeper for a split second before I could pull away. "Thank you," I said, grinning.

I handed him the packages I had for him. "I hope it's okay to open these in front of everyone."

"Why? Is one a sexy photograph of you?" His lips curved in a seductive smile, and for a moment, I wanted to give him a photo of me, my hair down, hopefully looking provocative, but then I didn't know how to do that.

He opened the first box. It held a black apron, with *I make this look good* scrawled in white across the top. "Thanks, babe. Already getting ideas for wearing it." He waggled his eyebrows.

Ripping the paper off the other package, he laughed too loud to not draw the attention of others.

"What's that?" Vince asked.

"A book ..." Walker turned it for all to see. "About having sex later in life." He smiled up at me, still perched on his lap.

"What?" Vince's laugh rang out. "I guess you are getting old."

Walker glared at his brother. "You wanna go, little bro? We can go, anytime. Say the word." Vince's smile only grew larger.

"It's related to my research. I was here to meet with a couple of ladies who are experts in sexual health, particularly in older adults."

Walker's parents exchanged a glance.

"The women, Miss Nat and Miss Nell were fun and warm. They were at that yarn bar the day we went back to Perry Harbor to shop. They recommended it. Said every man should have a copy." I shrugged.

Walker's mom eyed the book. "Yes, that's a good one. One of our recent favorites." She winked at his dad, who read the title and nodded. The two of them were like Cheshire cats as everyone else broke out in various degrees of giggles and shocked expressions. I felt so warm and content at that moment.

My phone rang with an incoming Facetime call.

"Excuse me. It's my parents." In an instant, fingers of cold dread crept across my middle. I stepped out of the room and into the study by the den.

"Joyeux Noël," they both said in unison.

"Um, Joyeux Noël," I stumbled. "Why French?"

"Oh, the primary language in the African country we'll be in soon is French," Mom said. "Best to learn it yourself than rely on an interpreter, so you should get started as soon as you can. We'll help you catch up once we're together."

I didn't want to learn French. Foreign languages didn't come easily. I'd taken Latin in high school, already preparing for medical school and the Latin-based terminology, and did well enough. French wasn't Latin. I pushed this new expectation aside.

"So, how are you? How are you celebrating today?" I said, struggling to keep my tone bright. It was Christmas. I wanted my parents, my family.

They opened with the normal conversation. The situation in the villages. The beauty of the city they were in.

Finally, Mom asked, "Where are you? That's not your apartment."

I looked around as if I'd forgotten where I was. "No. I'm at a friend's house. In Washington State."

"Washington State? Why there?"

"I came here to interview some experts," I blurted. Shit. There was nothing to do but keep going. "Um … I'm applying for a research grant from the Birch Foundation." I swallowed.

"You'll be able to do that from Africa?" Dad asked.

I shook my head. "It's a two-year grant. If I get it, I'll need to delay applying to GDNL." My heartbeat raced, imagining different reactions, from understanding and love, like Walker's parents had shown, to crushing disappointment.

Shocked silence rang through the phone, along with the image of their serious faces.

"Two years? Nora, you can't do that." My father's voice was tight.

"Dad, this is important to me."

"What's the topic?" he asked, his voice growing harder.

"Diagnoses in women typically associated with anxiety with no known cause. One issue is vulvodynia, so I was here to meet with some experts on sexual health."

"Sexual health?" My father's grey eyes bulged. He combed his hand through his thick and still dark hair, so much like the texture of mine. "Nora, that sounds fun, but please be serious. What we're doing is *saving lives*."

"I *am* serious." My voice shook, but I ignored it.

"Nora," my mother's face appeared on the screen. She pushed her glasses up and set her jaw like she always did when she needed to explain something to me about the world. "I know you enjoyed research when you were in school, but honey, it's time to do actual work now. Your father and I are counting on you. Don't let us down. Not when we're so close to the goal."

I swallowed. I didn't want to let them down. They paid for the STEM tutor and all those prep classes in high school. Because they did, I got scholarships and had less debt now. They helped with tuition, pushed me, and supported me. Not everyone had such supportive parents or the opportunities they gave me. I owed them.

"Your mother and I put our reputations on the line, Nora." My father's voice boomed from the side of the frame. "They're fast-tracking your application because you're our daughter. You want to embarrass us?"

"I never asked you to do that." It was a scream in my head but barely a whisper into the phone.

"Kenneth, calm down," Mom said. "Nora. You're away from home. You're not yourself. Listen to me. There will be time for research later. After a few years with GDNL, you may want to take a break and start a family. I understand that. You'll have time for research then. Now is the time to get in with GDNL. It will make working for them later much easier."

My chest tightened, and my palms sweat. Had she planned out my whole life? Did I have a lifetime of expectations still to meet?

"I wish I'd had this chance when I was your age," Mom said, "but years ago, they didn't let female physicians into the places we're going today. Now, you're a woman who can break down barriers for others. Nora, you aren't just saving lives, you're saving the dreams of all those little girls out there who want this. Don't turn your back on them."

My body shook, and I couldn't catch my breath. "I'm not turning my back ... on ... on anyone. I'm not trying to embarrass you. This is what *I* want. I want to do research."

"What *you want*?" my mother shrieked. "Nora, that doesn't sound like you. Where is this coming from?"

"Okay. This conversation is finished." My father's voice boomed again. "We'll talk when we've all settled down. Your mother's right. This isn't the girl we raised. This isn't you, Nora."

The call ended, and my shoulders sagged as I gasped for air. I felt the burn of tears but blinked them back.

They were right. I'd never spoken to them like that before. I was the good girl. The kid who toed the line. This Nora, who did what she *wanted* because it was fun or interesting, had never been me. I was losing myself here. *Or finding yourself,* a small voice whispered in the back of my brain.

"Nora, is everything okay?" Walker's gentle concern annoyed me in the den's quiet warmth. He shouldn't be the one asking that question. My parents should. But they didn't.

"I'm fine." Always fine. "I just need a minute." I rushed to the foyer and shoved on my boots.

"I'll come with you." He picked up his running shoes and walked toward the nearby bench to put them on.

"No." It came out harsh, and Walker blanched. "I'm sorry. I ... I need to clear my head. A short walk on the trail. Not far. I'll be fine." I closed the door behind me with a thud.

What was happening to me? I dialed my lifeline.

"Hey, baby girl. Merry Christmas. Did you meet the family? Still glad you stayed on that island with him?"

"Merry Christmas, Jamar." The tears overflowed at the sound of his voice.

"Hey hey hey, what's going on? What did that asshole do? I can be on a plane in hours, fully prepared to kick his ass. Where are you?"

Jamar was mostly talk, but if I really needed him, I knew in my soul that he would come. "No, no, not him. It's my parents."

I heard him exhale. "Tell me." I unloaded the story into the phone and onto his broad shoulders.

"I'm just ... I feel ..." I stammered. "I don't know what... It's my job to make life and death decisions all day long, and I can't decide how to feel right now. I'm all messed up, and that's not me. I don't know what to do. It's happened more than once on this trip, and it's freaking me out."

"Nora. Take a breath. In through your nose. Out through your mouth."

"Jamar, I don't think—"

"I didn't ask you to think. I asked you to breathe. Do it." I jolted at his words, but then I took measured breaths, calming my pulse and lowering my blood pressure.

"How did you feel this morning? Before you talked to them?"

"Fine. Happy. Walker is ..." How did I describe such a wonderful man and his family?

"Nora, nothing has changed since then. Your parents still want you to go to GDNL, and you still applied for a research grant that would keep you here for two more years. It's the same situation you've been in for a while. Look around you. Where are you right now?"

"The woods, a trail near the house."

"Can you see the house?"

I turned. "Yes."

"Good. What do you see?"

I saw warmth and welcome and a watching figure silhouetted in a window. I choked out my answer, "Gray board siding. Big cedar beams. Lights on inside."

"That's where you are. You aren't deciding about GDNL. You can't because you don't have all the information, including the outcome of your proposal. So be where you are at this moment. On that trail. In that house. It's all you can ever do. Be where you are."

My body relaxed. Nothing had changed since this morning. I'd already known they didn't want a delay with GDNL, and though I'd hoped they would see research as a viable reason to stay, I knew they would eventually accept it either way, not wanting me to let my colleagues down. I'd never asked them to fast-track my application. That was their choice. My breathing slowed, and I ended the call with Jamar.

Stepping back inside the house, Walker met me in the foyer, out of sight.

"Babe?"

I smiled. "Sorry. The conversation with my parents, we talked about my research and delaying GDNL. It didn't go well."

"What happened?" Concern etched his features, and my belly fluttered. He cared about me, and God help me; I cared about him. True feelings after ten blissful days.

But he lived in Texas. I lived in Nashville, hopefully. Jamar hadn't met him. I hadn't mentioned him to my parents. I shuddered at the thought of how they would judge him for being a race car driver. Some of the horrible things they'd say flashed through my mind. My head was a mess.

I had to get it together, find my way back to the real me who weighed options logically and thoroughly, then decided, usually correctly, based on facts rather than feelings and desires. I had to return to a world that made sense if I was going to figure out what to do about my parents and GDNL.

I shook my head. "It's not worth getting into."

He pulled me close. "What do you need, Sweetheart?"

Parents who give a shit about me. Like yours. "I'm good." I tried to smile as we walked back into the big room and settled in the chair again. Walker's caring touch and comforting caresses were luxurious, and I soaked it all in. Stored it away because I had to leave.

I didn't belong here with these people who loved and listened and showed up, and the longer I stayed, the clearer that became. This always had an end date, no matter how much I *wanted* more.

Self-sacrifice is usually necessary to do the right thing.

Walker deserved better than the mess I was. A woman who made life and death decisions every day for others but couldn't even stand up to her own motherfucking parents.

"Here. This is from Mom and Dad," he said, placing a small box on my lap. I looked over at them in the kitchen, and they waved as they pulled pre-prepped food from the fridge to make breakfast.

"But I didn't get them anything."

"It's fine. I'm sure they just wanted to include you."

Included, just like I wanted, like I belonged. I opened the box to find diamond earrings nestled in plush midnight-blue velvet. The sparkle made me blink. I'd owned nothing like this, ever. I noticed Emme and Michelle now wearing similar pairs.

"These are beautiful." I inhaled as I grazed my fingers across the clear stones. His parents gave me the same gift as the one they gave their other sons' *wives*. Tears burned at the edges of my eyes. *I wanted too much, and I shouldn't want.* My vision blurred. I had to get out of there.

"This is too much." I stood, fidgeting as one of my hands smoothed my hair. "I'm just a girl you met. We're having fun on a break from real life. I ... I can't accept them." I handed him the box and walked away.

34

WALKER

I FOLLOWED HER INTO THE BEDROOM, NOT LOOKING BACK at what I was sure were the worried glances of my family as her words *I'm just a girl you met* rang in my ears. Nora had never been just some girl I met. Not even that first day.

"Nora, keep the earrings. It's just a gesture."

"A gesture? Walker, they bought the same thing for Emme and Michelle. And they are enormous diamonds. The stones are larger than the one in my mother's engagement ring."

I sighed. "Look, I know it's a lot, but it isn't to them. Honestly, it was probably easiest to buy you all the same thing. Hell, one of their personal assistants probably picked them out. It sounds bad, but it's the truth. It really is a gesture. Please keep them. I think you want to."

"It doesn't matter *what I want*, Walker. How many times do I have to tell you that?"

"And how many times do I have to tell you it *does* matter? You are allowed to want things, Nora. You're allowed to complain about shitty things and be angry or pissed when something is unfair." What had her parents said to her? Whatever it was had hit her hard, and that made me angry. She was shaking. I wanted to fix it. I wanted to find her parents and knock their heads together. Instead, I shoved my balled-up fists into my pockets.

"You don't understand. Your parents are ... not like mine."

I drew a deep breath, trying to calm my agitation. "Then explain it to me."

She sighed and sat on the bed. "I can't do this. You make me want things I shouldn't, things I can't have."

"Sweetheart, talk to me. What do you think you can't have?"

"This life. *Your* life is so different." Her head shot up. "You do what you want. I barely understand the concept. You drive race cars for a living with people who have more money than God. People who could eradicate hunger in small countries, but instead, they race million-dollar cars and burn oil and waste resources all because they *want* to."

"Is that what you think of me, of what I do, what I did?" She wasn't entirely wrong, but her judgment still stung in the silence between us. "You think I'm a spoiled little rich kid who knows nothing about the real world? What work is? What sacrifice is?"

Her eyes met mine, and her face fell. "No, that isn't what I think. I didn't mean that." Her sincerity showed in her eyes, along with something else.

"Then tell me what you think," I said and kneeled in front of her.

"I think ..." She blinked back tears. "I think I should go."

"What? No. Not like this. Not after everything between us. Nora, tell me what's going on."

She crumpled further, and I wanted to hold her.

"I'm sorry, Walker. I didn't mean what I said. I know that's not who you are."

I couldn't stop myself. I picked up her hand and kept my voice low. "Sweetheart, what did your parents say?"

She straightened, feigning strength through the pain I saw plain as day. "They're disappointed I may not be joining them as soon as they hoped. Disappointed that I'm interested in research. Disappointed ... in me." She inhaled deeply and gave her head a slight shake. "It's fine. I didn't mean to make a scene." Why did she do that? Why did she hold back her feelings and pretend everything was fine? It wasn't fine.

I smoothed her beautiful hair back as she gazed down with something that looked like shame. "Nora, you didn't. And if you did, I wouldn't give a shit. I only want to be sure you're okay."

"I am."

She wasn't. And this closed-off person wasn't Nora. Not the Nora I knew, and I would swear on a stack of Bibles that the Nora I knew was the real one.

I didn't push, though I wanted to. I wanted to fight and shout and hold her and make up. I wanted so much with her, more than with any other woman before.

Slowly, I handed her the earrings, and she accepted the box with a weak smile, then held it gently.

"Are you hungry?" I asked and stood.

"Yeah." She closed her eyes. "Give me a minute. I'll put these on and wash my face." Again, she smiled at me, but this one was new. Fragile, resigned, sad. I didn't like it.

She stood, and I took her hand more firmly in mine. "I'll make you a plate. Come out when you're ready."

"Five minutes," she said and turned toward the bathroom, pulling out of my grasp. It was the first time she'd ever done that.

. . .

Nora was quiet. Not enough for anyone but me to notice. She wore the earrings, which drew my attention to the shine of her eyes. After a big breakfast, everyone took a walk on the wooded loop. The thick canopy of the trees was all the umbrella necessary to hold off the light rain. My brothers told her all the embarrassing childhood stories from holidays past. But they made her laugh, and she seemed to settle back to herself in the fresh air, even if it was a quieter version.

We played board games, *Code Switch* being our favorite, and I finally caught glimpses of my Nora. The bands constricting my heart, thankfully, loosened.

Later in the afternoon, we snuggled in the den, reading our new books, although she switched to her highlander romance novel after about thirty minutes, saying she *had* to finish it. The light almost hit her eyes as she said it.

Dinner was beef Wellington and all the sides. Mom discovered the dish years ago when they came to one of my races in England. Since then, it was reserved for special occasions. The new chef mom hired had made a spectacular version this time. Lighter, somehow, but still as tasty.

"Hallmark movie time," Emme announced.

"What?" Nora asked with a brighter smile.

"After dinner, we usually watch a Hallmark movie or two. I picked out a couple to stream before my nap earlier." Emme grinned, and Canyon groaned.

"Come on, Canyon," she said. "One is called *A Baby for Christmas*, and the other is *A Miracle Noel*. Babies and miracles are on brand for us this year."

"*A Miracle Noel*, that's it!" Nora bolted up in her seat. "I've seen it, and I was trying to remember the name a few days ago. It's a good one. I'd watch it again."

"If you've seen it, we'll pick another. There are plenty to choose from. Maybe one of the guys wants to pick." Now Emme was just teasing us.

"No way," said Vince.

Nora turned to me with her eyebrow raised.

"I don't watch," I said. "I'm on kitchen duty, or I'll chop some wood or clean a bathroom."

"Or run till I puke," Canyon added.

Vince slapped him on the back. "How far is that bro, a mile?" Canyon flipped him off as discreetly as possible.

"Come on, girls. We don't need the men for this." Mom stood and gave Dad a side eye with a grin.

"You don't have to go," I whispered. "We could turn in early."

"No, I want to. This is actually one of *my* holiday traditions." Her smile still wasn't quite there. I hoped a sappy movie would fix it.

As they watched, I heard talking and laughing often. Nora fit with my family. She fit with me. I had to keep seeing her. What we had was real, more real than anything I'd ever had before.

She'd scared me earlier but was back in my arms where she belonged.

"We have one more bottle of Beaujolais," I said as I pulled her close from behind while she undressed in our closet later. I wanted it to be *our* closet for a lot more days than the rest of the week.

"Let's save it for another time. Tonight, I want to feel you over me. Connected."

She was reading my mind. Again.

As usual, I started a fire before turning down the sheets. I stretched out in my boxers and waited, wondering which set of lingerie she'd choose for tonight. I was smiling like a fool thinking about it.

She appeared and stood beside the bed. The tie of her robe loosened, and she wriggled the fabric off her shoulders and down her body. She was naked in the firelight. No lace. No silk other than her pale skin and dark hair. And I loved her.

I swallowed at the vision of her moving onto the bed. God, I loved her.

Her lips trailed their way up my chest, and my fingers smoothed over the curve of her waist as I watched. Hovering over me, she kissed me with tenderness and something that felt like more.

I lifted to deepen the kiss, and she rolled, pulling me on top of her. Her hands grasped my hips and the fabric of my boxers as she helped me take them off. When I returned to her, it was all warm skin to warm skin. With my arms under her shoulders, I propped myself up to see her in the soft glow of the firelight. I loved her.

"You're beautiful, Nora."

She smiled and pulled me tighter to her heat. I wanted a taste and started to slide lower.

"No," she said. "Stay with me." She pulled me to her again, but the kiss wasn't the feverish fun it usually was. It was hesitant and a bit guarded.

Today had been emotional for her, more than any other day I'd known her. Maybe she needed this connection to take away any remaining sadness. I know I did.

I kissed her deeply and nipped at her neck and shoulders before teasing and sucking her sweet pink peaks. She moaned, and my hand eased lower to tease the patch of curls there. She slowly rocked into my palm, and I slid my fingers down to caress and stroke until I heard her breathing deepen. Her legs opened, allowing me to pet her wet folds.

"Condom," she said.

I didn't want to leave her for any reason. I wanted to be inside her bare, but something in her eyes told me tonight wasn't the night. I stretched for the nightstand beside the bed. Once I covered myself, I slid between her thighs. My arms returned to their spot under her shoulders, and I took in her beautiful face once more. I loved her.

Sinking into her heat, I held her gaze, but she closed her eyes as she moved against me, chasing her pleasure and letting me watch. She clutched at my ass, pulling me tighter to her as she moaned and panted her breath.

"Harder, Walker. I need you."

"Say that again, babe."

"I need you, Walker. Mark me like you did the other night. Please."

Fuck, that was hot. So, I did. I kissed and sucked and marked both her shoulders and collarbones as I pushed and ground into her. She got wetter and hotter until she tensed, and I knew she was close.

"Are you with me, Sweetheart?"

"Yes, don't stop. Let's ... together."

Two more thrusts, and she let go, triggering me.

35

WALKER

Again, I woke without Nora in my bed, but I could hear her voice. I slipped on my discarded boxers and padded into the bathroom. I found her on the closet floor, her laptop open.

"What's going on? Is everything okay?"

"I'll have to call you later," she said into her phone before dropping her hand to her lap. "I … I'm so sorry, but I have to leave today. There was an emergency, and the hospital is short-staffed. They asked me to come back early." She was lying.

I ran my hand through my hair and sighed. I wanted to beg her to stay. I wanted to refuse to take her to the airport. I was in love with this woman and thought I had a few more days to figure out how to make this work.

With me leaving racing, I'd be in the States. We could find a way. This didn't have to be the end. It wasn't just one night and another. I came alive with her, and she came alive with me.

"Nora."

Her eyes were dull, and her expression determined.

"I'm sorry. You've been so kind, but I have to go." She rose to her feet.

I'd been kind? What the fuck was happening right now?

"I'm booked on a noon flight from Bellingham today. If you could take me to that harbor, I can get an Uber to the airport."

"No, I'll take you from Perry Harbor." The words came out soft. I was stunned.

"Oh, okay. Thank you," she said and walked past me into the ensuite to pack. I stood still and watched her for a few beats, defeated. Last night, I thought we were connecting. But that look in her eyes, the intensity of it made sense now. She was saying goodbye.

With her bags packed and dressed in the tight red turtleneck and jeans she wore that first day, she rolled out to the big room where my parents sat drinking coffee in the early gray light.

"Good morning," Mom said brightly, then frowned. "What's this?"

"I'm afraid I have to leave. The hospital had an emergency. I'm so sorry to rush off. You've all been so welcoming, and it really has been wonderful knowing you."

She looked at the Van Gogh hanging on the wall, and I remembered the night in the museum and our first night here. Seeing the art and the world the way she did made it brighter. How would I possibly see it that way without her?

THE BOAT TRIP to Perry Harbor was silent, but my head was a loud cacophony of thoughts against the low hum of the boat's motor. I vacillated between thinking about how to let her go and trying to figure out what to say to make her stay. We were good together. So good. Why didn't she see that?

The forty-minute drive to Bellingham was polite. She thanked me for the trip and the museum. We both tried to talk about the happier times and laugh about our days together.

At the airport, I stopped at the drop-off area and got out to grab her bag for the last time. She took the handle, but I didn't let go.

"Tell me I can see you again. Tell me we'll figure this out. Don't walk away from me, Nora."

She blinked with a sigh and then looked at me. "What are we doing, Walker?"

I let go of the bag. "I didn't plan it, but *I'm* falling in love. It's that simple. And I don't want to lose you."

Unshed tears glistened. "This won't work. I can't be in love with you." The resolve was clear in her expression.

"The hospital didn't call, did they? You called them. You wanted to leave." She didn't deny it.

"Walker, I can't stay in this alternate universe any longer. It's too hard. I have to go back to my real life, where things make sense, and I know what I'm doing. I don't recognize myself here." She paused and came closer. "You are the best man I've ever known. I'm the one who can't do this."

"Is this the 'it's not you, it's me' bit? Fuck Nora. We're beyond that shit. This isn't some alternate universe. *This is real.* You know it is. I do too." I held her hand to my heart, the same one she was ripping out of my chest at the moment.

My last effort.

"You can't live your life for your parents. Living your life for the approval of others is letting them control you. I know that better than anyone."

She pulled her hand away. "Walker, my parents made sacrifices to pay for tutors to get me into the right programs so I'd get into a great undergrad and med school. I've never let them down before. I can't start now. It's not who I am. I just can't."

"They don't own you or your life because they raised you. You're a grown woman. Do what you want, Nora, please, for both our sakes. Do what you want."

She was quiet. Stoic. This must be the face she used when she delivered bad news at the hospital. She was a wall. And going up against a wall never worked out well.

I turned to the car and opened my door. "Tell me to stop, Nora, and I will."

Her face was still that wall. "I'm not stopping you."

My family mostly gave me space for the remaining days at the house. Nora left me and didn't look back. And I was leaving racing, the only career I'd ever had. It was safe to say my emotions were unpredictable for several reasons.

I'd tried to be casual about it. Think of Nora as a woman I picked up at the airport and brought home for the holidays because I didn't want to be alone. It was an intense time for both of us, and we clung to each other. That's why it felt like more, like love. I told myself I'd be over it by the time the decorations were down.

After too many drinks to a happy New Year with my brothers, I texted her. I'd agonized about what to say, writing it and deleting it a million times, but then went with the simple truth. I missed her.

She wasn't just a woman I picked up at the airport. She was different. Sincere in her affection, genuinely interested in the well-being of others, and modest about how rare and remarkable she was. In short, she was lovely. And beyond my reach. Some other lucky man would spend his life making sure she knew it. This man needed to move on.

I let Mick know I'd decided to retire effective immediately, and those first weeks had been busy. A trip through Europe. Photo shoots for the press releases. The painful recounting of all my wins and more recent losses on all the international racing channels. Social media was mostly kind, but sentiments that sounded like *washed up* and *too old* hadn't escaped my notice.

I let the activity distract me to the point where Nora felt like a beautiful dream sometimes, except for the very real ache in my chest. Even seeing Claire at a party on the arm of an oil billionaire only made me miss Nora more. There was no comparison.

Finally, on the ranch, I let the images of my past fade with days of hard work alongside my brothers and settling into my new life in Texas. I was where I wanted to be. But some images refused to fade, and they all had Nora in them.

36

NORA

New Year's Eve sucked. No other way to say it. Being impulsive led to heartache. Walker's text made it worse. He missed me. And I missed him with an ache I couldn't describe or ignore. I struggled to breathe with it sometimes. But all I could bring myself to text was that I missed him too.

I ghosted my fingers along my neck and collarbone, but the bruises from his lips were gone. Those first few days, I'd stood before the mirror, pushing against the marks to feel the memory of him there one more time.

Work had finally pulled me out of the deepest sadness. No more being impulsive. My parents taught me to think things through, always. Make good choices, they said when I was growing up. What they meant was don't do drugs, don't drive too fast, and don't eat food that's bad for you, like those Little Debbie snacks. Treats are dangerous because we don't forget once we've tried them.

I wished I'd listened better. You couldn't miss what you didn't know.

The weeks since leaving Hewitt Island hadn't been

great, but I was trying. I'd had another conversation with my parents that went about as well as the one on Christmas Day. As I expected, they said they would accept a delay if I received the grant. God, I hoped I got it.

Why couldn't my family be more like Walker's? I missed him. I missed them all. They were lucky. What they had was incomparable. I didn't realize families could be that way outside TV and Hallmark movies. Another thing that I'd miss now that I knew. Damn it.

"You want me to pick you up?" Jamar asked as he walked into the alcove behind the nurses' station at work. Tonight was the Birch Foundation dinner where they would announce this year's grant recipients, and he'd offered to escort me so I didn't have to watch Flores with his one true love while I sat alone. I'd told him Michael Flores was no longer anything more to me than a distant memory, but he insisted. I wondered if Walker would ever be just a distant memory. Did I want him to be?

"Sure. Thanks," I said.

"You look hot, Nora. Flores will eat his heart out," Jamar said as he took in the simple navy-blue cocktail dress I'd purchased for the event. I wore the diamond earrings Walker's parents gave me, and they sparkled against the backdrop of my long hair. I'd been wearing it down more lately. The hair and the earrings made me feel closer to Walker somehow, and that made me stronger. I hadn't yet been able to wear the delicate, lacy lingerie he'd bought for me. Too many memories for that yet.

"Thanks, Jamar." I hoped my grin looked genuine as we entered Alexander Hall, one of the entertainment spaces on campus. Muted tan walls and tan industrial carpet created a blank slate for the circular tables draped with black tablecloths and topped with fine china and crystal. Gold and white flower arrangements dotted the room, and the scent of lilies co-mingled with the food aromas coming from the catering area.

A small bar was located near the back, and Jamar and I headed straight for it. I needed a drink to calm my nerves. My entire future was riding on tonight, professionally and personally.

I needed something to focus on other than everything I missed about Walker, like his firm muscles, hint of a southern drawl, generosity, and laugh, not to mention his tongue. And I truly wanted to do that research. It might be the only thing that *could* distract me.

A young woman approached with a tray of miniature quiches. Instantly, something sparked in Jamar's eyes, and the same light shone in the server's as well.

I selected a quiche to taste and glanced between the two frozen people.

"Um, hi, I'm Dr. Johnson, Jamar." He stumbled over his words, which I'd never heard him do before.

"Melissa. It's nice to meet you."

"Are you a grad student?" Jamar asked quickly.

Melissa glanced at her tray, half full of bite-sized food. Grad students across disciplines often worked events held at Alexander Hall.

"I am," she said and stood tall. "A doctoral candidate in economics."

Wow. That would not be a simple path for me. Econ had been like another foreign language in undergrad. It clearly impressed Jamar, as he asked more questions. They talked, and I periodically took quiches from her tray, helping to legitimize her lingering with us.

After a few minutes filled with chitchat and meaningful

smiles, she returned to circulating in the crowd, but Jamar tracked her more than he probably realized.

We found our seats with two other grant applicants from the Biology and Chemistry Departments. I stumbled through conversation and small talk with my tablemates while I picked at my dinner, too nervous to eat.

"What's going on with you tonight?" Jamar asked, keeping his voice low. "Usually, you'd be interviewing these people. This quiet Nora is not you."

Not me. How did everyone know what *was* or *was not* me when I barely knew myself?

"I'm nervous, Jamar. I need this."

"You got this, baby girl."

Dessert and coffee were served, and it was time for the grant announcements. The foundation's president, Victoria Keating, opened with a review of the work the Birch Foundation had supported in the past, the program's vision, and overall goals.

My heart raced, and I heard Walker's voice telling me to take slow, deep breaths. The memory came with a sudden awareness in my core. God, I missed his hands on me. His smile. His support. All of him.

I had to move forward. He was there, and I was here. He was living a new dream with the support of his loving family. I was a mess who barely had a family. But with this grant, I could be more. Do more.

They announced the names and projects one by one, my mouth going drier and my heartbeat pulsing with each project that wasn't mine. I held my breath, and Jamar gripped my hand.

"From the Emergency Department, Dr. Michael Flores et al. with an examination of ..." The words that followed the name ran together and muffled as if I'd slipped underwater. Time stopped. I watched a drop of condensation slide down my water glass as I heard the blood rush in my ears.

Flores won the grant. I didn't.

The presentation concluded, and the university's student jazz ensemble took to the stage for the entertainment that would close the evening. Jamar's hand had squeezed mine where it rested on the table as they announced the remaining winners. A professor seated with us had won for chemistry, and we had offered our congratulations which helped to distract me for a moment. My head now spun with words that sounded muted and otherworldly.

"Are you okay?" Jamar asked from the seat next to mine.

"Yes." Always okay. "I'm ... going to miss you, Jamar." Resignation filled my tone.

He furrowed his brow. "What are you talking about?"

"GDNL. I didn't get the grant. I have no excuse now." I sniffed and attempted to shake off the sadness.

"Nora." Jamar's voice was soft but stern. "Do you *want* to work for GDNL?"

"It doesn't matter what I want. Self-sacrifice is usually required to do the right thing." The words were flat and automatic.

"That's true. But who decides what's right? Your parents? Do they have a magic book I don't know about? Or is it possible you can decide what's right by yourself?"

"You don't understand, Jamar. Your parents would do anything for you."

He nodded. "They would, they made sacrifices to give me opportunities they didn't have, and I appreciate it, love them for it, but they were also doing their job. It's what parents are *supposed* to do. Support you, encourage you, prepare you to find what *you love* so you can do that for the good of others. That's the *right thing* for you, what you love. And I think the *self-sacrifice* you need to make is to let go of this crazy-ass desire to please them."

"You don't understand."

"Yeah, you've said that. Say something else." His expression hardened as he sat back in his chair.

"Like what?" My hurt and anger spiked.

"The truth. Tell me what you want, Nora, *you*."

The truth. The truth was, I didn't *want* to ever work for GDNL. It would be illogical. I didn't want to travel. I didn't even like it. I never did. What I wanted was research. To devote my time and my brain to improving healthcare for women. *Make life worth living for those that still are.* Walker's words that night we danced at The Boathouse.

Jamar's face was stone. "I'd be saving lives," I whispered, no longer gleaning the strength I once had from those words.

"Who's life, Nora?" Jamar ran his hand across his brow like he did when he wanted to say more but was trying not to.

"Say it, Jamar."

"It's time. You've saved hundreds of lives. Now, save your own. Tell your parents to love you how you are or fuck off. Apply for another grant somewhere and do research. Do what *you* want for a change."

"What I want," I whispered to the ceiling. "Walker said the same thing."

"Listen to him. That guy, he changed you. I mean that in a good way. And it's not just that you're wearing your beautiful hair down. You feel things now."

"I did before. I wasn't a robot."

He raised his eyebrows. "Before him, you were an incredible doctor. No one was more devoted to their work. Hair braided tight. Perfect. But you were a robot doing what you thought your parents wanted, or the hospital administration, or the Birch Foundation board. Now, you're not just an incredible doctor, you're a woman. A woman whose life needs to be saved by groundbreaking research."

He was right. I was a robot, and I had changed. My shoulders sagged with the weight of the truth I'd tried to deny for too long.

"How do I tell them, Jamar? How do I let them down?"

"Let them down? Because they can't call the shots when you're a thirty-five-year-old woman? Nora, they should feel nothing but pride about you. If they don't, that's on them."

I gulped the last of my wine. "I need something stronger."

Jamar stood. "I'll get it. You take a beat and think about what I said." He pointed his finger at me before turning for the bar.

Moments later, a chair shifted on my other side, and I turned to see Michael Flores lowering to the seat. His unwrinkled gray suit cut to fit him perfectly, paired with a dark purple button-down shirt, highlighted the warm sepia tone of his skin and the light blue of his eyes. Light glinted off his silver Rolex as he settled an elbow on the table.

"Congratulations. Here to gloat?" My words were soft and bland.

"No. I'm curious about what your next move is. I doubt you'll let this setback stop you." He brushed a hand through his jet-black hair. His usual smug expression was replaced by what looked like genuine interest.

I huffed at the word *setback*.

"Birch was always just a stepping stone for you," he said. "You're not satisfied here."

"Huh, satisfied."

"That's what I said. The Emergency Department doesn't satisfy you." He leaned closer. "I couldn't satisfy you. You want more. More than I, this hospital, or even this foundation can give you. But there is a place, and you have to go find it now. It's not here. You and I both know it."

I met his gaze and his expression gentled. "I'm sorry how things ended with us," he said. "But there's a man out there who will light you up. And though I love Laura and want to marry her, a part of me will always be jealous of that man."

Jamar returned with my drink, and I raised my head as a tear spilled over my lashes. I wiped it away quickly, but he saw it.

"What did you say, asshole?" Jamar's eyes bore into Michael's.

"Jamar, no. What he said was true, and I needed to hear it. He was actually very kind." I smiled at him.

Michael nodded and rose with a flourish. "It was good to see you two, but Laura's getting tired, and I should make a few more rounds with my team. We'll want to get to work soon. Let me know your plans, Nora. Stay in touch. I'll help if I can." He reached out to Jamar. "See you around, man." Jamar shook his hand, though he kept his expression stern, protective.

"I should go too," I stood and smoothed down my skirt as Michael walked away.

"Think about what I said, Nora. Do what *you* want. You know I got your back."

Jamar hugged me, and briefly, I remembered Walker's

embrace. "You're right. I can't work for GDNL. It's not me." Saying the words out loud already had me feeling a little bit better.

"Damn straight."

I chuckled at my cocky friend, who was decent and smart and deserved a happily-ever-after if anyone did. "I'll get an Uber. You stay. Drink that cocktail." I spotted a certain beauty walking from the catering area toward the bar. I nodded in her direction. "Talk to Melissa. She's probably off now."

Jamar followed her movements. "She's a grad student." His voice was laced with caution.

"In economics. Not your department or even the hospital. No one will bat an eye. You're both adults. And you like her. She may be the smart, Black woman you've been looking for."

"Well, aren't you the romantic, suddenly?"

"I think I've always been a romantic. What's sudden is my awareness of it." The images of Walker flashed again in my mind, and this time, I held them close. I wanted my own happy ending with him, but I'd left him, hurt him. I had to find a way to fix that too.

My life was a mess, but at least I wasn't going to GDNL. I was going after what I wanted, and he was what I wanted more than anything.

I walked to the lobby to grab my coat and call an Uber. The stone floor and walls echoed my footfalls as I headed toward a bench with a view of the glass doors and the road where my ride would appear. The room's perimeter was lined with bronze busts and paintings of former university presidents and the original donor, Edgar S. Birch, who'd founded the school in the late 1800s. As I looked at their faces, I wondered if any of them had ever had trouble standing up to their parents.

"Nora?" I turned.

"Mr. Williams?" My brow furrowed.

He nodded with a chuckle. "Yes. I thought that was you."

It was Mr. Williams from the hotel in Seattle. My heart stuttered at the memory of my first breathtaking night with Walker.

"I wanted to apologize," he said. "That night in Seattle, I was exhausted and worried about our son and his new family."

"How is everyone? The baby, your daughter-in-law?"

"Good. Son's back at work, though I think he'd rather be home with Andrea and the baby. He's taking his family leave in a couple of months." He shifted on his feet. "But that night, I didn't get the chance to introduce you to my wife. We were so grateful for your kindness, and then you and your friend were gone."

My friend. Walker was so much more than that.

Mr. Williams gestured to the woman at his side. "This is my wife, Dr. Elizabeth Thomas."

I froze. "Dr. Thomas?" She came closer. "I've ... I've read some of your work while researching for this grant. Your paper with Dr. McGregor."

"Yes, well, I've read some of your work too."

I tilted my head. "What do you mean? I'm ... unpublished."

She smiled. "For now. First, I didn't know *you* were Dr. Nora Reynolds. It surprised me when we realized it earlier this evening." She cleared her throat. "I'll get to it. One reason I came here tonight was to speak to you. I'm part of an advisory review board for the Birch Foundation and read your grant proposal. Also, I knew you weren't getting this one. I guess women's sexual health just isn't that interesting to some people." She gave me a knowing smile.

My mind reeled. *She* was Dr. Thomas, a research leader in women's health and someone whose work had influenced me and my research hopes for a while.

"Your project is viable, and I was impressed with the interviews and preparation that went into your proposal. I recently took a position at a large university, and I'm transitioning my work there. I've received grant funding to conduct clinical trials with women on a new medication under review by the FDA. Sort of a female version of Viagra, but not really. As we both know, women's bodies are not the same as men's, and their sexual response cycles are different. This drug works differently than past contenders, so I have some hope. I have a couple of adjunct faculty positions to hire as assistants for my work focused on sexual health, particularly women's. I'd like you to take one of those positions."

Still stunned, I was silent as Dr. Thomas leaned in.

"Think about it. I know it's sudden, but I wanted to offer you the job *before* knowing our connection. And then when I realized, well, I have a good feeling about this Nora, or Dr. Reynolds." Her expression was kind and confident. "You could do a shift at the hospital now and then. I wouldn't expect you to give up practicing entirely. But you would spend most of your time researching and working with our graduate students."

I had to be dreaming. This was exactly what I wanted. I closed my eyes and replayed the words. *What. I. Wanted.*

"Where? What school?" I asked, a tremble in my voice.

"The University of Texas at Austin."

Talk about *a miracle Noel.*

She held my gaze, and I smiled because ... Walker.

37

WALKER

"It's lunchtime, man. Take a break," my brother Canyon said as he placed the roll of fencing wire in the back of the truck and checked his phone. "Emme's due any day now, and I can't be dead on my feet when she goes into labor. Let's go. We both could use a break."

I didn't want a break. I wanted to work and sweat and grind until the images of Nora in my bed and in my arms dulled.

"You go ahead. I'm not hungry," I said.

"Bullshit. Now that you're not on your race-car-driver diet, you eat more than anyone. You're moping, and it's pissing me off."

I faced him. "Pissing you off? Why the hell is that?"

"Because you're bringing me down. My fantastic wife is having my baby. A sweet baby girl that I am going to love and protect like I do her momma. This is my destiny, man. My dream. I'm living it, and your grumpy ass is ruining it."

"Sorry I'm ruining your dream." Sarcasm dripped from every word.

"I'm not leaving you out here without the truck, and I can't go to lunch without the truck. So, get the fuck in."

"Fine. Damn, man." Finding the toolbox, I dropped in the pliers I was using to twist the fence wire and patch the hole we'd found on our ride yesterday.

"Let's load everything up," Canyon said.

"Why? We're coming back in a couple of hours. This hole isn't fixed."

"Did you hear what I said about Emme? I may not be. I'm in go mode, man, twenty-four-seven. We'll leave it all in the truck. Easy."

Fuck, he was annoying, but the best way to shut him up these days was to give him what he wanted. Images of me giving Nora what she wanted invaded my mind, and I sighed for the millionth time as I slid into the driver's seat.

The ride to the ranch was quiet, except for Canyon rambling about some Valentine's Day gift he bought for Emme. I didn't want to talk about it. Didn't he see I was fucking dying? Asshole.

It had been over a month since that text where I tried to pretend her leaving hadn't gutted me. She responded with the same wish for a Happy New Year and that she missed me too.

The words that had comforted me then, given me hope, now sounded cheap and hollow. She'd walked away. I'd made it clear I wanted to see her again, and she'd cut me off. If she missed me so goddamn much, why wasn't she texting me, calling me? I hadn't changed my number. I kept my phone charged and on me at all times. Nothing from her. Too many nights, I sat up looking at an open text window and typing the perfect combination of words to bring her back to me, only to erase them all before I hit send. It was pointless.

She was back in her world, and I was in mine. Even

with my broken heart, I was glad to be on the ranch and finished with racing. It was the right decision, and I didn't regret it.

I parked the old farm truck in the gravel beside my uncle's house. Canyon hopped out and barely kicked the dirt off his boots before he was up the steps and yanking open the storm door. Why wasn't he going to check on Emme if he was so worried about her?

I shook my head, then glanced toward Vince's place and the nearby grading work where my house would soon be. He and Michelle left yesterday for a pre-baby-making vacation, Vince said. Once they returned, they intended to get serious about adding another grandchild to the brood. Fuck my life and my happy brothers.

I loved them, but a man had a breaking point. Looking at the empty building lot, I tried to focus on the future I could still have there. Maybe I'd meet someone else and have a family. Maybe I'd grow a new heart. Miracles happened.

I rounded the front of the truck and glanced at the rolling fields beyond Canyon's place. He and Emme moved into the house we'd all grown up in, and the same firm building mine had remodeled the original ranch home into a modern version, now baby-proofed from basement to rafters.

Those fields were the same ones I'd run through as a child. Fields where I'd dreamed about racing and what my life would become. They were winter brown, but I could see the beginnings of spring green Bermuda hay and imagined the purple flowers of alfalfa that would pop up low to the ground. I pictured Nora in blue jeans and cowboy boots, walking my way with the sun behind her. Her long, thick hair loose in the breeze. Her lush lips smiling.

I rubbed my chest at the familiar ache and headed

inside where I stopped short in front of the long kitchen table.

Nora.

I blinked, half convinced I'd conjured her in my mind as I watched her stand. Except she wasn't wearing jeans and cowboy boots. She wore a green dress that dipped low and came in tight around her trim waist, showing all her sexy curves. My hands twitched.

"Walker, you have a guest," Aunt Susan announced like it was no big deal.

"Walker. I ... I'm happy to see you. I've missed you," she said.

I was thrilled and heart-sick and pissed. "What are you doing here?" I asked, trying to keep my voice even.

"I, well." She glanced at my very pregnant sister-in-law, who smiled sheepishly and arched her back, pressing one hand into her side.

"Emme told me where to find you. I was hoping we could talk."

She took a few hesitant steps closer, and I wanted to grab her, kiss her, and tell her I loved her. Because I still did. Instead, I stood frozen, not yet trusting my own eyes and ears.

"Lunch is beef chili and cornbread. It'll hold," Aunt Susan said. "Why don't you two head out to the porch where it's quieter?"

Nora stepped toward the doorway I'd entered, and I reached for her hand out of habit. We both stared, and she slid her warm palm against mine like she did at the top of the escalator at the airport that day.

Out on the wraparound porch in the bright early afternoon, we sat on the swing at one end, breaking the contact of our hands. Immediately, I missed the connection.

"What are you building?" she asked, nodding to the cleared land in the semicircle of homes here at the end of the drive.

"My house." We both stared into the distance at the barn, corrals, and fields beyond.

"This place is beautiful and not too far from Austin," she said.

I nodded. This small talk was killing me. "Nora, tell me what you want?"

"You," she said without hesitation but still looking away. "And I want to do research." She ran a shaking hand through her hair that fell down around her beautiful face. "But mostly, I want to be with you."

I swallowed at the sound of the words I'd wanted to hear for too damn long.

"You left me."

She turned to me. "I shouldn't have. I was wrong. Can you forgive me?"

"This is my life," I said, and she nodded. "You'd move to Austin?"

"What if I already have? Well, not actually, because I'm still looking for a place to live. I don't have to be near campus since I'll only have a couple hospital shifts a month, and I'd like to be someplace like this, where the air is sweeter." Her words were quick, reminding me how she spoke of the things she was passionate about.

I blinked. "You moved to Austin to be with me?"

"No, well, not entirely. That would be a lot of pressure, and I'm just some girl you met. I was hoping to date you. To know you. See where it goes …" She shrugged. "And then … marry you and have your babies." Incredible words. More than I'd let myself imagine, but I hesitated to believe her.

Softly, I huffed. "Nora, you were never just some girl I met."

She glanced down, then up at me. "I took a position at UT Austin. You remember Mr. Williams from the hotel in Seattle?"

My mind hung on *a position at UT Austin*. I replayed the words as I watched her lips. "Um, sure."

"Well, Mrs. Williams is actually Dr. Thomas. A leading researcher in women's health, and when I didn't get the grant at Birch, she offered me a job with her here."

"Wait, you didn't get the grant?"

"No, Flores did. And I'm glad. Because I landed my dream job. I told my parents I wasn't ever going to work for GDNL, and I was moving to Austin to do research and hopefully win over the man I love. They weren't, *aren't*, happy, and may never speak to me again, but I can't live my life for them." She lifted her chin and met my gaze, looking sad and determined and hopeful all at the same time. "Someone wise once told me that doing things for the approval of others is letting them control me. What *I* want matters, and what I want is you."

Four words. *The man I love.* Everything else was like an echo after those four words. "You love me?"

"I do." She grinned and leaned closer. Like that night on the sofa in the hotel room when she crawled across to me, her lips were mere inches from mine, and my free hand came up to cup her cheek.

There was nothing to think about. All that mattered was her. Everything else, we would work out. I rested my forehead against hers and exhaled. "I love you too."

She moved quickly, pressing her lips to mine and climbing into my lap. Her knees bracketed my hips, and her heart beat strong against mine, struggling to leap out of my chest. I sighed at the feeling of holding her again. Like I could finally take a full breath. I cupped her ass and pulled her tighter to me. Holding her there, I broke the kiss and buried my nose in her soft coconut-scented hair. I was finally home. Whole.

"God, Walker, I missed you. Your voice. Your hands on me. I love you. I'm so sorry I left. Please forgive me."

"Ranch life can be hard, a little boring, or monotonous at times. Not much glamorous travel or month-long vacations. More simple pleasures. I plan to be a rancher for the rest of my life. Can you be happy here with me?" I asked.

"Walker."

"I need you to be sure. I can't lose you again. That's a wall at 200 miles an hour, and I won't survive."

Her voice was low. "I want the rancher, so I want the ranch. If you're happy here, I'm happy here. I'm here because of *you*. I love you."

I closed my eyes and breathed her in. "God, I missed you. Don't leave again."

"I won't. I promise." She sighed into my mouth before giving me a hungry kiss full of all the desire and unsaid things between us. I could tell her I loved her until the end of time, and I'm not sure I'd ever get it all out.

I heard the rush of footsteps land on the porch. "Hey, sorry to interrupt, but Emme's water broke. We're headin' out," my brother said, and I smiled at his panic-stricken face.

"Well, don't look so freaked out. You're getting your dream," I said.

"Yeah, well, from the looks of things out here, you are, too." He jogged down the porch steps.

My aunt and uncle rushed out next to Emme, and I felt Nora start to get up, but I held her to me, right on my lap.

Canyon already had his truck started. The overnight go-bag for the hospital rested in the backseat of the cab.

"Come on," he shouted as he jumped out of the truck again, rushing to Emme, walking down the stairs. "You okay, baby? Should I carry you?"

"No." Emme laughed. "Susan's timing my contractions. I just need you to drive."

"Should Walker drive? He's the pro. And then I could sit with you."

"I'm not a pro anymore," I said. "You got this, man. Plus, I'm a little busy right now. We'll come to the hospital later. Like hours later." I squeezed Nora's ass again, and she protested, but no one paid attention to us.

"The chili's on the stove. Be sure and turn it off when you leave," Aunt Susan said as she climbed into the extended cab of the Ford F150 with Emme. My uncle Hunt rode shotgun, his grin big.

The gravel crunched loud as they backed out and eased onto the concrete circle drive before Canyon floored it.

"You need a place to live?" I asked, watching them speed away.

She smiled, this one coy and teasingly deceptive, along with her innate sensuality that was only Nora. "Do you know anyone renting a room somewhere nearby?"

I kissed her again and whispered against her cheek, "Live with me."

"Really?" Her face lit with a hesitant smile and a sparkle in her eyes.

"Yes."

"Is there room?" she asked, still with a teasing gleam, and I remembered her questions about staying on the island with me.

"It's a big house." My lips curved into a grin.

"Is there a washer and dryer?" She frowned in mock seriousness.

"I think there is," I said.

"Okay."

38

NORA

Traffic was a bear today. It usually was, but I tried not to complain too much. Once I hit the rolling hills near the ranch, I loved my commute southwest from the sprawling UT campus. Plus, I planned to work frequently from home soon. Walker scrapped his original house plan, and his architect designed a new one. It included a study in a back corner with floor-to-ceiling windows that framed the flowing green land. The study at his parents' house on Hewitt Island was beautiful and serene, but this one was more so because it was mine, mine with Walker.

The research was everything I'd hoped for. Some of the grad students were more ready than others for the workload, the boring details, and the excitement or the disappointment of watching a new theory be supported or contradicted by our findings. But they were learning and growing, and I was too.

I pulled into the drive and opened the garage door. I swiped a hand along my braid as I hopped out of the car. Late summer heat in Texas did not allow me to wear my hair down as often as Walker preferred. I grabbed my backpack and slung it over one shoulder as I jogged inside.

"Hey babe," I called as the air-conditioning hit me. "Sorry I'm late. Traffic. Where are you, and when is everyone getting here?"

"I'm upstairs, Sweetheart. Bedroom."

I rushed past the large kitchen island, barely noticing all the foil containers, though my mouth watered at the smell of barbecue. Walker's uncle Hunt was world-class at cooking beef in all the ways.

I dropped my bag in the study, away from the rooms that would soon fill with family, friends, and caterers for tonight's housewarming party. Hustling up the back stairs near the kitchen, I noted these walls could use one more coat of paint. A few white spots bled through the calm blue-gray color. The contractor would return on Monday, and we'd get it on the punch list.

We'd moved all our furniture in this week, but that didn't mean we were done. It would take some time to fill a house with four bedrooms, a study, a den, and a bonus room. We had a kitchen table and chairs, which had been mine, a TV that had been Walker's, and a sofa that we bought new. We had to start somewhere.

Most important for tonight, we had outdoor furniture and a covered deck with several ceiling fans to keep the hopefully cooler evening air moving for the party.

The plan was for this to be our first night in the house, but our new bedroom set hadn't arrived yet. I tried to hide it, but I'd been disappointed with the news.

Since there had only been a building lot when I *came to my senses and admitted I loved him*, his words, moving in with Walker meant moving into Walker's space at his aunt and uncle's house. We had the entire upstairs since Susan and Hunt slept in the primary suite on the first floor, giving us some privacy, and the initial awkwardness of meeting them at the coffee machine in the morning faded soon enough.

"Babe? What are you—" I stopped short as I crossed the threshold of our bedroom. The lights were on even though fading orange sunlight poured through the picture window on the other side of the room. Our furniture was here, the king-sized four-post bed perfectly appointed with a crisp white comforter and sheets and pillows in a pale blue that matched the walls.

"I thought it was delayed," I said, looking at Walker.

"I lied. To surprise you. Again, sorry, but not really."

I looked at him sideways as he stepped closer. "Just make sure all your little deceptions lead to good things, Walker Hewitt."

He nodded. "I'd never lie to you, not when it mattered. I hope you know that."

"I do. I expect you to keep it that way." I squinted at him to make my point before letting my joy at the surprise show on my face. "So, we can sleep here tonight?" My mind was already flooding with images of him and me and that big comfy bed.

"Yep." He kissed me with enough heat to make me rethink the party.

I pulled out of his grasp before I stripped right there. "Let's go to your uncle's and grab our things. We can shower here." I winked.

"Yes, ma'am," he said, and I chuckled, turning toward the doorway.

I caught my breath at the large photograph hanging on the inside wall, the elderly couple from the Angus Hayes Gallery in Seattle. It hung in the center, lit perfectly by a light in the ceiling like the space had been designed for it, like the Van Gogh in his parents' house on Hewitt Island.

Surrounding it were smaller shots. The ones of us at

the Pike Place Market. The color and darkness of those photos contrasted with the large black-and-white photo that captured the substance, sensuality, and magic of two people who'd truly loved each other most of their lives.

"Walker …"

"I love you, Nora," he said from behind me as I gaped at the couple. They were embracing, his front to her back, with confident, mysterious smiles among the wrinkles, age spots, and thinning hair. Her shoulders were bare in the silky tank she wore with flowing linen pants, and his chin rested on one at the base of her neck. His lips curved just above her skin, exposed by her short, stylish haircut. It was sweet and intimate, with the gleam in their eyes hinting at the continued passion between them. It was like the image of their younger selves was still there, if only in their lover's eyes. It was magic.

Walker wrapped me in his arms like the man in the picture, and I felt his lips below my ear. "I love you like that man loves her. That's our goal. To love each other through everything life throws at us, no matter what. Passion and trust and anger and forgiveness and everything in between. To know we'll be okay because we love like they do. To smile and laugh in our seventies, like they are. …
Marry Me."

I turned in his embrace. "What?"

He knelt on one knee. "Marry Me."

I was speechless as he held out a ring. A single bright stone on a delicate platinum band. Perfect, and I watched as he moved slowly to place it on my finger.

"Tell me to stop, Nora, and I will."

"I … I'm not stopping you."

His kiss was as magical as our first one in the downtown Seattle train tunnel. But unfortunately, his family really was coming soon. So, we walked to his aunt and uncle's house, deciding to shower and change there before we packed a few things to bring to *our house* for our first night.

Walker wore jeans, a dark blue T-shirt, and the same alligator boots from that day in the airport. Eight months ago. A lifetime.

I wore a long sundress and the matching alligator boots he bought for me. He liked me in cowboy boots, and I liked the way he looked at me. I twisted my hair in a loose bun on top of my head, which usually signaled to Walker that he could take it down once the air cooled with the evening breeze. He loved to take down my hair, and I joked that growing up, he must have had a thing for Rapunzel. He laughed but never denied it.

The food was delicious, and the house was full of family, friends, and congratulations on our new home and our engagement. Vince and Michelle were laughing with a group gathered at a high-top table near the pool as the outdoor string lights came on. Michelle was trying to inconspicuously not drink alcohol. A sure sign of a new baby in the works.

Emme and baby Sarah sat on the covered deck. Margot and Preston sat nearby, taking turns holding her like the dotingly proud grandparents they were.

They'd spent most of the summer on their beautiful island in the cool sunshine of the Pacific Northwest, and Walker and I had visited as much as we could between the ranch and getting Dr. Thomas's lab operational. I loved it there in our room in *the big house*. It was perfect.

A roar of laughter and high-fives rang out from the side yard. Walker and Canyon were playing cornhole with some kids from the Boys and Girls Club, where Walker volunteered. He was teaching karting to a few middle schoolers, and they'd formed a solid bond. Walker encouraged the kids to challenge themselves, know their limits, and celebrate their growth rather than wins.

I smiled at my life as folks from church, from the cattle auction house, and from the symphony, all mingled like old friends while the night bugs sang in the growing dark.

This was my family. I gazed at the shimmering stone on my left hand for the hundredth time tonight. It was illogical that someone could feel this good, this complete. But I did.

"I'm ready for bed, gorgeous," Walker said later, snaking an arm around my waist and pulling me into the study as the caterers cleaned up the last of the dishes in the kitchen. "I've been half hard all night watching you."

My belly always flipped when he said stuff like that. This man was it for me in every way.

"Walker, not yet." I giggled. Something I was doing a lot more of these days.

He groaned. "Come upstairs. Five minutes. Give me a little taste under that skirt, then I'll let you go."

"This is not my first rodeo with you, cowboy. You won't let me go."

He ran his hand through his hair. "You're right. Okay. But how much longer? That dress of yours showed your shape more than you knew when you were standing in the setting sun. Young Reverend West had to look away."

I startled. "Are you joking? Is this one of those things like Carly might catch us naked in front of the fireplace?"

He shook his head. "He's a man of God, but he's still a man. I can't fault him. He did look away after all."

"Why didn't you tell me? Shit. They'll never let me help with the corn-maze fundraiser if they think I'm a hussy."

Walker chuckled. "Hussy? Do you hear yourself, Dr. Reynolds?"

"Babe, I'm all in here. Emme said the corn-maze fundraiser was the social event of the season. It's a priority."

"It'll be fine." He kept snickering as we walked back into the kitchen.

"We have about fifteen more minutes, Mrs. Hewitt, then we'll be out of your way," one server said.

"Oh, I'm not—" I started, but Walker cut me off. "That sounds good. Thank you."

I looked at him. People had called me Mrs. Hewitt in many places since I moved to the ranch, and I guess I'd have to break the habit of correcting them.

"It's only a matter of time, Nora. I'd marry you tomorrow if you'd let me. I'd marry you yesterday if I could," he said, pulling me in for a hug.

"Do you need me here?" he asked. "If not, I think I'll head upstairs. File my nails. Open some wine." He waggled his eyebrows. Since February, he'd ordered a case of a particular Beaujolais from a high-end wine shop in Austin every month. "Maybe do some reading," he said. I still loved his fuck-hot glasses, and he knew it.

Finally, I closed the front door behind the caterer and took in the empty house as I roamed the space, turning off lights. No rush. We had all night. We had our whole lives.

Up the stairs and into our bedroom, I found glowing white pillar candles on the dresser and bedside tables. Texas summer was too hot for a fire. Candles were a romantic substitute.

Walker sat on the bed, his lower body under the sheet, his bare chest above, filing his nails in his sexy glasses like he had our first night.

"I love you," I said. "I may have that first night. You touched me, and I knew I'd never be the same." Silence stretched between us for a moment.

"Come to bed, Nora."

I walked over to him, took the emery board, and removed his glasses, setting them both on the bedside table. I sifted my hands through his chest hair and smoothed along the ridges and planes of his hardworking muscles. He'd filled out more since our first night. He was strong and solid. He grasped my wrists and pulled me down over him. His lips found mine in a slow, drugging kiss as his hands skimmed up my legs, bringing my dress with them.

Settling my knees around his hips, he sat forward so I rested on his lap with our lips still locked. My heat pressed into the solid ridge of him under the sheet. His hands cupped my face, and his lips released me before he removed the heavy combs and pins that held my thick tresses off my neck.

He sifted his fingers through it. "I love you too," he said. "I definitely fell that first night when you let me undo your braid and brush your hair. It was satin across my fingers, and I pictured doing that for the rest of my life."

Again he kissed me as the sweetness of our words surrounded us. With tender slowness, Walker lifted my sundress off and leaned back to take in the lace as I sat over him. "Oh, the pale pink. My favorite." His grin held the sexy promises he always kept.

Lifting me, he rolled to lay me next to him, and the movement shifted the top sheet. He was naked and hard, and he was mine. Together we worked to remove the lace he loved between fervent kisses. Then he stretched out beside me.

"Are you ready for me?" His fingers traced my folds, now soaked. His smile was sweetly wicked, and I loved it. "Oh, that's so nice, babe." I still loved his words of praise.

He moved between my legs and opened me to him, kissing along my thighs. I moaned as his warm mouth covered me before licking and sucking and making me even more eager.

"Walker, come here." I reached for him, and he moved to kiss along my stomach and breasts as he lined himself up with my body.

"Eyes open, babe," he said, and I nodded. He slid inside, filling me as he looked into my soul.

"I love to be inside you like this, with nothing between us." He whispered across my lips as he held my gaze and slowly rocked, the base of him hitting my clit in the way we both knew would make me scream. So many intimate things we'd shared about our bodies, the positions, the touches, the scents, and tastes, but nothing else connected him to me like this. Good old-fashioned missionary. Face to face, him above me, eyes open and locked with mine as he loved me.

EPILOGUE

Walker

The Following Christmas

Wine gets me hard. Well, wine and thoughts of Nora, open to me, her scent filling my nose, her moans and sighs filling my ears. With her taste on my tongue, the fruit and tart of a particular wine are like nectar for the gods. I'll never get enough. I took a sip from my glass on the side table.

No man should worry about his dick as long as his tongue works. That's damn right. I'd stay in shape, take care of myself, and hope my dick worked into my seventies or eighties. But if it didn't, I knew my tongue would. I had a lifetime ahead with this nectar of the gods.

The woman of my dreams appeared from the study, stretching and exposing a thin strip of satin skin below the bottom of her silky tank under an oversized flannel. It was one of mine. Fuck, she looked good in my shirt. Soft and warm and everything I needed.

She liked to work in the mornings at home on the

ranch. Rancher's hours start early, and with us on similar schedules, it meant I had her sweet curves in my hands all evening most nights. But here on Hewitt Island, I remembered our first days together last year and the feel of lazy mornings wrapped around her with nothing to do but worship her body. I wanted more of that. Tomorrow's usual solstice tradition of staying in bed all day couldn't get here fast enough.

"Hey there, Mr. Sexy Glasses," she said with her provocative smile, my favorite one of them all.

"Come here, Mrs. Hewitt. Give me a kiss." In the cozy den next to the study, I closed my book and sat forward in the cushy club chair. The fire crackled and sizzled in the background as a chilly rain fell outside, turning the sea water and distant island evergreens to shades of blueish gray.

She stalked toward me. "That's Dr. Hewitt to you."

"Yes, ma'am," I said and winked as she bent for a quick kiss. I pulled her closer with one arm and pressed my lips to her soft belly. My other hand rested on her hip. She wasn't showing yet, but I couldn't wait to see the bump there.

"How's my little man?"

"What makes you think it'll be a boy?"

"It has to be. I need to start with a boy, something I know about." I shook my head. "If we had a little girl first with her momma's smarts and blue eyes, she'd own me, Nora. I'd give her anything she wanted. I'd be a terrible father."

"Babe, you'll be a wonderful father, no matter what. And you forget. *I* own you." Her eyes held a wicked gleam. She did own me. No question.

We were married two weeks ago at a small nearby resort with an intimate wedding space on the water. Fresh evergreen boughs and white twinkle lights decorated the simple hall, and Nora, in a flowing white dress, stole my breath.

In a final show of billionaire flourish for his last son's wedding, my father flew in all the guests from literally around the world on private planes. The wedding planner's team arranged for temporary luxury glamping sites to be constructed on a farm in Perry Harbor and scheduled a fleet of seaplanes to transport everyone to the remote island resort for the ceremony and reception.

I didn't want to know about the army of personal assistants and staff it took to plan, organize, and arrange that event. I'd been away from all the pomp and show of wealth, and I didn't miss it. Plus, all I could think about that day was the extraordinary woman I was spending it with.

My brothers and their wives were there. Aunt Susan, Uncle Hunt, and a few of the longtime ranch hands. Nora's friend Jamar and his fiancée Melissa, Mr. Williams and Dr. Thomas, and even Angus Hayes and his husband, since he agreed to take our formal wedding portraits.

With the F1 season finished, Mick and a few of the guys from my racing days made the trip, including Lorenzo, who took the driver's seat and owned it in his first year.

Nora's parents came from Africa. They loved their daughter, and even though the relationship remained challenging, I hoped our wedding day would start a new phase for them. With time and now, the addition of a new little life, maybe they could all put the past behind them.

We didn't know she was pregnant at the wedding. She peed on a stick two days ago when she said her boobs hurt, and that was that. No one else knew yet. Just us. Here in this house, where it all began.

Nora ran her hand through my hair, and I looked at my wife before pulling her down to straddle my lap.

Her eyes went wide. I was hard as stone, and I held her tight against me.

"Oh, that feels good," she said and settled into position. "What have you been doing out here?" She raised her eyebrow in question.

"Reading … about oral sex."

"What?" Nora chuckled.

"This doctor guy wrote a book about making sure you come first. He had a few techniques we haven't tried yet." I kissed her neck. "He has a book about blowjobs too, but I don't think you should read it. If those got any better, you'd probably kill me."

"Walker." Another giggle as my hand roamed her back.

"I want to take you on this carpet, right here in front of the fire," I said and scooted us forward to the edge of the chair.

"That sounds perfect, but—" she held out her arm to show me the special watch on her wrist, "we have company."

"No, we don't," I said. "It will take them at least ten minutes to get here. I can do this."

"Not this time."

"Come on, babe," I pleaded, then kissed and sucked her neck the way she liked, making her squirm against me the way I liked. I'd been staying away from her magnificent breasts since she said they were sore. So, I doubled my efforts in the other places that got her hot.

"Hal, who's here?" she said, her voice ringing out strong and confident.

The disembodied voice filled the space. "Walker and Nora. Margot and Preston approaching on drive. Canyon and Emme, and Sarah at cabin one. Vince and Michelle at the lap pool."

Shit, Mom and Dad were approaching on the drive. "The shower it is." I scooped her up and jogged to *our* bedroom.

"It's starting. Hurry!" Emme called from the TV room in the big house. This was my last televised interview. A sort of *one-year-later where are they now* type deal for ESPN2 and SkySports.

"I'm five months pregnant. This is hurrying," Michelle said as she entered the room with Vince hot on her heels like if she stumbled, he'd be there to catch her. And I couldn't even give him shit about it. I knew the feeling, and Nora had been pregnant for about a minute.

Michelle and Nora popped popcorn like it was a damn Hallmark Christmas movie, and my brothers were practically salivating at the chance to give me shit. I wasn't the lone interviewee on the show. This was not a big deal, but maybe it was since it was their last glance at me, the race car driver.

The guy in the black swivel chair spun to face me on the screen. "You are one of only a few people from the US to break into the sport. You won two championships in your career, and you're credited with initially training Lorenzo Messina, the best new driver this year. With that kind of success, how have you transitioned to life after racing?"

I talked about ranching, working with my brothers, and marrying the love of my life. Emme nudged Nora at that comment.

"Your wife is a researcher at a university."

"Yes." I smiled off camera to where she had stood watching at the side of the sports show's set.

"Some have said you can never truly leave racing behind. As part of such an elite group of drivers, you don't have any interest in returning to the sport, training others, perhaps taking on a leadership role at some point?" he asked.

"Do you know what my wife researches, Todd?"

The interviewer checked his notes and raised his eyebrows. I could always tell when people realized how lucky I was. "This says *women's health and sexuality later in life*."

"That's right. When I was in F1, I was one of twenty people on the planet who had that job. Now, when my wife needs help with her research, I'm the only person on the planet with that job. I think my future's brighter than ever." Todd chuckled and took a beat before getting the discussion back to racing.

Michelle laughed. "Nora, I can't believe you let him get away with saying that on international TV."

"Why?" she asked. "He's right. News flash, everyone, we have sex. Good sex. Hot sex. Try new things and love every minute. Why are people scandalized when they learn that a couple in love, a now married couple, has sex? It's illogical."

I grinned to myself at Nora's *mini-rant*. That's what she called them. I'd like to see my brothers razz me about this one. I don't recall hearing their wives make such a statement.

"You puff out that chest any more, and it's going to explode," Vince said while I kept smiling. Fuck, I loved my wife.

The interview ended, and Mom stuck her head in the room, baby Sarah in her arms, and announced Carly had dinner ready. They'd arrived a couple of hours ago, and already she was holding the tiny pink explosion of baby girl in a steel grip. Mom had boys. So, she would get every female gender-leaning item until that little girl could stand up and choose for herself.

Canyon and Emme were relieved that my folks were here for the solstice this year. They would keep the baby tonight and tomorrow so the new and exhausted parents could have time alone for the day. There was plenty of breast milk in the fridge, clearly marked. So much had changed since last year.

"Hey, Mom, after dinner, I'll run and get the pack-and-play for Sarah to sleep in tonight," Canyon said as we all walked past the brightly lit tree to take our seats at the large dining table.

"That's not necessary. We've been sitting in the nursery for a while, and I think she likes it. Let's give that a try. The crib is the same as the one she has at home."

"What nursery?" Emme asked, and we all looked at Mom.

"The one back there." Mom nodded toward their bedroom with a secret smile. Emme and Canyon led the way. Nora's expression was questioning, and I shook my head.

"Oh, my goodness, Margot, this is beautiful," Emme said, disappearing into Dad's office.

What used to be my father's office, then a trophy room was painted a pale green with little evergreen trees and what could only be called woodland creatures in various spots. The color, the wood casing on the windows, and the cedar bead board low on the walls turned the space into a magical forest. The ceiling was painted a darker blue with white stars scattered to every corner.

A new crib sat on one side of the room opposite a dresser with some sort of pillow on top and a fancy rocking chair with a footstool. A beanbag was next to a low bookshelf already filled and a basket holding brightly colored toys.

"Where'd the trophies go?" I asked.

"We had them packed up," Dad said. "We'll ship them to you, or we can store them. But this little angel needed a special room, and this was the one closest to your mother."

Nora smiled and smoothed her hand across her flat belly. I'm not sure she even noticed she was doing it.

"You like it, babe?" I asked, keeping my voice low. "I think there's space for a few cribs in here."

"I love it." She looked at me with tears gathered at the edge of her lids, so I kissed her.

"It's a new kind of trophy room," Dad said. "We want to be the best grandparents ever. That's what I'll be most proud of in the coming years. This is the start."

Nora swiped a tear, and I pulled her into my arms. "Hey, don't cry."

"You remember that first day we met?" she asked. "When we were separated on the train?"

I nodded. "I didn't like being apart from you after only a few hours, and I hadn't even kissed you yet. It was all I could think about."

"We were texting, and I said I thought you had it all."

I brushed a piece of hair behind her ear. "And I said no one had it all. I wanted enough."

"Walker, you, us, and this family are so much more than enough."

"For me too, babe."

GET TO KNOW PERRY HARBOR! Start this steamy series today.

Your Two Lips (Perry Harbor Book 1)

If you can't have true love, have great sex

Finn Bakker has had enough one-night stands with wealthy tourists on this picturesque PNW island and is ready to find real love, settle down on the family tulip farm, and add his own dream, a mountain biking resort.

Emily Rutherford has money and a new start, but she can't have the love and family she craves. She'll make the most of it, exchanging love for all the passion she can get.

When the strong beauty teams up with the rugged farmer in a benefit mountain bike race, they come face to face with their own weaknesses on and off the bike.

Friendship with passion just for now. But life and family have a way of crashing into the best-laid plans. She won't take away his chance for the future he imagined. He can't imagine a future without her. Can they find a way to heal the scars of the past, or will she kiss his two lips and walk away?

A friends to lovers, he falls first, steamy, mountain biker romance set in the beauty of a PNW coastal island community. It's about family, responsibilities, and being true to the thing that makes us whole, love.

ORDER *Your Two Lips* now on Amazon.

Thank you for reading *Formula One Noel*. I hope you loved Walker and Nora as much as I did. Join the Hewitts for more Christmas fun with some folks you already know in the Bonus Epilogue. To access all bonus materials visit:
www.christinabraver.com/bonus.

Want the inside scoop on all things Perry Harbor and my misadventures in writing? Sign-up for my newsletter via my website:
www.christinabraver.com. Unsubscribe at anytime.

As much as I try, I'm not perfect. If you find an error, please email me at:
author@christinabraver.com.

ALSO BY CHRISTINA BRAVER

Perry Harbor - The Bakkers

Available on Amazon

Your Two Lips (Book 1) Finn & Emily

Your Sweetness (Book 2) Lucas & Jo

Your Heart (Book 3) Tess & Drew

Perry Harbor - The Boathouse

Your Turn (Book 4) Rhys & Nicole

Perry Harbor Related Standalones

Formula One Noel (Book 2.5)

A Steamy Holiday Romance - Walker & Nora

Vegas Baby (Book 4.5)

A Steamy Holiday Romance - Grant & Hannah

Coming Fall of 2023

AFTERWORD

I am not a doctor or a sex therapist, but the issues of women's health and sex positivity across all ages of adulthood have always been of interest to me. This book touches on a couple of heavy topics, gender inequality in healthcare and real sex information and techniques, but it also highlights the good news that sex doesn't have to stop at fifty, or sixty, or seventy!

If you want to read more, your public library is a great place to start. Here is a list of books I highly recommend. I read all of these in preparation to write this book and honestly, I think everyone should read them, no matter your gender identity or orientation. There is something to be learned. Perhaps we can become better lovers and better people.

McGregor, Alyson J., *Sex Matters: How male-centric medicine endangers women's health and what we can do about it*, Quercus, 2020.

Nagoski, Emily, *Come As You Are: Revised and Updated: The Surprising New Science That Will Transform Your Sex Life*, Simon & Schuster; Updated edition, 2021.

Kerner, Ian, *She Comes First: The Thinking Man's Guide to Pleasuring a Woman*, Harper Collins Publishers, 2004.

Kerner, Ian, *Passionista: The Empowered Woman's Guide to Pleasuring a Man*, William Morrow Paperbacks, 2008.

Blank, Joani (Editor), *Still Doing It: Women & Men Over 60 Write About Their Sexuality*, Down There Press, 2000.

Price, Joan, *Better Than I Ever Expected: Straight Talk About Sex After Sixty*, Seal Press, 2005.

ACKNOWLEDGMENTS

Thank you to all the wonderful people who made this possible.

To my sister, Tracy, and my mom, Christine, for first giving me the means to become a writer.

To Brent Archer, my fabulous writing sprint partner who helped me plot and kept me writing, and Nicole Knightly for great plot advice.

To Dr. Grant L., Dr. Kimberly M., and Mitchell H., the subject matter experts who helped me create authentic characters and events.

To Amelia S., Kim S., and Maryanne K., my beautiful book betas, who bravely read this entire manuscript first.

To all my friends who have supported and encouraged me along this journey. You know who you are and I know who you are. Thank you!

To my kids for supporting me and saying they were proud.

Special thanks to C for being my Subject Matter Expert on Formula One. You are a human Google.

To my husband and very own beta hero who first said the words "You should write a book."

ABOUT THE AUTHOR

Christina Braver writes steamy, small-town, contemporary romance set in the Pacific Northwest. Her stories are about real people and real love with the guaranteed HEA we all need.

She's been reading romance for decades and loves to escape into stories about strong heroes with softer sides and independent heroines with a bit of sass.

She strives to support allyship in her writing and portray diversity in everyday life. She believes together, we will save the world.

When she isn't writing, Christina can be found reading in her favorite corner chair, sipping wine and laughing too loudly with friends, or cooking dinners that always take twice as long as the recipe suggests. She lives in Seattle with her husband who shares his bourbon, and two teenagers that keep them both on their toes.

And just like her favorite latte, her books have some steam. If that's not your regular brew, you may want to change your order. Enjoy!

Made in the USA
Monee, IL
01 November 2023

45604925R00174